Old Scores

Old Scores

Aaron Elkins

OPEN ROAD
INTEGRATED MEDIA
NEW YORK

Copyright © 1993 by Aaron Elkins

ISBN 978-1-4976-4316-1

This edition published in 2014 by Open Road Integrated Media, Inc.

345 Hudson Street

New York, NY 10014

www.openroadmedia.com

Old Scores

Acknowledgments

New writers are usually amazed at the willingness of experts from various fields to answer the questions of inquisitive novelists. Sometimes even old writers are amazed. It is with pleasure that I acknowledge my debt to the scholars and authorities who so patiently and good-humoredly helped me (and Chris Norgren) get out of one jam after another.

Georgina Adam, Paris correspondent of *ARTnews,* lucidly explained some of the more inscrutable aspects of the current French art scene; Chiyo Ishikawa, Assistant Curator for European Paintings, Seattle Art Museum, enlightened me on an esoteric sticking point concerning Rembrandt's early career; John Henry Merryman, Sweitzer Professor of Law Emeritus, Stanford Law School, did his formidable best to keep me intellectually honest on issues of forgery and authenticity in art; and Professor John R. Price, School of Law, University of Washington, filled me in on laws of succession, particularly in France, and on several other tricky legal subjects as well. Straightening out my French required three people—Albert Jekenta and Louise Lillard, formerly of the Beverly Hills Unified High School District, and Bob Kirk of Seattle. My sincere appreciation to all.

The Barillot Museum in Dijon is wholly fictional, and is not meant to represent the Dijon Fine Arts Museum, which is indeed very fine.

CHAPTER I

"My treat," Tony said, reaching over my extended hand to pick up the check. "This is on me."

Oh-oh, I thought. Watch out now.

This is not to imply that Tony Whitehead is a devious type, or one in whom every generous action implies some ulterior motive. It's just that Tony usually doesn't do things without a reason. Sometimes it's to your advantage, sometimes it's not. And it's been my experience that when he picks up the tab—it's not.

Tony is my boss, the director of the Seattle Art Museum (or SAM, as we insiders call it). I'm Chris Norgren, the curator of Renaissance and Baroque art. We were lunching a few blocks from the museum in the stylish, dark-wood elegance of a trendy new dining spot called Palomino. Our table was at a railing overlooking the spectacular glass-and-granite atrium of the Pacific First Centre building four stories below. As befitted a restaurant that described itself as "a Euro-Seattle bistro," Palomino was neoeclectic all the way. The furnishings were vaguely Art Deco, the wall hangings and open brick ovens vaguely Country French, the massive round columns and mauve walls vaguely Aegean.

It was all very handsome and inviting, and certainly of the moment, but it wasn't a choice I would have expected from Tony, who prided himself on ferreting out little hole-in-the-wall "finds" under the Alaskan Freeway. He'd surprised me by suggesting it. And made me wonder what was up.

Not that I didn't trust him, you understand. As a matter of fact, I do trust him. And I like him a lot. He works hard and he has high standards for himself and his staff. He's a skilled administrator and a formidable Trecento scholar, and more than once I'd seen him stand up for his people when the chips were down. He'd been particularly kind to me at a critical time in my life.

All the same, there was an occasional whiff of snake oil in his nature, and he had a history of getting me involved in things I should have known better than to get involved in. Always for the greater good of the Seattle Art Museum, of course, or in the interests of art itself. But not always in the interests of my personal comfort and convenience.

"How was the meal?" he said amiably.

"Delicious," I said. Which was true. I'd had a spit-roasted-chicken pizza, thereby taking advantage in one dish of both the Milanese *girarrosto* that roasted the fowl, and the alder-fired Roman pizza oven. The famous apple-wood-fired oven had made its contribution in the form of bruschetta, delicately charred chunks of Italian bread coated with olive oil, garlic, and bits of sun-dried tomato. I hadn't figured out a way to try the hardwood grill, too, but whatever I'd had was excellent.

"How about some dessert?"

"No, thanks."

"Why don't we have some salad? You know, a palate-cleanser."

I agreed. We ordered green salads. Did we wish fresh Gorgonzola and walnuts on them, the black-shirted, black-trousered waitress wanted to know. We didn't. Would we care for another glass of wine?

"Go ahead, Chris," Tony said expansively. "No hurry getting back. We've got all the time in the world."

"No, thanks, Tony. Gee, I wonder why I have this feeling I'm going to need a clear head."

"Ha, ha," he said reassuringly, "not really. Although, you know, there is something I wanted to tell you about. Don't look so edgy, Chris. I think you're going to find this interesting."

I didn't doubt it.

He reached for the bruschetta and tore off a piece. "As it happens, there's a collector who wants to give us one of his paintings," he said off-handedly. "It'd fall in your bailiwick if we take it."

"What painting?" I asked warily.

"Oh, it's just a portrait. By, what's his name, you know, Rembrandt."

Well, there in a nutshell was why no one had ever accused Tony of not knowing how to get someone's attention.

"What's-his-name-Rembrandt," I said thickly, once I got my voice going again. "Tony, this is ..." I frowned. "What do you mean, *if* we take it? Are you kidding me?"

"Well, we do have a small problem. The man we're talking about is René Vachey."

"René ... ?" I stared at him. "And he just ... just up and offered us this old Rembrandt he happened to have lying around?"

Tony continued his placid chewing. "That's about it. One of his lawyers called me this morning to tell me about it."

"Just like that? Out of the blue?"

"Just like that."

I sat back against my chair, not sure just what my feelings were. "Mixed" would be as good a way as any to describe them, I guess. A Rembrandt portrait. Any red-blooded curator of Baroque art who says he wouldn't be salivating for it sight unseen would be lying through his teeth. I mean, after all, Rembrandt is—well, *Rembrandt.* The fact that SAM didn't own a single one of his paintings was something I regarded as almost a personal affront, but I'd long ago given up the idea of getting one any time soon. And now, suddenly, there it was, in my mind's eye, gilded seventeenth-century frame and all, hanging in the Late Renaissance and Baroque Gallery on the fourth floor, in pride of place on the west wall. I was dazzled.

At the same time, the mention of the donor's name had made me thoroughly leery. I'd never met the elderly René Vachey, but I knew who he was. A successful French art dealer as well as a collector, he was one of the art world's more eccentric characters (and take my word for it, that is saying something), unpredictable, controversial, notorious. To some, an unscrupulous and self-serving scoundrel; but to many others a welcome gadfly in a field cram-full of self-puffery and faddishness. I could see both points of view.

The most spectacular of his escapades had occurred about ten years earlier, when the morning shift at the Musée Barillot in Dijon had walked in to discover to their horror that six of the museum's most-prized possessions had vanished during the night, frames and all. Among them were paintings by Tintoretto, Murillo, and Goya. The usual tumult followed. The police were called in and got to work grilling museum employees and other suspicious characters. Photographs and descriptions of the stolen works were given to Interpol. Accusations of lax security were flung at the museum director, who responded by wringing his hands and bemoaning the sad state to which French morality had degenerated. He also fired his security chief.

Then, exactly four weeks later, René Vachey opened a public exhibition of works from his own excellent collection, mounted in his own gallery, three blocks from the museum. This was something he did occasionally, but this time there was a difference. Featured proudly and prominently in their original frames were the six pictures missing from the Barillot.

More tumult. Vachey, one of Dijon's most prominent citizens, permitted himself to be arrested and charged in what was almost a public ceremony. Afterward, he held a news conference well-attended by the Parisian press corps (whom he had taken care to invite). Yes, he said, he had taken the pictures from the museum, or rather caused them to be taken; the responsibility was entirely his. But *stolen* them? No, he had not stolen them. To steal, he pointed out, was to take the property of another, was it not? But whose property *were* these paintings? Did the Musée Barillot *own* them? He thought not, and he thought he could prove he was right.

Now I ought to point out that we are not talking about timeless works of art here, despite the famous names. Artists are like anyone else; they have off-days. Usually they themselves destroy or paint over their less successful efforts, but often enough these works survive. And there are certain small European museums, and some American ones, too, that have capitalized on this, picking them up relatively cheaply and amassing collections rich in great names but lacking in great works. This is not my favorite approach to developing a museum, based as it is on the belief that the average museumgoer is too dumb to know or care what he or she is looking at as long as the label says Picasso or Matisse. Worse, that's precisely the kind of museumgoer it helps to create. ("Ooh, look, a genuine Picasso! Isn't that *beautiful?*")

Anyway, the Musée Barillot, I have to say, was just such a museum. In fairness, it could hardly have afforded a first-rate collection of paintings. Containing a modest collection willed to the city by a wealthy physician named (surprise) Barillot at the turn of the century, it had since received little support beyond that required for maintenance. It had, in fact, made almost no acquisitions since the late 1940s. Just how it had managed to acquire the pictures in question was something that was buried in the remote past. They had hung there as long as anybody could remember, that was all.

And it was just this point that had started the clever Vachey thinking. He did some research, tracing them back to their appearance in the country in about 1800 as Napoleonic loot from Italy, Germany, and Spain. With thousands of other plundered artworks they had been destined for the Louvre, but they were among those the experts pronounced unworthy of basking in *la gloire de France* and had found their way into the French art market. Eventually, one or two at a time, the museum in Dijon had picked them up in the early years of the twentieth century. They had done so legally, paying the going price, and they had the papers to prove it (although it had taken them a while to locate them in the dusty vaults of a bank in Beaune).

Vachey shrugged this off. How could paintings or anything else be purchased legally from sellers who had no right to them in the first place? But French law didn't see it that way, and a much-publicized court case ensued, with Vachey cheerfully questioning the French legal system's authority to rule in cases involving non-French property.

Yes, cheerfully. For the whole thing was a sensational stunt. There had never been a question of its being anything else. Certainly these second-rate products of first-rate artists had no financial or aesthetic appeal to Vachey. His own collection was infinitely more valuable than the Musée's. He had simply decided to call attention, somewhat ahead of its time, to the enormous and tangled question of Who Owns Art?—and perhaps to make some waves and ruffle a few feathers in the sober, snooty French art establishment along the way.

This he did brilliantly, for three well-publicized weeks, until the court began to make threatening noises. In the end, the paintings went back to the museum, as Vachey had always claimed—and I believed him—was his intention. He also paid the museum's legal expenses and voluntarily donated from his own collection, as a goodwill gesture, a fine Goya charcoal study that was worth more than all six "stolen" pictures put together.

From beginning to end, he had clearly considered the whole affair an enormous lark. Whether you conclude his basic motives were altruistic or self-serving depends on who you talk to. There was little doubt that he accomplished something useful by focusing attention on an important issue. On the other hand, he also became for a while the world's most celebrated art dealer, which couldn't have been bad for business. But whichever way you felt about that, the fact remained that he did it by burglarizing a museum, and anytime you load pictures in and out of trucks you subject them to frightening risks, especially when you do it through windows—in a hurry and on the sly. I've already said that these weren't among the Western world's great masterpieces, but Tintorettos are Tintorettos, and as far as art people are concerned, you don't mess with them to prove a point.

He'd also caused an art museum, and by extension, art museums in general, to look foolish, and that was what was worrying Tony and me right now.

So that was the man who wanted to give us a Rembrandt. Who knew what he was up to this time? The only thing I was sure of was that any gift horse from René Vachey required a long, hard look in the mouth.

"This picture," I said to Tony, "what does it look like?"

The salads had come. Tony began on his. "I told you," he said. "It's a portrait. Oil on canvas."

That struck me as a rather laconic description from a man who can get every bit as overheated about old paintings as I can.

"But what kind of a portrait? Of whom? Group or single subject? What kind of condition is it in? How much restoration has there been?"

Tony hunched his shoulders and chewed, the implication being that his mouth was too full of arugula and fennel to reply at the moment.

I leaned forward, eyes narrowed. "You haven't actually seen it, have you?"

"Well, not exactly—"

"Have you?"

"Well, no, nobody has."

"Not even photographs?"

"Well, n—"

"So we don't really know for sure it's what he says it is."

Tony swallowed and put down his fork. "Hell, we don't know for sure it exists. This could be some hoax, some game he's playing. It probably is."

I sat back and looked at him, thoroughly deflated. "So why are we even talking about it? Why are we bothering?"

"Because," Tony said, "he just might be on the level. What do you want me to do, tell him we're not interested? Tell him to go find some other museum for his lousy Rembrandt? Tell him to go ahead and give it to the Met?"

"No, I guess not."

"Of course not. How'd you feel if the next time you walked into the Met, *your* Rembrandt was hanging on *their* wall?"

I laughed. "Not good."

"Well, neither would I. So let's not jump to conclusions."

"Agreed. But something's clearly fishy here, Tony. Look, why would Vachey donate anything to us? Why not some other museum? Why *not* the Met? That'd give him a bigger public arena, if that's what he's after. Or why not a French museum, where at least he'd come away with some tax benefits?"

"Makes you wonder, doesn't it," Tony agreed.

"We've never had any kind of association with him, have we?"

"Well, in a way, yes. You know who Ferdinand Oscar de Quincy was?"

It wasn't a name you'd be likely to forget once you'd heard it. "Sure, he had your job back in the fifties."

"That's right. Well, before that, in the forties he was with MFA & A. You remember what that is, don't you?"

I nodded. MFA & A—Monuments, Fine Arts and Archives—was the U.S. Army unit that, with major British assistance, had tracked down so much of the stupendous German art plunder of World War II and gotten it back to the museums and individuals it had been taken from. It had been the biggest and most successful recovery of stolen art in history, a well-deserved feather in the cap of the U.S. military. Afterward, most of MFA & A's experts, like

Rorimer of the Met, and like de Quincy of SAM, had returned to the museum world from which they'd been recruited.

"Anyhow," Tony said, "according to Vachey, de Quincy was personally responsible for getting a dozen of his paintings back to him, and he swore then that he'd repay him someday by giving something worthwhile to de Quincy's museum." He shrugged. "That's us."

"What took him so long? It's been almost fifty years. De Quincy's been gone for forty."

"You've got me. According to his attorney, Vachey's getting on in years, he's getting sentimental. Wants to set his accounts in order before he passes on. He's taking care of old obligations, settling debts, redoing his will, all that kind of thing."

I picked abstractedly at the salad. What I'd heard so far was not abundantly convincing. From what I knew of Vachey, I didn't think he was the sentimental type, or at least not sentimental enough to give away something worth millions just to discharge a half-century-old obligation. There was surely something peculiar going on here, something we hadn't been told.

"Tony, let's assume the painting does exist. Let's assume it's really a Rembrandt. How positive are we that he's got legal ownership? How did he come by it? What does the provenance look like?"

Now provenances are tricky things. A provenance is the pedigree of a painting, the record of its ownership from the time it left the artist's hands. Since paintings change hands often, works as old as the ones we were talking about tend to have long provenances. Often they have gaps; for one reason or another, pictures disappear for a while and then turn up again, often fifty or a hundred years later. When this happens, there are always questions. How, after all, can people be absolutely certain that a long-lost Titian that is discovered in the living room of an Atlanta townhouse is the very same picture last seen or heard of in 1908 when it disappeared from the wall of a church in Pisa? (Answer: they can't, not absolutely.)

Even when there aren't gaps, there are often questions about authenticity or ownership. But a reasonably solid-looking provenance, capable of being at least partially verified, is a necessary place to start. Without it, no museum curator in his right mind would touch a so-called Old Master.

"There isn't any," Tony said.

My fork stopped halfway to my mouth. "No provenance?"

"Not to speak of, no. He says he got it from, well, from a junk shop in Paris. It was grimy, almost black. Naturally, the seller had no idea what it was."

"Well, how does *he* know what it is?"

"He says he knew the minute he saw it. He bought it, had it cleaned, took a good look at it, and satisfied himself that he was right."

"What do you mean, satisfied himself? Are you saying he authenticated it himself?"

"That's it."

I laughed. "Come on, Tony, this is a joke. An art dealer authenticating his own picture? What kind of authentication is that? Especially René Vachey, for God's sake."

He shrugged. "What do you want me to say?"

"Well, what do the French experts have to say about it?"

"I told you, nobody's seen it. He's setting up a big show at his gallery, and this is going to be the centerpiece. Critics, press, everybody's invited. I hear it's already making a huge flap over there. He's practically challenging the experts to prove his attribution's wrong, and people are starting to choose up sides before they even see the damn thing. Vachey has a lot of enemies, and, as usual, he's right in the middle of it. He called Edmond Froger a *dilettante ignorant,* in *Le Monde.*"

"Oh, wonderful."

Tony shrugged. "Well, the guy *is* a horse's ass."

This was starting to have an ominously familiar ring. Several years before the Barillot affair, Vachey had gotten together about fifty of his own paintings to form a well-publicized exhibition called the Turbulent Century: 1860-1960. It ran for a month at a gallery he owned in London, and was scheduled to go to Switzerland, Belgium, Holland, and back to France. In all these places, eager museums had been squabbling with each other for the privilege of getting it. This was quite a show, including works by Gauguin, Seurat, Braque, and Picasso.

Except it didn't, not according to some reputable critics and reviewers who pronounced most of the collection to be questionable or downright spurious. Others, equally distinguished, supported Vachey's claims of authenticity. Battle lines were drawn. There was another flap, with epithets a lot more colorful than *dilettante ignorant* being hurled back and forth. In this one, Vachey remained back in Dijon, away from center stage, enjoying the fireworks while the experts fought it out. In the end, the museums scuttled for cover and pulled out with much huffing and puffing. Not, however, before they—and by extension, art museums in general, and by further extension, art experts in general—had been made laughingstocks. There were a lot of people who thought that just might have been the iconoclastic Vachey's aim in the first place.

And right now I was starting to wonder if it wasn't time for us to think about scuttling for cover ourselves.

"He can't expect us to accept the offer without seeing it, can he?" I asked. "Because if so—"

"No, you've got yourself an invitation to the opening. You can examine it to your heart's content. Okay?"

I considered. The odds were about a hundred to one against the trip accomplishing anything. An unknown "Rembrandt" discovered in a junk shop by a man with an offbeat sense of humor and a quirky history, to put it mildly. No provenance, no reliable authentication. Not a very good bet. On the other hand, for a hundred-to-one shot at this particular reward, yes, I was willing to take a trip to Dijon. Which is a very lovely little town, I might add.

"Good," Tony said heartily, "so it's settled. I'd better send Calvin along with you. He's at the Return of Cultural Property Conference in The Hague, anyway, so he can pop over to France easy. He can take care of the paperwork details, check the fine print, that kind of thing—his French is even better than yours. That'll leave you to concentrate on the painting."

"Fine." Then, after a second: "What do you mean, you'd *better?*"

Calvin Boyer was the museum's public affairs officer, formerly known as the marketing director. I enjoyed his company—well, most of the time—and he seemed pretty good at what he did, whatever it was, but I couldn't see his being much help in this.

"Well, you know," Tony said, just a little cagily, "you're absolutely tops at what you do, and you know that I trust you completely to handle anything that comes up—"

"Right. But?"

"But, you know, sometimes you're, well, you're not too swift when it comes to people. And Vachey is a very tricky customer."

"Oh, I'm gullible, is that it?"

This was an old complaint from Tony, who was given to wondering aloud how a naive soul like me had survived as well as I had among the sharks of the art world.

"I'm just saying you maybe trust people a little too much," he said. "You're not suspicious enough, you don't have a devious mind. You take people at face value, you don't always look under the surface of things. This is not a criticism, Chris."

It sure sounded like one to me, and I started to climb up on my high horse, but caught myself in time. As a divorced man whose very first clue that his marriage wasn't everything it might have been came when his wife moved in with another man—this was after she'd been seeing him for a year without my noticing a thing—I figured I was in no position to tell Tony about how sharp I was at seeing under the surface of things.

Besides, I have a friend named Louis who from time to time has told me pretty much the same thing Tony just had. Louis says that I tend to resort to the secondary repression of ego-threatening perceptions for fear of bringing to the surface the primal hostilities and id functions that I long ago denied by means of primal or infantile repression.

At least I think that's pretty much the same thing Tony said. Louis is by trade a Freudian-Marcusian psychotherapist, and not always as lucid as Tony.

"Calvin's an M.B.A., Chris," Tony explained further. "You're an art historian."

"Okay," I said, not quite grasping his logic, but letting it pass. "Actually, I'll be glad to have him along. And he can help work out the logistics for getting the painting analyzed. We'll want to have Taupin, from Paris, run it through infrared and X ray, don't you think? And there's that outfit in Lyons—what's its name?—that can do laser microanalysis. I've got it somewhere."

"Mm," Tony said, and pushed his salad plate away. He'd finished his salad. I'd hardly looked at mine. "Come on, let's head back."

We took the escalator down to the lobby, passing under a

"Baroque" stone arch that had come from a 1920s theater that had once stood on the site. Once out on Fifth Avenue on a mild October afternoon, we threaded our way through shoppers, bemused tourists, and fellow late-lunchers getting back to work. While we walked, Tony told me more.

The Rembrandt, it seemed, wasn't the only centerpiece of Vachey's show. Vachey, no piker when it came to gall, was actually claiming to have come up with a *second* "newly discovered" painting; this one by the Frenchman Fernand Léger, who was, with Picasso and Braque, one of the foremost proponents of Cubism in the early years of the twentieth century. The Léger, it was understood, would be going to a French museum, as yet unnamed.

"Is that right?" I said. "Where'd he find this one, at a garage sale in Toulouse?"

"Strasbourg, actually," Tony said. "A flea market," and then he couldn't help laughing. "Now don't jump to conclusions here, Chris. Whatever else you can say about Vachey, he has a hell of a record for stumbling on masterpieces nobody even knew were out there." He started counting them off on his fingers. "There's that Constable that's in San Francisco now, remember? And that Francesco Guardi that wound up in, where was it, Budapest, and don't forget the Lebrun—"

"Well, yes, I know, but—"

"All those authentications were verified later—beyond any doubt, Chris. Sure, he's made a few that didn't hold up, but that much you have to admit."

"I suppose so," I said. "Well, there's one thing to be thankful for, anyway."

"What's that?"

"I was just thinking: He might have given the Rembrandt to a French museum and stuck us with the Léger." I put my hand over my heart. "Whew, it's too awful to contemplate."

I say such things primarily for the fun of annoying Tony, who has a thing about me being too enamored of my specialty. He thinks I need to be more eclectic. He says I put the Old Masters up on a pedestal (he's right), and that I look down my nose at anything after the eighteenth century (he's wrong, but not wildly wrong).

But this time he wouldn't bite. He merely gave me one of his superior, pitying looks and went on with his story. According to the terms, both pictures were to be displayed for two weeks at Le Galerie Vachey, after which they would go to their respective new owners. Vachey would pick up all transportation and insurance costs. He would even provide a continuing fund to cover future conservation and insurance.

"So what do you think, Chris? Too good to be true?"

"By half," I said.

In Seattle, you can't walk very far without passing an espresso bar, and most of us are addicted to the stuff. Tony and I, exercising our iron wills, ignored two of them, but finally succumbed at the third, a plant-filled, conservatory-like Starbucks on Fourth near Union. We got on the end of a line of five or six people at the counter.

"Uh-uh, no, it *is* too good to be true," I muttered while the barista went through her steamy routine at the espresso machine. "There's a catch somewhere."

"Um, there is a sort of catch," Tony said.

I looked at him sharply. I didn't like the sound of that *um*. "What catch?"

"Two catches, you might say."

"What catches?"

"Well, remember what you were saying about getting that X-ray and microscopic analysis done?"

"Yes—oh, Bussière, that's the name of the lab in Lyons. I have the number in—"

"No dice," Tony said.

"What?"

"No labs. No X-ray, no ultraviolet, no cross-sectional analysis, nothing but the naked eye. You can look at it all you want, but no scientific stuff."

"Why not, for God's sake?"

"That's the way he wants it, Chris."

"But *why?* Tony, come on, he knows it's a fake, that's the only possible reason."

"Not necessarily. He says they're fragile. He's worried about damaging them."

"With X rays? That's ridiculous, you know that."

"Apparently he doesn't."

I shook my head. "I don't buy it. You know what it is? He's got a good fake, that's all, and he's giving it to us because he thinks Seattle is probably located just west of Dogpatch, and what could we know about art? He thinks he can get it by us, and after he does, he's going to announce that it really *is* a fake, and so once again he'll show us all up for the greedy, ignorant idiots we are—don't ask me what his point is this time."

Tony listened to this harangue, visibly and somewhat smugly amused. "And could he?"

"Could he what?"

"Get it by you?"

"By me?" Oddly enough, the question caught me by surprise. "I don't think so," I said honestly, after a moment.

"So there's no problem."

"Well, yes, there is. First of all, there's the question of why he won't allow tests—he knows damn well they won't hurt the picture, and he knows equally well that museums *always* run them before they buy something."

"True, but we're not buying anything, are we? He's giving it to us."

"What's the difference? Why not allow them? And there's a second problem. Sure, if it isn't real, I think I could spot that, but a lot of other so-called experts have thought the same thing and wound up making big mistakes. What if I made a mistake?" I shook my head. "I don't like seeing us put anything in our collection without adequate testing."

"But you're not a 'so-called' expert, Chris," Tony said simply. "If you tell me it's a fake, we won't touch it. If you say it's real, that'll be plenty good enough for me. We'll take it in a flash."

I was flattered, even touched. I cleared my throat. "Thank you, Tony. I appreciate that."

"Besides, we can test the hell out of it after we get it here."

"Right," I said, laughing. Tony wasn't the sentimental type either.

Tony smiled in return; somewhat weakly, I thought. "Well, actually, even that's not true, Chris. You see, this is a restricted gift."

"A restricted gift? You mean we're not allowed to sell it later? Even if we decide we don't like it?"

His expression was one of bottomless forbearance. "Chris."

"Tony?"

"Museums are not in the business of 'selling' works of art," he said softly. "You know that."

"Oh. Right. Sorry. I don't know what I was thinking of. I meant we're not allowed to de-accession it?"

I suppose I was getting back at him for getting me into this—for despite all my reservations, I knew perfectly well I was in it up to my eyebrows.

"That's better," he said, fractionally mollified. "But not only can we not de-accession it, we have to agree to keep it on permanent exhibit—well, for five years, anyway—properly labeled *as* a Rembrandt, and displayed in a manner befitting a Rembrandt."

He exhaled, long and soberly. "So, my friend, if we decide to take it, we better be damn sure it *is* a Rembrandt ahead of time."

In themselves, restrictions like these are not extraordinary. Donors are always sticking little riders on their bequests that tell you what kind of case something is to be displayed in, or when or where it's to be placed, or what should be next to it, or how it ought to be lit. That, as far as it goes, isn't usually objectionable. These things are gifts, after all, and the people donating them usually love them every bit as much as we do. Why shouldn't they care about what happens to them after they go to a museum?

But this was different. The proscription on testing made it different; the absence of provenance made it different; above all, the presence of the unpredictable René Vachey pulling the strings made it different.

"You mentioned two catches," I said. "Was that the second one?"

"Actually, no; that was still part of the first."

"What," I said, gritting my teeth, "is the second?"

"Um, it'll hold. I'll tell you about it when we get back."

Um again. "Tell me now."

"Patience. Let's have our coffee first."

"Tony—"

"Here, Chris," Tony said generously as we got to the cashier, "let me pick up the tab. This is on me."

CHAPTER 2

I knew that whatever else was coming was going to be bad because Tony invited me into his office when we got back to the museum, then further suggested that we step out on his private terrace. It is well known among the staff that this little terrace, for whatever reason, is Tony's locale of choice for dealing with recalcitrant curators. Maybe he thinks the unspoken threat of winding up, crushed and broken, on the pavement of Second Avenue five stories below helps soften us up.

"Terrific view, isn't it?" he said, elbows on the railing. "You can really feel the pulse of the city from here."

"What's the other catch, Tony?"

He sighed. "The, uh, timing of Vachey's showing is a little unfortunate, I'm afraid. And he insists on your being there."

"As long as it's not next week," I said, smiling, then stopped abruptly. "Tony . . . it's not—"

But his look told me that it was.

I grabbed him by the arm and peered at him. "Not Sunday. Tell me it's not Sunday."

"Would that I could," he said sadly.

"Oh, Christ. Tony—"

"Actually, it isn't Sunday, it's five p.m. Monday, but you can't get from here to Dijon by five o'clock the same day, what with the time difference, so you'd have to leave Sunday. Saturday night, to be on the safe side. I know it's a nuisance—"

"Nuisance! Tony, I put in for this time off three months ago. You know how—wait a minute, why couldn't I go check out the painting earlier? I could be in Dijon tomorrow. I could be back by the weekend. I could—"

But Tony was shaking his head. "Nobody gets to see the pictures before the showing. That's the deal."

"All right, what about after? I could go in a couple of weeks, see them then."

More head shaking. "No. For one thing he wants you at the opening Monday. For another, we have to make our decision by the end of the following day. You get twenty-four hours to examine it and come to a decision. Otherwise it's off and he goes someplace else with it."

"You said I could examine it to my heart's content," I said bitterly.

"To your heart's content as long as it's inside of one day."

The image of Tony lying crushed and broken on the pavement of Second Avenue, five stories below, flitted briefly through my mind. "Tony, this is absolutely crazy. There are too many conditions."

He surprised me by agreeing readily. "Way too many. Vachey's playing some kind of game; that's obvious. And, look, if you get out there, and you wind up having doubts about the picture, or his motives, or anything else that tells you we ought to keep clear of this, then that's that. Case closed."

"Doubts? Are you kidding? Of course I have doubts. Even if it turns out to be real, how do we know it's not stolen? Who knows where he got it? Or how? I mean, come on, a junk shop? The guy must think we're complete rubes."

Tony let me rant on for a while, but he knew as well as I did what I was really griping about. When I finally wound down, he put a sympathetic hand on my shoulder.

"This is sure screwing up your love life, isn't it?"

"Boy, you said a mouthful," I said ruefully.

* * *

The truth of the matter was that my love life wasn't in any too good shape to begin with. I was in love, yes. With a bright and beautiful woman named Anne Greene. And she was in love with me; I had no doubts on that score. Anything we did together was sheer pleasure. We could talk earnestly for hours, brimming with interest and animation, and then laugh because we couldn't remember what we'd been talking about. On walks, on drives, on bicycle paths, at concerts, at art shows, in bed—as long as it was with her, everything was full of warmth, and laughter, and peace. I dated no other women, and she dated no other men. Not because we had an explicit understanding, but because that was the way we liked it. We'd each found the right person. Why keep looking?

So what's the problem, you say? Your own love life should be that good, you think?

There was, in fact, only one difficulty, one small impediment: We happened to live 6,200 miles apart, give or take a few hundred one way or the other. I was in Seattle, and Anne was in Kaiserslautern, Germany. True, it is possible to have wonderful experiences under those conditions. But it is not possible to have frequent wonderful experiences. Or frequent anything.

On the other hand, it may not be all bad. My friend Louis (the psychotherapist) wondered recently over a glass of Orvieto if I hadn't gotten myself into so bizarre a fix on purpose, to avoid the repetitive, counterproductive conflict between erotic energy and social utility; that is (I think), between love and work. Repressive desublimation, it's called, and apparently it is the grease that makes the wheels of industry and commerce go 'round.

But with all due respect to Louis, I didn't buy it; I'd never given much thought to the wheels of industry and commerce—and I missed Anne like crazy.

Anne was a captain in the U.S. Air Force. She had been something called a community liaison officer, but recently, with the cutting back of European military forces, was made an education officer, responsible for developing programs to help servicemen find their way back into the work force in the United States.

I had met her a couple of years earlier when I was in Europe helping to organize an exhibition of paintings. At the time, my personal life was in shreds. I was in the throes of a miserable divorce; sulky, hurt, and thoroughly down on the female sex in general. Anne had come along just when I needed her and had helped me to see things straight again. During the six weeks I was in Europe we'd become close, and closer still when I left.

Since then we'd spent a fortune in telephone bills, and seen each other perhaps eight times. All right, exactly eight times. Fortunately,

I have the kind of job that gets me to Europe two or three times a year, for a week or two at a time, and Anne had taken two long, marvelous vacations with me in the United States. Eight times in two years is once every three months, on the average. About right for getting together with your brother-in-law; a little sparse for relating to your meaningful other.

The trouble was, Anne was as dedicated to her career as I was to mine. And being a fully credentialed Late-Twentieth-Century Male—sensitive, supporting, and enlightened—was I about to suggest that she give up her job and come live with me in Seattle? Not me. Even though I did earn considerably more money than she did. Even though her Air Force career was hardly a "career" if they could switch her from community liaison to educational services overnight, without bothering to ask her opinion about it. Even though she could easily enough find interesting work in Seattle, but what the hell was I supposed to do in Kaiserslautern? No, sensible as such a decision might seem to you—to any right-thinking person—I wouldn't think of bringing it up.

Not for a minute.

And so we got along on our once-every-three-months schedule— worried, but not overly worried, about how it would all eventually work out. For the present, it was the best we could do, and we were grateful for what time we did have together. Which is not to say that there weren't problems sometimes—such as the one I had just gotten myself into by volunteering (or did I volunteer? With Tony, you're never sure.) to be aboard a plane to France on the following Sunday.

Sunday, you see, was the day on which Anne expected to find me waiting at San Francisco International Airport at 1:00 p.m. She would arrive then on a military charter flight from Frankfurt, having convinced her superiors that her presence was essential at a job-reentry conference to be held at McChord Air Force Base, near Tacoma, on the following Wednesday. That gave us—would have given us—three crisp, glorious November days to drive slowly up the northern California and Oregon coasts to Puget Sound. We would stay—would have stayed—at inns I knew of, with woodburning fireplaces and huge windows looking out on rocky headlands and crashing surf.

Now I'd be lucky to get back from France by Wednesday night, which would leave just three days for us to be together before she had to fly back to Germany.

Not feeling good about it, I called her from my office at 2:00 p.m., 11:00 p.m. German time. The phone rang twice before she picked it up.

"Hello?"

I knew from the velvety timbre of her voice that the telephone had awakened her. I imagined her pushing herself up on her pillow, short brown hair tousled and warm from sleep. I felt my own voice soften.

"Anne, it's Chris. I'm sorry I woke you up."

"You didn't, not really. I was hoping it was you when I heard it ring." She sounded excited and happy. My heart sank a little more. "Chris, guess what, there was room for me on an earlier flight. I'll be in San Francisco at seven o'clock in the morning. That'll give us the full day together, do you realize that? We could—"

I sighed and got it out. "Anne, I can't make it Sunday."

"You can't—is something wrong? You're all right, aren't you?"

"Yes, I'm all right. It's just that something's come up at work. I'll be gone till late Wednesday. . . ." I explained; not very coherently, I'm afraid. "Anne, it's not as if—" I faltered. Not as if what? Not as if I were more interested in chasing down the Rembrandt than I was in seeing her? Well, I wasn't; it was just that . . . I didn't know what to say, so I let the sentence hang there.

"We'll still have three days together," I told her. I hoped I sounded more exuberant than I felt. "All we'll miss are the first four."

Right. Just the long, looping, lonely curves of U.S. 101, with the rockbound sea on our left and those sweeping, forested bluffs on our right. Just the brooding offshore monoliths of Bandon and Cannon Beach, shrouded in blue-gray fall mists. Just the lighthouses at Yaquina and Heceta Head on their bleak, wave-pounded promontories. Just the shout-out-loud pleasure of having an entire, endless week ahead in each other's company.

Having only the three days killed all that. You can't have an endless three days. From the beginning, you can hear the clock ticking.

"I know," she said.

"We'll drive the coast next time," I said. "It'll still be there. So will those inns along the way."

"Did you make the reservations?"

"Yes. I'll cancel them," I said glumly.

"No, don't cancel them. I think I'd like to make the drive by myself. I'll rent a car."

"It's over a thousand miles."

"That's all right. It'll be nice to look at the sea. And I can use some time by myself. I want to do some thinking."

That didn't sound exactly ominous, but it didn't suffuse me with joy either.

"We'll talk when you get back to Seattle," she said.

That sounded ominous.

"Anne, this is just one of those logistical problems, it's nothing serious. They happen, that's all. Remember when you couldn't make it to Antwerp last year?"

"Of course I remember. I know this isn't your fault."

"So what is there to talk about?"

"I don't know. I'm not making sense. I'm still half-asleep. I'm sorry I won't see you till Wednesday."

"Me too. You still have the key to my place?"

"Uh-huh."

"I'll leave some things in the refrigerator for you."

"Thank you."

"Anne?" I hesitated. "Everything's all right between us, isn't it?"

"Of course it is," she said, sounding surprised. "Don't worry, we'll work things out. Chris?"

I waited. I realized the back of my neck was tense.

"I love you. Very much." The softness was back in her voice. I felt most of the tightness melt out of my neck.

"I love you," I said sincerely. "I'll see you Wednesday."

I hung up, reassured but not totally.

What was there to work out?

* * *

A few minutes later I called Tony's administrative assistant. "Lloyd, I need some airplane tickets." I gave him the details.

"Will do," he said. "Pronto mucho."

"Oh, and I'd like to go first-class, please. Or business-class, if you can't get that."

This was taboo, as I knew very well. First-class seats were standard if you were transporting, say, a Van Gogh or a Caravaggio—one seat for you, one for the picture—but mere human beings traveling on museum business flew K-class. Generally speaking, I had no objection to the policy; this was the first time I'd asked for an exception.

There was a pause before Lloyd answered. "I'll have to clear that with Tony."

"Fine," I said. "He owes me."

CHAPTER 3

"You want my best guess?" Calvin asked, looking up from a copy of the *Executive Gift Catalog,* which I'd gotten for him from the seat pocket on the plane. Calvin Boyer is the only person I know who actually orders things from these catalogs. I can personally affirm that on his office desk is a palm-sized digital clock, an electronic chronometer that can time up to three functions simultaneously, that his Porsche has a customized shift knob of hand-rubbed walnut and richly gleaming brass with CWB engraved on it, and that he ordinarily travels with a handy-dandy pocket calculator capable of saying "Where is the toilet?" in seven languages (something he didn't need on this trip, having lived in France until he was eleven). Even now I could see the dark glint of the multifunctional navigator's wristwatch, with "safety-ratcheted bezel," on his wrist.

Despite these and numerous other oddities of personality, Calvin is a likable guy, lively and upbeat, and even bright in an obtuse sort of way.

I turned from the window. "Sure," I said. "What's your best guess?"

We were seated side by side in the comfortable, plush chairs of a FrenchRail TGV, that sleek, silent, 180-mile-per-hour train that is usually the fastest and always the most comfortable way of getting from Paris to any other important French city. I had landed at Charles de Gaulle Airport a couple of hours earlier after a reasonably pleasant thirteen-hour flight from Seattle—the first-class seat didn't hurt any—and gone directly to the Gare de Lyon to meet Calvin in time to make the 5:19 for Dijon.

"I think these paintings of his are fakes," Calvin said. "Both of them. The Rembrandt and the other guy too."

"Léger," I said. "I agree with you."

"I think he's on another one of his crusades. He wants to show the world that art experts are fundamentally full of crap. I'm telling you."

"Could be," I said, then smiled. "You wouldn't think he'd have to go to so much trouble to make that particular point."

"He thinks the pictures are so good," Calvin continued, "that he can get them by you and most of the other pros—as long as nobody starts analyzing pigments or whatever they do in the labs. And as soon as some of you guys commit yourselves and say they're genuine, *then* he's going to get them scientifically tested himself, and the results are going to show that they're fakes after all, and that he put one over on you and half of the art world."

"Thereby demonstrating that art experts are fundamentally full of crap," he concluded with more verve than was strictly necessary.

"I heard you the first time, Calvin."

"Hey, nothing personal, pal. My advice to you is not to commit yourself one way or the other."

"I have to. We have to either accept it or turn it down by the end of Tuesday. Day after tomorrow."

"Hey, that's really tough," he said, his interest returning to the page. "Whoa, what about this? 'A double-sided calculator-clock desk folder. Flip it up, and it tells the time, flip it down . . .'"

Calvin's hypothesis was pretty much the one that I'd come up with last week in talking with Tony. Since then I'd refined it a bit. I imagined the feisty and more than slightly crackpot Vachey had in mind another one of his media extravaganzas. According to Tony, the French art experts and critics were already quarreling over the authenticity of the "newly found" paintings, and no one had even seen them yet. After the public unveiling at tomorrow's exclusive but highly publicized reception they would very likely be at each others' throats, and Vachey himself would have center stage once more. I assumed he had some kind of big finish in mind, and Calvin's guess that he himself would eventually submit the paintings to a scientific examination and then trumpet the results was as good as anything I could think of.

I had even come up with a reason for his donating the paintings to a couple of museums instead of simply announcing and displaying his "finds" and letting the critics respond on their own. He had cleverly reasoned, I thought, that museum officials, rapacious entities that we were—or that he thought we were— would be so blinded by our acquisitiveness that we might very well be a great deal less skeptical and more suggestible than the professional, presumably more objective (ha!) art critics.

I turned thoughtfully back to the darkening window. We were about twenty minutes into the trip, just breaking clear of the seemingly endless outskirts of Paris. Miles of grimy railroad yards had been succeeded by blocks of drab and graceless apartment buildings, which were followed in turn by anonymous factories, warehouses, and auto-wrecking yards, and then by great, sinister tracts of weedy, bulldozer-rutted land pockmarked with oily puddles. In the murk of dusk it had all seemed even more depressing than it actually was, but now we were in open country at last; plowed fields and ancient fortified farmhouses and rolling, wooded hills. In an hour we would be in Dijon.

I sighed, wondering just what we were getting into.

Calvin looked up once more. "On the other hand," he offered helpfully, "maybe they're real and this isn't a setup at all."

"True. Which is why we are speeding over the French countryside at this very moment. But if they're real, why is he so against scientific tests?"

"Yeah," Calvin said.

"You know, there's another possibility, Calvin; a variation on the make-the-experts-look-like-jerks theme. What if this Rembrandt is the real thing, and Vachey is laying on all these conditions to make us think it's *not* real? Not allowing any tests . . . giving us only one day to make our decision . . . Anybody with any sense would conclude Vachey's trying to put one over on us, right? So let's say we play it conservatively and refuse the painting because we doubt its authenticity. Then Vachey goes ahead and proves it *is* authentic—"

"And we wind up looking like saps." He glanced at me admiringly. "Jeez, Chris, you got a devious mind."

I laughed. "Tell that to Tony, will you?"

* * *

When we got to Dijon, Calvin headed instinctively for La Cloche, the town's most elegant hotel, while I went to the inexpensive Hôtel du Nord a few blocks away—not because I was repentant about the first-class seat to Paris (I wasn't), and was trying to save Tony money (I wasn't), but because the du Nord was where I had stayed the first time I saw Dijon, when it was the best I could afford. I had liked the simple ambience, liked the people who ran it, and been coming back ever since. Actually, Tony had tried to get me to book a room at La Cloche too, his philosophy being that penny-pinching in the matter of hotels reflected badly on the museum. But I wasn't penny-pinching, I was just reliving my youth.

Once I'd showered, I joined Calvin for a light dinner at a café a couple of blocks away, but I wasn't much in the way of company. I was washed out from the long trip, lonely for Anne, and nursing a mild case of first-night-in-a-foreign-city blues. And according to my biological clock (showily confirmed by Calvin's snazzy wristwatch), it was noon Seattle-time and I'd been up all night.

But Calvin hadn't. He'd only come a few hundred miles, from a conference in The Hague, and was full of his usual high spirits. Despite my telling him that unless things had changed, nightlife in Dijon was nonexistent, he went off to see for himself. If there was any to be found, I had no doubt that he would find it. Notwithstanding an unimpressively geeky build, a darty manner, and what seemed to me to be a striking facial resemblance to Bugs Bunny, Calvin did extremely well in singles bars, discos, and the like. It was because he was a good dresser, he claimed.

As for me, I had no interest in singles bars or discos. I went up to my room on the top floor of the du Nord, thinking dejectedly about Anne driving north from San Francisco, solitary and reflective. She'd be in the beautiful Mendocino headlands by now, or maybe as far as the giant redwood country if she'd been in a hurry and taken Highway 101. But why would she be in a hurry?

I sighed, and for a while I stood with my elbows on the high sill of the casement window, looking mindlessly out into the night, over the slate roofs of the medieval university just across the way, and the harsh Gothic towers of the cathedral of Saint-Benigne a few blocks beyond. When I realized I was falling asleep on my feet,

I pulled off my clothes, managed a few sketchy strokes with my toothbrush, and fell heavily into bed. Tomorrow was the big day, culminating in the opening of the show at Vachey's gallery. But first, at 11:00 a.m., I had my own private interview with René Vachey, arranged with considerable difficulty before I left Seattle. I intended to meet him head-on about his refusal to allow testing. And if I couldn't get him to change his mind, well, I was damn well going to know the reason why.

CHAPTER 4

Once upon a time the power of the dukes of Burgundy matched that of any ruler in Christendom, including the king of France. Those days are long past, but the splendid ducal palace still stands (it is now Dijon's city hall), and the streets around it—Dijon's *ancienne ville*—are filled with elegant two- and three-story townhouses, built anywhere from the sixteenth to the eighteenth centuries, and scrupulously maintained. Walk six or seven blocks in any direction, and you might be in any prosperous French city; modern, bustling, anonymous. But to be in the *ancienne ville* is to be immersed—architecturally, at least—in a vanished age of refinement, wealth, and quiet charm.

Vachey's townhouse was located here, in the heart of the Old City, three blocks from the Palais des Dues, at 39 Rue de la Préfecture. Like most of the houses on these streets, it had a brief historical-society tablet on its facade, MAISON DE GERLAND, it in French, BUILT 1682-1686 FOR ANTOINE DE GERLAND, COUNSELOR TO THE AUDIT OFFICE AND DEPUTY TO PARLIAMENT. This was the only sign on the building except for a tiny brass plaque, no larger than an apartment house nameplate, beside the entrance archway. LE GALERIE VACHEY, it said simply, almost pretentious in its lack of ostentation.

When I walked through the open archway, actually the old coach entrance, I found myself in an enclosed, cobbled courtyard, open to the sky, in which a coach-and-four would have looked right at home, but that instead held two glossy, dove-gray Renaults parked at an angle in one corner. At the back of the yard was the facade of the house proper, two stories high, classic and well-balanced, with tiers of tall French windows peeking out from a well-trimmed network of ivy creepers just beginning to drop their leaves.

The entrance to the building was by way of a gracefully scalloped flight of stone steps at the top of which a dour, waspish man of fifty appeared, peering mistrustfully at me through the open doorway.

"Dr. Norgren?" he inquired brusquely. I assured him I was.

"Enchanté" he muttered, which doesn't carry quite the weight in French that it might in English. He was Marius Pepin, secretary to René Vachey, he told me in nasal, distracted French. He extended his hand, but let it fall away just short of touching, as if his thoughts had gone on to other things halfway there. I didn't take offense, because he seemed like a man with a lot on his mind, but still it wasn't what I'd call an exuberant welcome.

I had been keeping Mr. Vachey waiting for some time, I was sternly told—presumably this was the cause of M. Pepin's anxiety—and would I kindly hurry along in, please, as Mr. Vachey was in the midst of an extremely busy day and did not like being kept waiting.

I apologized (I was all of three minutes late, having turned the wrong way at the corner) and followed him into the house and up the wide stairway. Vachey's living quarters, Pepin told me while scurrying ahead, were on the lower floor, with the gallery situated above. Mr. Vachey awaited me in his study, adjoining the gallery. I was to excuse the confusion and disorder resulting from ongoing preparations for the show and reception that evening.

Whatever spasm of hope that gave me of catching a glimpse of the Rembrandt on my way in was quickly dashed. Most of the gallery portion of the floor was blocked by a set of folding, linen-covered partitions at the rear of the stairwell, so that I could see nothing beyond the landing on which I stood. Here, in a sort of bay, were a few well-displayed paintings by French artists of the Cubist movement: Derain, Duchamp, Villon, Delaunay, others I wasn't sure of. There was also a set of glass doors. Pepin went directly to them, pushed one open, murmured a few obsequiously respectful words to someone within, then stood aside and motioned me in.

Stepping by him, I found myself in one of the most fantastic rooms I'd ever been in; big, gorgeous, and dauntingly ornate, the kind of place most people get to see only in a museum, and only in a first-rate museum at that. I almost expected to run into a polite little velvet cord stretched across the entry foyer. But of course there was no cord, and in I strode, past Pepin, stepping directly onto a nineteenth-century Aubusson carpet (wincing curatorially as I did) that was laid on the worn parquet floor. The walls were sheathed in Venetian Renaissance paneling, rich with fifteenth-century urban scenes done in wonderfully detailed marquetry. I'd never before seen so much in one place. One of the panels had *1489* on it, inlaid in yellowed ivory.

Against one wall was a Boulle commode from about 1700; a glittery, complex tour-de-force inlaid with curling arabesques of brass, ivory, tortoiseshell, and I who knew what else. There was a massive old fireplace with a worn coat of arms cut into the stone in low relief, plump Louis XVI chairs, bronze and marble sculptures everywhere, table lamps made from eighteenth-century Sèvres vases, handsome old books bound in gold-tooled leather. Dominating the room was a huge, old desk that people had probably been killed for; made of cherrywood and polished brass, and topped with a thick, rosy slab of marble that had been carved, with unimaginable patience, into wispy filigree around the edges.

Behind this imposing piece, ensconced in a weird red armchair with a frame that seemed to be made completely of wicked-looking elk antlers—getting in and out of it without being impaled must have taken practice—sat a sunny, smiling man who didn't look in the least upset about being kept waiting for three minutes. Nor did he look notorious, crackpot, or any of the other things I've been calling Vachey. He was, in fact, a positively amiable-looking man in his mid-seventies, a bit stringy in the neck, but deeply tanned and healthy-looking, with a close-cropped pepper-and-salt beard and sharp, friendly, intelligent eyes. He was dressed in a white shirt and flowered tie with an old cardigan over them. On his feet, which I could see through the desk's kneehole, were worn leather slippers. Around his neck hung a magnifying glass on a cord. He closed a thick, well-used looseleaf book when I came in, and watched with apparent enjoyment while I goggled at the room.

"So, what do you think of my study?" he asked in French.

"It's magnificent."

"Yes, yes, I suppose so." He cocked his head this way and that, like a chicken sizing up its surroundings. "But my God, I can tell you, it's hell to dust." This was followed by a peal of merry and transparently genuine laughter. I liked him right off, which hadn't been part of my plan.

"How do you do, Monsieur Vachey? I'm Christopher Norgren. I'm sorry about being late."

He waved this off, stood up and shook hands with a formal little bow, and motioned me toward a chair.

I sat, first checking for antlers.

"Some coffee?" Vachey said. "An apéritif?"

"No, thank you."

On the Rue de la Préfecture, a noisy truck rattled slowly by. The sound easily penetrated the French windows near Vachey's desk. So did a whiff of exhaust. Surprised, I glanced up and saw that the windows were ajar.

"Yes?" Vachey said. "Something worries you?"

"Well, I—" I gestured at the centuries-old paneling, the old books, the furniture. "Aren't you concerned about their condition? I'd have thought—"

"That there would be an up-to-the-minute climate control system installed here? Self-correcting temperature and humidity sensors; locked, ultraviolet-blocking windows?" He smiled. "Back there, in the gallery, for the paintings, there are such wonders. But here, this room, this is not a museum, this is where I work, monsieur. Everything in here was made to be used and enjoyed. In here, everything ages as God intended it to age, myself most of all."

He settled back in his own menacing chair. "Now, what exactly may I do for you?" he asked agreeably.

I cleared my throat and went into a well-rehearsed opening speech of thanks for his donation to the museum.

There is a persistent and touching faith among American travelers to France that the way to win the Gallic heart is to make an honest effort, no matter how humble or inadequate, to address the natives in their own tongue. Not so, in my opinion. In Germany, yes. In Italy or Spain, yes. But in France, they are likely to gaze at you with this hurt, disbelieving look—roughly the expression you might expect from a cow that has just been unfairly hit between the eyes—while you innocently mutilate their beloved and beautiful language, as anyone who is not a native speaker inevitably must.

This is a lesson I seem to have a hard time learning, and, as usual, I started off on the wrong foot, in flowing but mangled French, even though I knew that Vachey, having lived in London for some years, was fluent in English. My presentation was received in pretty much the stunned-cow manner described above, enlivened by an occasional wince when I came to some of the trickier diphthongs. Nevertheless, he listened patiently, although now and then he would flap a hand in an amicable get-on-with-it gesture.

Awkwardly, I got on with it. "As much as we appreciate this noble and generous gesture—"

Flap went the hand, accompanied by an indulgent chuckle.

"—we find ourselves with several questions of some pertinence to any eventual decision—"

Flap, flap. I couldn't blame him. The language does this sort of thing to me. I love listening to myself speak it. It seems to be at its worst when I'm nervous, and I was nervous.

"I wonder, do you think we should try English?" he suggested gently. "Don't you think we'd get done sooner?"

By this time I was glad to oblige, and I came straight to the point. "Mr. Vachey, I'd like to talk to you about your prohibition of scientific testing—"

"Oh, but that isn't subject to negotiation, I'm afraid. There can be no scientific analysis of any kind." This was said not in the least harshly.

"But you must realize that raises questions—"

"No, no, I don't believe in it."

"But—"

"Mr. Norgren, the true connoisseur doesn't rely on chemistry and microscopes to tell him what is art and what is not. Surely you agree?"

I did, as a matter of fact. "Well, yes, but it isn't a question of relying, it's a matter of using all available means—"

"No, I'm sorry," he said apologetically. But firmly. "I'm sorry, but that's the way it must be."

"But surely you know that if we accept the picture, we'd have it analyzed later in any case."

"Of course. When it's yours, do whatever you wish," he said serenely.

I shook my head in frustration. "But then why—"

He wiggled a finger. "No," he said pleasantly, and smiled; a charming, raffish little grin. "No, Mr. Norgren."

And that seemed to be that. Vachey sat smiling at me, hands clasped and at rest on the desktop. Dissatisfied as I was with where things stood, I was reluctant to press any harder. There was always the possibility that the surprisingly sweet-tempered but famously unpredictable M. Vachey would tell me to forget the whole thing. And I didn't want that to happen.

"Tell me," he said with interest, "why do you make such a point of tests?"

"Why do I—?"

"What can science tell you that your own two eyes cannot?"

I settled deeper into my chair. Were we negotiating after all? "Well, as I'm sure you know, no reputable museum adds a major work to its collection without taking every available step to ensure that its attribution is accurate."

"Ah. You want to be certain of its authenticity, is that it? You fear I might have attributed it wrongly, that it might not be a Rembrandt at all, might even be a forgery?"

I hesitated. Vachey was beaming at me, but I didn't really know how touchy he was. "Yes," I said neutrally.

He took it with a pleased little laugh. "And you don't trust your own knowledge, your own experience, to tell you?"

"I trust them, but . . ." I decided to take a chance and level with him. "Frankly, Mr. Vachey, what's weighing on my mind —on our minds—is your outright refusal to allow any scientific analysis. None of us can come up with a valid reason for that."

He smiled. "You don't believe me when I tell you I'm convinced it harms the pictures?"

I took a breath. "No, sir."

He tipped back his head and laughed; genuinely, as far as I could tell. Then he jabbed the magnifying glass in my direction. "Well, tell me something, Mr. Norgren: Just what is wrong with a forgery?"

I stared at him.

He looked back at me, his eyes keen and alert, and very much amused. He was having a good time. "It's a simple question. What ... is wrong . . . with a forgery?"

But of course it wasn't a simple question. The affable Vachey was trying to lead me somewhere, and I didn't know where, and I didn't know why. "A forgery is a deception," I said guardedly. "It pretends to be something it isn't."

"Ah," he said happily. "Something better than it is?"

"Yes, of course."

"No, not of course. Let me ask you this: What if a fake were so well done that it couldn't be told from the original—what then, eh?"

He was leaning attentively forward, his small, lively hands still clasped on the desk's beautiful marble top. Clearly, this was a subject that he found engaging, but I didn't like it at all. Why was he going on about undetectable forgeries? Was this just something he enjoyed talking about, or did it have something to do with the Rembrandt?

"It would still be a fake," I said uneasily.

"And no *reputable*"—teasing emphasis here—" museum would have anything to do with it. Correct?"

"Right."

"But why not? If what we appreciate in a work of art is its artistic, its aesthetic, quality, then why is a copy that cannot be told from the original—except in some chemical laboratory—any less worthy of our esteem?"

This was a hoary old question. Any student who has taken a course in the philosophy of art is likely to have spent some time on it. Weighty thinkers have written whole books on it, but every time some long-worshipped fake is revealed for what it is, the subject noisily surfaces again. Every major museum has gone through the miserable experience of having to announce that one or more of its famous treasures is in fact a fake. Reattribution, we call it in Museumspeak, and not so long ago the great Metropolitan Museum of Art itself reattributed over three hundred of its art objects, all of which disappeared ignominiously into its cellars, never to be seen in the light of day again. It's even happened to SAM.

And consider one of my own favorite paintings, Rembrandt's

beautiful, glowing *Man with the Golden Helmet,* with its place of honor in the history of Western art. It was praised by the experts and loved by millions. Until a few years ago, when along came a nasty new technique called neutron photography, which smugly proved that it hadn't been painted by Rembrandt at all, but by some unknown contemporary. At which news the art world promptly went into one of its periodic blue funks. I didn't take it too well myself. I was grumpy for days afterward.

Why, exactly? Had a beautiful object ceased to exist? No, it was still right there to be looked at. Had discrediting it made it any less beautiful than it was before? Of course not; it was the same painting. Did it prove that it was any less masterfully painted? Not at all. Did it make me love the painting itself any less than before?

You better believe it.

Well, why? That was the question Vachey was asking, and I didn't know any wholly satisfactory answer. "I think," I said slowly, "that aside from the dishonesty involved—"

He pounced cheerfully on this and brushed it aside. "Dishonesty? That's a different issue, is it not? It doesn't affect the aesthetic properties of the object. It doesn't make it more or less beautiful in itself."

True enough. "But there's more to it than aesthetics," I said. "When a Van Gogh or a—a—" No, at this particular juncture I just couldn't make myself say Rembrandt. "—a Titian turns out not to be that at all, it means it's no longer a link to the artist. Its connection to him—to his time—is false, or rather, nonexistent. It tells you nothing about him, says nothing from him to you."

His expression was both scornful and amused. "Ah, so it loses its value as a sacred relic? Is that what you're saying? Well, well, so it's religion we're talking about, Mr. Norgren? Cultism?" His eyes, a striking smoke-gray dappled with flecks of hazel, sparkled with enjoyment.

"Mr. Vachey," I said with sinking heart, "why are we talking about this at all?"

He regarded me with calm good humor. "But we are simply having an interesting philosophical discussion. I am arguing that the distinction between a work of art and a perfectly rendered imitation has nothing to do with the aesthetic value of the work.

It is in the mind of the viewer. A provocative point, to be sure, but purely hypothetical."

I almost believed him. Vachey had a wonderful capacity for making you believe that talking to you—about anything at all—was the most delightful thing he could imagine. Maybe it was. But there were hard-to-describe overtones, too, that gave you the feeling that he was putting you gently on, that he was enjoying his own private little joke—not exactly at your expense, but over your head, so to speak. In any case, I couldn't quite make myself believe that we had been having a friendly discussion apropos of nothing in particular.

"Mr. Vachey—"

One of the two telephones on the desk rang. He picked it up, listened a moment, and said: *"Oui, merci bien. Cinq minutes."* He replaced the receiver. "I'm so sorry. Another appointment. Is there anything else?"

"Yes, several things. What exactly is the hurry? I don't understand why you're so adamant about allowing us only one day to decide."

"Frankly, I thought it would make for better, shall we say, theater."

I couldn't help laughing.

"Would you really be happier with more time?" he asked.

"Of course I would."

"All right, take it."

"Take it?" I said, stunned.

"I'll give you the entire week. Until Friday. I'm seeing my lawyer in a few minutes; I'll have the pertinent clause changed."

"That's fine," I said.

Not that it made much practical difference. If I was going to be limited to a visual inspection, there was nothing I could learn in three days that I couldn't learn in three hours. By the time Friday came, I hoped to be long back in Seattle. All the same, his concession was interesting.

"Anything further?" he asked.

Encouraged, I pressed on. "Well, yes, there is. I don't suppose there's any chance of my seeing the painting before the opening tonight."

"Correct, there is not." He gave me his happy, expectant smile.

I hadn't thought so. I paused. Tony thinks that in delicate situations I have a way of insisting on clarity when things might be better off with a little fuzziness, a little room for maneuvering. I suppose he has a point, because I decided to go out on a limb now. Who could tell, I might even win another concession.

"Sir," I said, "I'd like to be frank. I think you have something up your sleeve. I feel it would be in our best interests to examine that painting before it's publicly unveiled. If you're not willing to do that, then we'll just have to—well, we'll have to—"

"Oop-oop-oop." Up went the forefinger again. "Now, Mr. Norgren, don't say anything we will both regret." He leaned forward with a kindly look in his eye. I think it was kindly. "You've been very tolerant with an old man so far, and I appreciate it. Bear with my foolishness just a little longer. You won't regret it, I promise you. The Rembrandt aside, I expect the evening to provide some—well, amusement, shall we say; a welcome little *frisson,* something to get the blood going on a dull October evening. Surely you wouldn't want to come all this way, and then not even . . . ?" He smiled. His eyebrows arched in friendly encouragement. He was a charmer, was René Vachey.

And he was right. Yes, I was leery, even more leery than I'd been when I'd walked in, but I was fascinated too. Just what was he going to try to pull off?

"Well—I'd like you to understand one thing," I told him, proving Tony right once more. "If you're expecting any public comment from me tonight, or tomorrow for that matter, or the day after that—"

He frowned. "Public comment? Of what sort?"

"Of the sort that puts me out on a limb by referring to your painting as a Rembrandt. Or as not a Rembrandt. As far as I'm concerned, the attribution is undetermined until there've been adequate tests. That's what I'll have to say to the press or to anyone else who asks."

This time, I thought, I'd gone and put my foot in it. Goodbye, Rembrandt. If there was a Rembrandt.

But Vachey responded with more of his genial laughter. "Mr. Norgren, say whatever you like to whomever you wish. I wouldn't have it otherwise. Now then: is your mind at ease?"

I was being gently dismissed. "Of course," I said, standing up.

Not by a long shot, I thought. I hadn't come close to getting

Vachey to change his mind about the testing. And I sure as hell didn't know the reason why. But I'd be lying if I said I wasn't hooked. You bet I wanted to know how this was going to turn out.

When I got back to the Hôtel du Nord, I checked *frisson* in my pocket English-French dictionary just for the hell of it. *Shudder, chill,* it said. *A pleasurable sensation of terror or gloom.* Great.

I went to bed and spent the afternoon sleeping off the rest of my jet lag. One thing was clear anyway: I was going to need my wits about me.

CHAPTER 5

"Okay, I got a question for you," Calvin said from the sofa against the far wall.

"Mm?" I was squinting into the mirror over the bureau, trying to insert, hook, and cinch the last of the various studs, straps, and clasps involved in getting oneself into a black-tie outfit. The reason I was squinting was that the du Nord, despite its many virtues, had a French hotel's typical disdain for illumination. There was one 25-watt floor lamp (at the opposite end of the room from the mirror), and two miniature bedside "reading" lamps lit by thickly frosted little bulbs in the shape of candles and with about the same power. That was it. This garretlike gloom added a certain dusky charm to the room, but it didn't make finding yourself in the mirror any easier.

It was 5:25 p.m. At 6:00 we were due at an elaborate pre-opening dinner in the famous old kitchens of Dijon's ducal palace, rented by Vachey for the occasion. Afterward, the privileged guests were invited to a reception and private showing of the paintings at Vachey's gallery. Calvin had come to my room to pick me up, since my hotel was two blocks closer to the gallery than his was.

"Let's hear it," I said. "What's the question?"

"Okay, what are you going to do if you go look at it tonight, and then you spend all week looking at it, and you *still* don't know for sure if it's a forgery or not? You going to recommend we forget about it and drop the whole thing?"

"Oh, I don't think it's a forgery, Calvin. I think Vachey's too sharp for that."

"What? You didn't agree with me yesterday they were forgeries?"

"I agreed they might be fakes. There's a difference between a fake and a forgery."

Calvin looked at me, willing to be amused. "Ok, I'll bite. What's the difference between a fake and a forgery?"

"No, I'm serious. A forgery is something somebody does on purpose—paints a phony Rembrandt, doctors it to make it look old, and then palms it off as the real thing."

"And that's not a fake?"

"Well, sure, it's one kind of fake, but there are other kinds of fakes that aren't forgeries at all, and those are the tough ones. Look, Rembrandt had hundreds of students, and in those days, part of the training was to make copies of the master's paintings. The harder they were to tell from the original, the more pats on the back they'd get from Rembrandt. So there are thousands of copies—perfectly legitimate Rembrandt copies—still floating around. They also had to copy his techniques in their own paintings. So there are also a lot of pictures around that aren't really copies of anything he ever did, but that are in his style. These things are all the right age for Rembrandt, they're done on the right kind of canvas or panel, they use the right pigments and binders, they even use his brush strokes."

"Jeez," Calvin said.

"That's not all. Rembrandt would stand there, right at their shoulders, and make corrections, a lot of them, right on their work, so quite a few of these paintings really are five or ten percent genuine Rembrandt. Well, sort of."

"Maybe, but they don't have his signature on them."

"But they do. In those days, any decent piece that came out of a workshop could have the master's signature on it. So we're talking about a lot of paintings that were sold as Rembrandts not three centuries later, but right out of the studio, while they were still damp. They have 350-year-old provenances."

"Jeez," Calvin said.

"Jeez is right." I finally got the bow tie properly aligned and slipped into my jacket. "Let's go. We don't want to miss anything."

Out on the Rue de la Liberté, the main commercial street of the Old City, it was a mild evening and the sidewalks were filled with shoppers and strollers. The Rue de la Liberté was Tony Whitehead's kind of street, eclectic as they come. Rough, half-timbered buildings from the fifteenth century stood cheek-by-jowl with elegant, mansard-roofed, nineteenth-century townhouses. Even the shops at street level had some odd juxtapositions. At the corner of Rue de Chapeau, for example, was Moutarde Maille, busy purveyor of mustards, on the very premises where messieurs Grey and Poupon first got together for business in 1777. Two doors down was an equally thriving McDonald's, busy doling out *beignets d'oignon* and *frites,* along with the occasional hamburger.

Strolling along, our tuxedos and patent leather shoes not drawing a second glance, I continued giving Calvin the bad news about fake Rembrandts.

"And then, of course, you can't forget about the crooks who came along centuries later and forged his signature on some of the old student paintings that he *hadn't* signed. That's all they had to fake, was the signature. A lot easier than a whole painting. And a lot harder to detect, since the rest of the picture checks out technically."

"No, no, something's wrong here," Calvin said. "Okay, maybe they check out as far as the materials and stuff go, but these are just art students, right? And we're talking about Rembrandt here, right? I mean, *the* Rembrandt. You're telling me it's that hard to tell the difference?"

I laughed. "Rembrandt had some pretty fair students: Fabritius, Aert de Gelder, Hoogstraten, Dou, Bol, Maes ..."

Calvin regarded me doubtfully, which was understandable. This was hardly a Who's Who of the world's great painters to most people. But to the educated person (you or me, for example), they were artists of the first rank.

"Take my word for it, Calvin, we're talking about some world-class painters here. And they didn't necessarily stop when they got out on their own. De Gelder was still turning out paintings in Rembrandt's style fifty years after Rembrandt died. I wouldn't want to bet my life, or yours either, on whether some particular painting was a Rembrandt, or a de Gelder in the style of Rembrandt. Not just from looking at it."

Calvin gave all this some thought. "Well, then," he said brightly, "I'd say you've got yourself a problem."

He didn't know the half of it. There are probably more dubious Rembrandts around than paintings by anyone else except maybe for Corot. According to Department of Customs records, 9,428 works by Rembrandt were imported into the U.S. from 1910 to 1950 alone. That works out to better than one every other day. Four a week, fifty-two weeks a year, for over forty years. Let it suffice to say that the figures are somewhat in excess of Rembrandt's actual rate of production. There is never a time when three or four of them are not the center of controversy. And that doesn't count the number, at least equal, in Europe. Or the U.S. Customs figures since 1950, which I didn't know and didn't want to know.

And even that wasn't the worst of it. To put it simply, these were not auspicious times to be too positive about Rembrandts. The *Man with the Golden Helmet* wasn't the only one that had run into trouble lately. The Art Institute of Chicago's well-known *Young Woman at an Open Half-Door* had recently been reattributed from Rembrandt to Hoogstraten.

Rembrandts, in truth, were the art world's equivalent of the African elephant and the mountain gorilla. "Endangered" was putting it mildly. Under the high-tech probings of modern science, formerly undisputed Rembrandts had been falling right and left. In 1921, there were 711; in 1968, 420. And by the time the international, fearsomely scholarly Rembrandt Research Project (referred to by grim curators behind closed doors as the Rembrandt Police) completes its long and unrelenting task of extirpation, it's expected there will be only 300 or so.

And only a little while ago came the dismaying news that even the beautiful, hauntingly evocative *Polish Rider*, pride of the Frick Collection, is apparently not what it seemed. It's not a happy period for those of us who used to be so sure we knew our Rembrandts.

"I'd say I had a problem too," I said.

"Okay, back to square one," Calvin said. "What do you do if you stare at this thing from now till Friday and you still can't make up your mind?"

I shook my head. "Calvin," I said, "you've got me."

We arrived a few minutes late at the Rue Rameau entrance to the palace courtyard in the midst of a swirl of dark, expensive cars dropping elegant couples at curbside like luminaries at a Hollywood premiere. A few tourists hung about on the sidewalk, not sure what they were watching. Across the street, more comfortably placed at outdoor cafe tables in the Place de la Libération, locals observed the goings-on over carafes of burgundy or chablis. There was even a French TV team that coaxed aside some of the incoming guests (it didn't take much coaxing) for a few words on camera.

The pomp and ceremony came as no surprise. Calvin had spent some time that afternoon with Madame Guyot, Vachey's gallery manager, and learned that we would be dining with an illustrious crowd indeed. Among the hundred invitees were France's most influential art critics, editors, and reviewers, along with some high government officials, including the Minister of Culture himself.

The show, Calvin had told me, was a much bigger affair than we'd thought. In addition to the Rembrandt and the Léger, there were another thirty-four Dutch and French paintings on display; the cream of Vachey's collection. Many were familiar to me. Some were justly famous. As far as I knew, none of them had any controversy attached to them. And all thirty-four would be donated to the Louvre on Vachey's seventy-fifth birthday, the following year—his way of expressing gratitude to the splendid country that had allowed him, the son of an illiterate Lithuanian immigrant, to achieve success far beyond the most fantastic dreams his father had had for him.

Calvin and I, evoking no interest from onlookers or TV people, made it unimpeded through the courtyard to the palace wing that held the old kitchens. There our invitations were taken, and we were bowed through the massive oak door by a liveried flunky straight out of a Thomas Rowlandson drawing—knee britches, lace cuffs, and all.

"This," Calvin said with approval, "is going to be fancy."

* * *

Possibly it seems odd to you that a fancy dinner, thrown by a cultivated and flamboyant man like Vachey, for an exalted crowd like this, should be held in a kitchen, even a palace kitchen. If so, that's because you don't know the kitchens of le Palais des Dues et des Etats de Bourgogne.

These were probably the greatest kitchens the Western world has ever known, surpassing even those of Louis XIV at Versailles because the Sun King, whatever his other attributes, didn't come within miles of the dukes of Burgundy when it came to good eating. It was here, in these kitchens, that the great culinary traditions of Burgundy—of France, really—began in the fifteenth century, with the legendary banquets of Philip the Bold.

They didn't eat in the kitchens in those days, of course, but the old ducal dining rooms are gone now, or rather they, along with the rest of the palace, have been converted to the personal offices of the mayor of Dijon, which is a good deal for *le maire,* but a bad one for the rest of us. Fortunately, with proper French respect for gastronomic history, the kitchens have been preserved, and are still used as a reception and dining area for affairs of state and high society.

They were more than large enough for Vachey's hundred guests, consisting of a huge chamber with pitted stone columns, somber Gothic arches, and a floor of worn stone slabs that looked as if they'd been in place since Philip had laid them down in 1433, and probably had been. Back then, they had been able to roast not merely one but six whole oxen at the same time (and often did), but the six gigantic, vaulted fireplaces along the smoke-blackened walls, each with its own enormous chimney, had since been knocked down to open up even more space.

Inside, people were sitting down to tables of four or six, smooth and elegant in their gowns and tuxedos. Eyes shone, laughter trilled, voices were keen and excited—many of them raised in lively dispute. I heard Vachey ardently praised on one side of me, passionately damned on another. It was impossible not to feel the sense of anticipation in the air, and of privilege. This was the *corps d'élite* of the French art establishment; they knew it very well, and they also knew that they had been invited, almost by right, to an event that would be covered in the world press the next day, and possibly, given Vachey's reputation for dramatics, for some time to come.

Almost as soon as we got inside and paused to get our bearings, I noted a telltale, glittery bulge in Calvin's beady eyes. Following his line of sight, I saw a table at which sat a stern-looking middle-aged man and woman and a flashy younger woman with a wandering eye of her own—Calvin's type, all right—who looked as if she might be their daughter. The fourth chair was vacant.

"Go ahead, Calvin," I said.

He didn't bother pretending not to know what I was talking about. "Well, no, there's only one chair, Chris, and I wouldn't want to leave you—"

"Calvin, will you please go? There are bound to be some other people here I know. I can renew old acquaintances. Besides, I hate it when you drool."

"Well, if you really think so . . ."

And off he went. I didn't think he'd get very far right under mama's and papa's baleful gazes, but with Calvin you could never tell. I was on my way to join a French art professor I knew slightly when a snatch of conversation caught my ear over the general hubbub, probably because it was in English, not in French, and in heavily Italian-accented English at that.

"But aren't the very distinctions themselves simply the old, worn-out objectivist reifications?" the lilting, high-pitched voice was asking. "Surely you agree, ah-ha-ha, that terms such as 'real' and 'false,' 'authentic' and 'inauthentic,' are outmoded constructs whose validity was never more than contingent at best? Surely we can reject out of hand the notion that any field of existence has a 'reality' outside of its own system of reference?"

It may be that there were several people in the world who were capable of uttering such a statement, but I, personally, knew only one: the many-faceted Lorenzo Bolzano, collector-son of a collector-father, adjunct professor of the philosophy of art criticism at the University of Rome, and European editor of the staggeringly abstruse *Journal of Subjectivistic Art Commentary* (to which I had yet to encounter a single, solitary subscriber). The learned Lorenzo was surely the wackiest scholar I knew, with views ranging from mildly laughable to stupefyingly incomprehensible. Hearing his voice wasn't altogether a surprise. Lorenzo, like his father before him, was a longtime and no doubt highly valued client of Vachey's gallery, and I'd thought he might be on the invitation list for tonight's exclusive affair.

And here he was, astride, unless I was mistaken, one of his favorite metaphysical hobbyhorses, the mind-bending notion that there is no valid distinction between an original work of art and a forgery. If you're thinking, so what, that was merely the same thing Vachey had been telling me that morning, then you've missed the gist of Lorenzo's speech. (Don't blame yourself.) Vachey had been probing into the elements of perception that affect our attitudes toward art and forgery. An unsettling topic, considering the situation, but not unreasonable in itself. Lorenzo was carrying things a giant step further, maintaining that there was simply no difference—literally no difference—between authentic art and counterfeit art, and that any distinction we tried to impose was purely artificial, with no aesthetic, empirical, or other foundation.

Did he really believe it? As far as I could tell: yes. That and a lot of other equally goofy ideas. Or maybe he didn't quite believe them, but he was so in love with the words and the crazy, convoluted philosophical mazes they led through that it was the next best thing to believing them.

But if he was a crackpot, he was an amiable crackpot, fun to argue with, unfanatical, obsessed not so much with his cockeyed theories as with the pleasures of argument. He could even be lucid and down-to-earth for long periods—sometimes minutes at a time—and was, moreover, one of the gentlest, sweetest-tempered people I knew, always a pleasure to run into. And there he was, gesticulating over his plate, gawky and hollow-chested, bald and beaky-nosed, his button eyes shiny with the excitement of discourse.

He was at a table with two other men, both of whom I'd met before. One was the stout and self-important Edmond Froger, director of the Musée Barillot, and part-time art critic for the *Revue Critique d'Art.* The Barillot, you may remember, was the small Dijon museum from which Vachey had temporarily stolen—excuse me, had caused to be taken—six paintings, about a decade earlier. That incident, while amusing to many, had never struck Froger's funny bone, and his continuing antipathy to Vachey was no secret. What he was doing there as Vachey's guest was anybody's guess.

The other person was Jean-Luc Charpentier, a member of the *Chambre des Experts d'Objets d'Art,* one of several influential French societies of independent, certified art experts who valuated art objects and issued certificates of authenticity for dealers and auction houses. The *Chambre des Experts* was one of the more prominent of the *chambres* specializing in nineteenth- and twentieth-century European art, with Charpentier's specialty being the latter.

A resolutely crusty and sharp-tongued man, he was at this moment devoting his attention to the *pâté de campagne* that had been laid out on the tables ahead of time, grumbling in an undertone to himself, or maybe to the paté, as he spread it on a slice of bread. Listening to Lorenzo for too long affected different people different ways, and talking to the chopped liver didn't really seem that extraordinary.

As always, a little inattention wasn't bothering Lorenzo. "If, on the other hand," he went blithely on, "we take as our starting point a postexistential, that is to say, a subjectivist and therefore multidimensional perspective, then we see, ah-ha-ha, that 'reality' is no more than a convenient metaphor for a many-layered . . . Christopher! Ha, I heard you would be here!"

He shouted this with a transparent joy that did my heart good, and jumped up, lanky arms outspread. After a clumsy Mediterranean embrace (Lorenzo wasn't any better at it than I was), he herded me to the one vacant chair. "Come, sit, join us!"

Froger grunted at me and extended a hand as I sat down. Charpentier merely grunted.

I watched regretfully as the waiters cleared away the paté before I'd had a chance to taste it, but cheered up when it was followed immediately by hefty but delicate salmon quenelles in a bearnaise sauce, with an artfully arranged border of curled, rosy shrimp. A round of Clos Blanc de Vougeot was poured—Vachey certainly wasn't cutting any corners—and we fell to. In Burgundy, one is expected to pay attention to the food.

But Lorenzo was one of those people who preferred talking to eating regardless of where he was, and in a minute or two he was back at it, gesturing with his fork as if to hurry the luscious dumplings down his gullet.

"Well, then, Christopher," he said, "you're just in time to settle an argument for us."

I laughed, not averse to a little Lorenzian hairsplitting. "What's the argument?" So far I hadn't heard any argument. Just Lorenzo.

"The issue is," he said, "do we defer to a false objectivist contextualism—"

"Objectivist contextualism," I heard Charpentier mutter, head down. Now he was talking to his quenelles.

"—contextualism that persists in confusing its own paltry, artificial system of reference with the universal dynamism of—"

"No, that's not the issue," Edmond Froger said with a burst of impatience. He leaned forward over the table, beefy and aggressive, perceptibly taking over the conversation. "The issue is, what is our friend Vachey up to?"

Lorenzo, who was actually quite easy to cut in on, once you found a place to do it, blinked and fell silent.

"Consider," Froger said. "This is a great day for France, yes? Everyone knows that tonight he will announce the donation of the greatest paintings of his collection to the Louvre. Unquestioned masterpieces all; I admit it freely. A magnificent gesture and worthy of unqualified admiration if that were all there was to it. But what does he do? He decides to use what should be an uncontroversial demonstration of generosity to 'reveal'—that is his word, gentlemen—two previously unknown 'masterpieces' that are by no means unquestioned. These he has kept a jealously guarded secret until tonight. Why has he kept them a secret?"

He paused to eye us all, one by one. No one offered an answer. We knew a rhetorical question when we heard one.

"And he refuses to permit any . . . scientific . . . testing of them whatsoever. *Whatsoever.* I ask you. Why?"

He lifted his wine to his mouth, drinking while he chewed. Small eyes watched us over the rim of the glass.

"I will tell you why," he said, as I hadn't doubted that he would. "They are inauthentic, that is why. Forgeries. I said so from the beginning, I say so now, and I do not doubt that I will say so after they are 'revealed.' I am not an underhanded man; I have said it openly, isn't that so, Jean-Luc?"

"Don't drag me into this, Edmond," Charpentier said crankily. "I'm not as accomplished as you are. I still find it necessary to see works of art before I judge them."

Charpentier's face went along with his manner: wild, beetling, devilish eyebrows that made him look as if he were scowling even when he wasn't; liverish lips that always seemed to be poised on the edge of ridicule or scorn; and a great, fierce, ruddy gunnysack of a nose, frequently used for contemptuous snorting. Despite all this,

I must admit that I had always found him good company. Things rarely remained dull very long with Charpentier around.

Froger eyed him for a moment. "Pah," he said. "The trouble with me is that I say what I think, I don't pussyfoot around just because someone might be offended. Vachey knows very well what I think. It's a matter of public record."

So it probably was. Froger didn't miss many chances to denounce Vachey in the monthly columns he wrote for the *Revue*. I can't say that I blamed him, given the circumstances.

"And just what is he after, our man Vachey?" Froger went on. "Let me tell you what is in his mind." He finished his quenelles, swallowed some wine, and made some pontifical throat-clearing noises while he arranged his thoughts to tell us what was in Vachey's mind.

Oh, I almost forgot to mention: This was, of course, the same Froger Tony had referred to as a horse's ass the other day. One of his more acute assessments, in my opinion.

"To begin, he is an uneducated man, our Vachey," Froger instructed us. "Rich, of course, very rich, and admittedly self-taught to a certain extent, but deeply jealous of those, like ourselves, who have a more profound understanding of art, a better-trained and more disciplined eye. It is the natural envy of the self-made man toward those whose tastes have been developed and refined through the generations. What was his father?" He laughed. "A cutter in a belt factory. A *Lithuanian* belt cutter!"

Lorenzo, who saw no contradiction in being one of the wealthiest men in Florence and a full-fledged egalitarian at the same time, objected in his mild way. "Oh, well, I don't know that I would say—"

On flowed Froger, pompous and oracular. "And so he lays his plans, he licks his chops, he sets his snare. He will show the world who is the smarter. Gentlemen . . ." He paused dramatically. ". . . do not be fooled. Do not fall into his trap. It is you I address in particular, Mr. Norgren."

"I beg your pardon?" My attention had lapsed a bit. Like Charpentier, I was still concentrating on the quenelles. (I wasn't conversing with them yet, however.)

"This so-called Rembrandt," he said. "You're not seriously thinking of accepting it, I hope."

"I might," I said. "I'll decide after I have a chance to study it tomorrow."

He shook his head, writing me off as a lost cause. "And his so-called Léger, to whom is he donating that precious masterpiece? Has he told you?"

"Told me? No."

"You don't know?"

"No."

"I understand he intends to give it to a museum here in France," Lorenzo put in.

"Not if I have anything to say about it," Froger said grimly. "I will do everything I can to prevent it. What the Seattle Art Museum in America does is not my affair. It is France I care for, France, which has always been the custodian of the torch of civilization." His voice quavered with emotion. "I will not stand idly by and see the museums of France mocked and ridiculed. I will not stand by and see our nation's luster tarnished yet again by this buffoon Vachey." His heavy fist thumped the table. Dishes jiggled. Echoes of "La Marseillaise" throbbed in the warm air.

It was too much for Charpentier. "God in heaven," he muttered. "Torch of civilization" . . . "our nation's luster." He wiped his lips with a napkin. He wiped his fingers. He flung the napkin to the tablecloth.

Froger looked at him coldly. "You find the phrases objectionable?"

"My dear Edmond. Who, precisely, placed the torch of civilization in France's care? Where was France's luster' in 1940, when—"

"This," said Froger, turning redder, or rather purpler, "is no way to speak in front of . . . l'étrangers." He cocked his head toward Lorenzo and me, in case anyone wasn't sure who the "étrangers" at the table were.

Charpentier laughed indulgently. "Mr. Norgren, what is your symbol?"

"My symbol?"

"The symbol of your country, your national emblem, the living creature that represents America."

"Oh. A bald eagle."

"An eagle. And yours, Mr. Bolzano?"

"Ah, well, that is not so easy to say, ah-ha-ha. The name 'Italia' derives in all probability from the ancient Romans' term for 'land of oxen'—"

"Yes, good. Eagles, keen of sight and fierce. Oxen, powerful and resolute. Of course. Naturally. And ours?" Charpentier asked Froger? "What is France's?"

Froger eyed him malevolently, his mouth clamped shut, but Charpentier waited him out.

"*Le coq,*" Froger finally mumbled through set lips.

"Precisely," Charpentier said dryly. "*Le coq.*" He picked up his napkin again, shook it out, and replaced it on his lap. "What I would like to know," he said, dropping his chin so that he peered out at us from under those tangled eyebrows, grumpy and droll at the same time, "is just how we can expect the world to take seriously a country that chooses a chicken as its national symbol?"

Lorenzo and I managed (just barely) not to laugh, but the conversation took a decided downturn anyway. Froger was miffed and stayed miffed. Charpentier had but one more contribution to make, informing us in a by-the-way tone that the term *chauvinism* derived from one Nicholas Chauvin, a patriotic nineteenth-century Frenchman. After that he dropped out of things too, to continue communing with his meal, and even the endlessly effervescent Lorenzo couldn't seem to figure out how to get things going again.

The main course didn't help any. Served with a show-stopping, velvety burgundy from the hallowed Romanée-Conti vineyards just down the road, it was Burgundy's best-known gift to fine cuisine, tender and fragrant with the thyme, shallots, and red wine in which it had been simmered.

Coq au vin, what else?

CHAPTER 6

A fter that came the traditional French salad of lettuce with vinaigrette dressing (gorgonzola and walnuts were not options), followed by some local cheeses with which to "finish" the wine, as they say here, and a very pleasant practice it is. Then a chocolate souffle that I was too full to eat, although it hurt me to look at it sitting there in front of me; and finally small, welcome cups of potent black coffee.

Charpentier and Froger were just heaping prodigious amounts of sugar into their coffees—this being one of the few serious defects of the French palate—when someone at the head table, which was located at one end of the room under four mullioned windows paned with ancient bull's-eye glass, called for attention.

A moment later, Vachey's thin, sprightly figure arose at the center of the table. Trim and natty, if a bit archaic in an old-fashioned white dinner jacket, he waited for the chairs to finish scraping on the stone floor as people turned to face him. His eyes, darting over his audience, were no less twinkly than they'd been that morning in his study, maybe more so. For a moment his glance rested warmly on me, and his eyebrows lifted in a quick greeting before he addressed his audience.

"My dear friends," he said in French, his voice lively and distinct, "thank you for joining me on this happy occasion. I know that you are impatient to see, collected publicly in one place for the first time, the most beautiful of the works of art which it has been my privilege to safeguard. ..."

Sauvegarder, I liked that. Not "own" or "acquire," as so many collectors would say, but "safeguard." I knew Charpentier agreed, because I saw his head dip in a minuscule nod of approval.

"... and, of course, the wonderful, newly discovered masterpieces by Rembrandt and Léger, so fortuitously rescued from a dusty and dangerous obscurity."

"Masterpieces," Froger huffed under his breath.

Some people applauded Vachey. Others peered at him in flint-eyed silence. The assemblage seemed to be made up of Vachey-haters and Vachey-lovers in about equal measure, or possibly with the haters having a slight edge. I was getting less sure all the time of which camp I belonged in.

Vachey then asked the Minister of Culture, a smiling but manifestly wary woman named Irène Lebreton, to stand up. With her at his side he publicly pledged to the Louvre, effective on his seventy-fifth birthday, all of the paintings that were on view that evening, "with the exception, of course, of the Rembrandt and the Léger." While flash-cameras clicked and whirred—the photographers and TV people had set up shop in a cleared area in front of the table—Madame Lebreton shook hands with him and accepted politely but guardedly on behalf of the nation. With gifts from Vachey, people knew they had to stay on their toes.

There was further applause, a little more enthusiastic than before, as the minister returned to her chair, stopping first to lean over, shake hands, and say a few words to a smirky, overweight young man who sat on Vachey's other side.

This, Lorenzo told me, was Vachey's son, Christian, who was not currently the apple of his father's eye. He had recently squandered almost all that was left of the fortune he'd inherited from his mother, Vachey's dead wife, in a seamy venture into bauxite mining in Venezuela. Before that it had been a Tanzanian cement factory, and before that a seaweed processing plant in New Caledonia. There was a conviction for tax evasion in his past, and well-founded rumors of associations with the Mob in both France and the United States. For the last decade he'd spent half of each year in Miami, but six months ago he'd given up his house there—two steps ahead of the law, according to Lorenzo—and returned with his tail between his legs to Dijon, where he'd been living on his father's sufferance ever since.

Lorenzo's expression as he explained all this told me that Christian wasn't one of his favorite people. I can't say that he looked especially likable to me either, but I drew no conclusions. Who knows, maybe I wouldn't have looked so likable myself if I'd just had to sit and watch my father give away a few hundred million dollars' worth of what might otherwise have been my own inheritance. I supposed he had a right to look a little sour.

Vachey lifted his hand to quiet the applause. "As to the paintings by Léger and Rembrandt—"

"If they are by Léger and Rembrandt," Froger said, ostensibly to those of us at his table, but his robust bass carried around the room. "For myself—permit me to doubt."

Vachey laughed, seemingly genuinely amused. "That is one point of view, Edmond. I suspect others share it, but I hope you will change your mind after you've examined them."

Froger watched him sullenly, hands clasped on his substantial belly, thick fingers splayed out. "We'll see."

Vachey bowed in his direction. "However, you are certainly right in reminding us that, other than by myself, they have yet to be authenticated. That will soon change, I am sure. As many of you know, Dr. Christopher Norgren of the Seattle Art Museum—"

I stiffened. I'd made it clear to him that I wasn't going to commit myself, and I meant to stick to it. I wasn't going to let him put any words in my mouth.

"—one of the world's foremost Rembrandt authorities—" Lorenzo shot me a wry glance. "Congratulations, Christopher."

I shrugged and kept my peace. I couldn't very well be expected to quibble with every word Vachey said.

"—has come to Dijon in connection with my offer of the Rembrandt to that fine museum. Like you, he will see it tonight for the first time. He will examine it at length tomorrow, at which time I look forward keenly to his evaluation of—"

"Monsieur Vachey," I said, "by the end of tomorrow, it is my expectation that, as an emissary of the Seattle Art Museum, I will be able to provide you with our response to the generous proposal which you have made, but I can say with assurance that I will be unable to come to a conclusion regarding the authenticity of the painting; that is to say, whether or not it can be attributed without qualification to Rembrandt van Rijn. That, as you know, cannot be accomplished without the aid of analytical techniques that are prohibited under the conditions of your bequest."

Sorry about that. I was speaking French, remember. And I was nervous.

My remarks caused a buzz, which I don't think was due solely to amazement at my command of their language. But Vachey himself accepted them affably. "Of course, forgive me. Now then. As to the Léger—"

"The so-called Léger," Froger said with a sneer, pretending to address Charpentier, but his booming voice sounded as if it were coming from the bottom of a well. If he wasn't enjoying himself, he was doing a good imitation of someone who was.

With no sign of rancor, Vachey joined in the mild laughter that followed this. He wasn't having a bad time either. His mood was buoyant and playful; he was practically purring.

"Monsieur Froger, will you do me the honor of coming up here with me?"

Here comes the *"frisson,"* I thought.

"What?" Froger had been caught off guard. He eyed Vachey suspiciously and cleared his throat. "I'll remain here, thank you."

In his place, I'd have been worried too. Whatever Vachey was up to, and I thought I knew, it didn't seem probable that Froger was going to like it.

"As you wish. It is a source of regret, ladies and gentlemen, that relations between Monsieur Froger and myself have not always been cordial. For this I take responsibility. A certain act of mine some years ago"—his voice was grave, but he couldn't keep that sparkle out of his eyes—" was an inadvertent cause of distress to our fine Musée Barillot and its excellent director, Monsieur Edmond Froger. Now I wish to make amends. I do so in the spirit of atonement and the hope of future friendship."

Froger looked as if he doubted it. I doubted it too.

"It is my pleasure to announce," Vachey said, "that the great painting you will see tonight, *Violon et Cruche,* by Fernand Léger, is hereby offered to the Musée Barillot of Dijon as an unrestricted gift. I hope they will honor me by accepting it."

He beamed tranquilly at Froger.

Talk about horns and dilemmas. It hadn't been five minutes since Froger had made it amply and publicly clear that as far as he was concerned the painting was a fake and Vachey was a charlatan, so what could he do now but turn it down? But what if Vachey had sandbagged him, as had suddenly begun to look highly possible? What if it turned out to be genuine? Refusing it would lose Froger the Léger and make him look like a chowderhead besides. Accepting it would get him the painting, but he'd still look like a chowderhead, and a toad-eating one at that. Assuming Vachey's aim had been to put his old adversary in an impossible situation, which I didn't doubt for a minute, it was a masterful stroke.

Froger started stammering. "It's not—I can't—that is to say, it's not my decision to make. My board of directors, which is to say—"

He sputtered to a stop and just sat there, getting redder and angrier, puffing up before our eyes. His features, dainty for his size in any case, seemed lost in the ample flesh of his head, like a too-small face painted on a balloon.

"As for your commendable concern for its authenticity, Edmond," Vachey continued smoothly, "we are fortunate in having with us one of France's preeminent experts in the oeuvre of this towering twentieth-century French master. Monsieur Charpentier, I'm sure we all look forward to your opinion of the Léger—pardon, the alleged Léger—with breathless anticipation."

Charpentier, loading a second small cup of coffee with sugar, looked up puckishly. "Oho. I see. Is this why I was invited? I must perform for my dinner?"

"You were invited because I couldn't imagine unveiling a major Léger without your presence, Jean-Luc, that's all. But it goes without saying that your opinion would be welcome."

"That's most gratifying," Charpentier said, "but my opinions are my livelihood, such as it is; unfortunately, I can't afford to give them away." After a second he added: "Have I ever asked you for a free painting?"

Vachey laughed. "No, and you wouldn't be likely to get it, either. All right, your professional opinion, then."

Charpentier, who had lit a cigarette, took a drag on it and slowly let the smoke drift from the corners of his mouth, scowling thoughtfully at Vachey all the while. "You are asking my professional opinion?"

"Of course. At your usual exorbitant fee."

"Just a moment," Froger said nervously. "I don't know if I'm empowered to authorize funds to—"

"Which it will be my pleasure to pay," Vachey said. "Naturally."

Froger fell silent, chewing his lip.

"I must say," Charpentier said to Vachey, "I'm surprised to be asked."

"Ah, you above all, Jean-Luc. With you, at least no one is likely to assume you are biased in my favor."

There was some history between them, because several people laughed. Charpentier himself, possibly mellowed by the thought of his unexpected fee, allowed himself a smile. "That's true enough, anyway. Very well, then, why don't we have a look?"

"Indeed." Vachey nodded his thanks. "In fact, ladies and gentlemen, why don't we all have a look? My gallery is at your disposal until midnight. There is cognac, champagne, and coffee." He smiled. "And, if you like, a few pictures to pass the time."

* * *

Most of the guests chose to walk the three blocks from the palace to Vachey's gallery. It was an odd sort of postprandial stroll: a straggling, elegant procession composed of groups of three and four threading slowly through the moon-washed Square des Ducs with its pensive, homely statue of Philip the Good, then turning left along the prettily medieval Rue de la Chouette, and right at the Rue de la Préfecture. We moved in a leisurely, relaxed fug of cigar smoke and winey breath, but the conversation was anything but relaxed. People were vigorously dissecting the events of the evening so far, speculating on what was yet to come, or otherwise discoursing learnedly.

A few yards ahead of me, for example, Calvin was launched on a confident exposition of the difficulties of authenticating art.

"Now take Rembrandt, for example, Nadia," he was telling his admiring new lady friend and her not-quite-so-admiring parents. "Do you have any idea how many brilliant students Rembrandt had? There was, let me see, Hoogstraten, Dou, er, Bol ..."

And in my own group, while Charpentier and I walked along in silence, Lorenzo was trying to calm a huffing, chafing Froger by loftily telling him to put aside pride and accept the painting if Charpentier verified it—or even if he didn't, as long as Froger himself found it beautiful. Why should he care whether it was encumbered with such artificial, misleading labels as "real" or "false," which changed nothing whatsoever, being as they were mere perceptual constructs, transitory and equivocal? All one had to do was look at things postexistentially, that was all.

For some reason, Froger did not appear to be soothed.

I wasn't feeling very soothed either. In just a few minutes I was finally going to be seeing the picture, and I was steeling myself for the worst; the worst being that it would turn out to be a colossal dud, nothing more than one of those "Rembrandts" that pop up in the art market every few years with an almost tedious regularity. If they aren't gobbled up by some eager, naïve collector, they are soon denounced, and then hurriedly withdrawn by the profusely apologetic dealers or auction houses that had them up for sale— only to surface again in a year or two, usually through other dealers, sometimes in other countries.

Surprised? You thought that, once a painting was proven to be a fake, that was that? That there must be some legal requirement that it be destroyed, or properly labeled, or *something* to protect unwary future buyers?

Sorry, but no such thing. Fakes are not illegal. You can copy all the Rembrandts you want. You can sign his name to them, you can crackle and darken them so they look old, you can put bogus seventeenth-century stamps and inscriptions on the backs. All perfectly legal as long as it's all in good fun. You can even go around telling people they're the real thing. What you can't do is try to *sell* them as such. That's why prudent forgers never sell their own work directly to the public; it's too easy to prove fraudulent intent. But dealers are another matter. They can be duped like anybody else, after all, and they can hardly be routinely charged with intent to deceive if some of their offerings turn out to be bogus. If the Met can make mistakes, why not them?

So where do you think all those exposed fakes that you're always reading about wind up when all the hoopla dies down? Back in circulation is where. After a suitable time, of course. And eventually, many of them end as the proud property of rich, gullible private collectors all around the world. Not that I thought of Vachey as gullible; not by a long shot. If his new Rembrandt was a phony, and if there was any duping going on, René Vachey was the duper. Guess who that left as the dupee.

At 39 Rue de la Préfecture, a pair of Vachey's minions stood at the door of the house, under Pepin's fussy, darting supervision, to examine our invitations and direct us up to the gallery, or rather to make sure that we didn't stray into Vachey's ground-level private quarters. Upstairs, the folding, linen-covered partitions had been moved back, opening up a sizable reception area in which the guests milled about, sipping brandy or coffee.

Naturally, the only thing I could think about was having my first look at the Rembrandt, but the entry to the main part of the show remained blocked by a table drawn up against the partitions. All that was open was the section on the landing, near Vachey's study: Villon, Duchamp, and the other Cubists. And I didn't have much interest in those. Near the table, Vachey was energetically conferring with his secretary, Marius Pepin, and with a round, fluffy, excited woman in her sixties who Calvin told me was Clotilde Guyot, Vachey's gallery manager. Evidently, the exhibition wasn't quite ready to open.

Restive and eager to get on with it, I snared a balloon glass of cognac from a passing waiter, found a corner by myself, and waited. I'd already prepared myself mentally for being face-to-face with the Rembrandt—the alleged Rembrandt—and I didn't want to have to talk to anyone before I did. The truth is, I was too jumpy for rational conversation, but that didn't bother Calvin, who located me and rattled happily on for what seemed like half an hour. I think he was generously describing for me the attributes of the young woman he'd dined with, or maybe of some of the other women there, but I couldn't swear to it either way. I gulped at the brandy and waited.

At long last there was a businesslike rapping from the front. The table blocking the entrance was moved to the side. Madame Guyot raised her great, pillowy white arms for silence and turned her sunny pink face on us.

"Ladies and gentlemen," she announced breathlessly, "it is my privilege to welcome you to the Galerie Vachey tonight, and to thank you all for coming, and permit me to invite you in to view the paintings, and—wait, please—kindly do not carry your beverages into the exhibition." This was emitted in fluttery French that lacked discernible pauses (no wonder she was out of breath), after which she stepped hurriedly out of the way and behind the table, just in time to avoid being trampled by the herd.

Calvin and I, caught near the entrance with nothing to duck behind, were less fortunate. We were borne helplessly into the gallery, where more partitions necessitated an immediate choice; either go right, into the French wing, which had the Léger, or left into the Dutch wing, where the Rembrandt alcove was. Calvin was swept off to the right with the greater part of the crowd, bobbing along in the flow like a plastic cup in the surf, but I managed to fight my way to the left, where I found myself in a corridorlike space about ten feet by thirty, low-ceilinged and lined on both walls with an orderly procession of seventeenth-century paintings by Dutch masters.

I caught glimpses of a Honthorst, a Bloemaert, a Cuyp, all superb and more than enough to capture my attention under ordinary circumstances, but at the moment they couldn't have interested me less. Like most of the others, I made singlemindedly toward an alcove at the end of the corridor, where the partitions were draped with lush, green velveteen; obviously the place of honor, although its main wall was out of sight, around the corner of the corridor.

But at the last second, I got cold feet. Slipping into a nook just before the alcove, I let the others push by. Now that it had come down to it, I found that I didn't want to look at it, not yet. The moment of truth was at hand, and I wasn't quite ready to face it. For despite the reservations I'd been expressing to Tony and Calvin, and despite the distressing doubts currently being raised about the entire Rembrandt oeuvre, I knew I wasn't really going to need a whole day of analysis, or even an hour. All it was going to take for me to know if the picture on that wall was the real thing was one good, hard look.

I'm not saying that was always the case—not by a long shot, it wasn't—but when it was a painter that I knew as well as I did

Rembrandt, and when I'd just done some heavy boning up, as indeed I had before I left Seattle, then I wasn't going to need very much time—or laser microanalysis or thermoluminescent discrimination, for that matter—to tell me what was what.

Sure, I'd want them for confirmation, but if it took more than three minutes to reach a conclusion, my own conclusion, for myself, I would be extremely surprised. If there was a Rembrandt in that alcove, I would know. If there wasn't, I would know that too.

I let the hubbub in the alcove die down a little, waited for a few people to come out, then took a breath and pushed around the corner. The painting leaped out at me, three feet from my face, brilliant and vivid from its recent cleaning, a handsome portrait of an elderly man. I peered at it, eyes narrowed, mind cleansed of everything else, focusing every ounce of concentration, everything I'd learned from fifteen years of scholarly absorption in Baroque art. I put the buzzing around me out of my mind. I scrutinized the brushwork, the palette, the thousand nuances of style and technique.

After a couple of minutes, I let out my breath and stepped back. I didn't know whether the hell it was a Rembrandt or not.

CHAPTER 7

Well, it wasn't that simple. Not that it didn't look enough like a Rembrandt; the problem was, it looked *too* much like a Rembrandt—but it was the wrong Rembrandt. Not the wrong person, I mean, but the wrong style.

In the seventeenth century it had been a famous witticism that Rembrandt's paints were so thick that you could pick his portraits up by the nose. (His grumpy response had been that he was a *painter,* not some damned dyer.) Ever since, those clotted gobbets of color had been hallmarks of his work, along with the astonishingly free, incredibly sure brush strokes, the somber, reflective atmosphere, the pensive subjects emerging from dim, vague scrubs of shadow into pools of golden light.

When you hear the words "Rembrandt portrait," that's what comes to mind, right? Well, that's what I was expecting too. Reasonably enough. That's what every newly discovered Rembrandt portrait of the last fifty years had looked like, and every phony one too. That was the Rembrandt I'd spent three entire days boning up on.

But this was different, this was in the style of the artist's youth, before he'd become the Rembrandt most of us know, the most famous painter in the world. No fat globs of paint, no looping, spontaneous brushwork. This was early seventeenth-century Dutch painting—in effect, Dutch painting before the mature Rembrandt changed it forever—at its best: clean-lined, highly finished, crisply realistic. And that's what made it so intensely surprising.

Paradoxically, you see, it is the later, greater Rembrandt who is most frequently and most successfully faked. Many a second-rate painting has passed as a Rembrandt if the ochers, browns, and yellows have been slapped on gluily enough, the outlines adequately blurred, and the whole thing done with moody flair. But to imitate the precision of the early Rembrandt takes discipline, not to mention well-honed skills, and those have always been in shorter supply than flair.

So all the prepping I'd done involved Rembrandt's mature style. It had simply never occurred to me that I might be dealing with a spurious early Rembrandt. Naturally, I was thrown for a loop. Who wouldn't be?

And okay, all right, I admit it. Possibly I was—um, er—just a wee bit overconfident going in.

The picture before me was of a weathered, dissipated-looking man in his sixties, with a long nose and a scant, grizzled beard. He gazed sadly out from under a capacious black hat with an enormous plume held on by a glittery gold chain, and a dull-metal gorget over a black tunic. Seedy and stoic, and a little cunning too, his face was the kind you might see today in an inner-city grocery store at eight in the morning, picking over a grimy handful of dimes and quarters to make sure there was enough for a quart of tawny port.

Once believed to be Rembrandt's father, this particular old derelict shows up in at least a couple of dozen oils and etchings done around 1630, not only by Rembrandt, but by many of the Leiden painters, trumped up in sham finery of one kind or another—turbans and fancy helmets, caftans and pseudo-Biblical armor. In this one, according to the white title card beside the picture, he was supposed to be *Un Officier*—a military officer.

As always, he was grave, introspective, and vaguely dazed by all the frippery. Rembrandt had put him in so many pictures that I'd never gotten them all straight. And I'd forgotten which of them had fallen into the "doubtful" category over the years, and which were still believed to be by Rembrandt. They vary hugely in quality, from clumsy sketches to highly finished pieces. And this one, which I didn't remember having seen in the standard *catalogue raisonné* of Rembrandt's works, seemed to me to be right up there with the best of them.

Was it possible that I was really looking at a Rembrandt, then? An unknown Rembrandt? Could something like this have survived unrecognized for almost four hundred years? I realized with a shock that I was half-convinced, maybe more. If Vachey hadn't laid down his prohibition on testing, then I think I might have been wholly convinced.

No, not quite. Those earlier, unsettling "philosophical" remarks of his about forgery and art kept flitting through my mind, which didn't do anything to ease it. Nor did his sticking it to poor Froger earlier, not that Froger didn't have it coming. I couldn't see where I or SAM had it coming, but who could tell with a quirky guy like Vachey?

The thing was, just because it was good enough to be a Rembrandt, that didn't make it a Rembrandt. At the very top of their form, some of his finest contemporaries or best students might conceivably have done something as good as this too. Gerrit Dou, say, or Rembrandt's own teacher Pieter Lastman.

Searching for the signature, I found a simple monogram near the top right margin, where the dull, stony green of the background lightened to an oily yellow: RHL, with no date. That would stand for Rembrandt Harmenszoon Leidensis, which was the way he signed his paintings in the early 1630s, while he was working in Leiden. It was not until 1633 that the name "Rembrandt" first appears on his paintings in the artist's elegant, familiar script.

So the use of the youthful monogram was right on target; there was nothing about it to make me doubt. On the other hand, there wasn't anything there to make me believe, either.

The problem was that the first thing a crook does when he wants to push some handsome old painting by a lesser-known artist as a handsome old painting by a famous Old Master is to get rid of the original signature and put on a false one. All such fakes have signatures. Without them, they have an almost unwinnable battle to be accepted as anything better than "School of X," and crooks don't go to all this trouble to settle for that.

No matter if the painter in question didn't usually sign his name, or if the forger had no idea what the artist's signature looked like. There are, for example, pictures in several private collections, and even one that used to be in a museum, that bear the proud signature *El Greco*—despite the established fact that the painter invariably signed his pictures with his real name, Domenikos Theotokópoulos. In Greek.

So I didn't know anything that I didn't know before.

* * *

By now, the noise, heat, and jostling of the mob in the alcove had started to get to me. I made my way out and back into the reception area, my mind bouncing all over the place. That painting was going to need more study, the back as well as the front, and I couldn't very well do it in that crush. Or even if I could, I didn't want to. Tomorrow I'd have it to myself, and have all the time I wanted with it.

I'd gotten a well-deserved comeuppance in there, and I was no longer sure about being able to carry out the task I'd come for. What did I do if, as Calvin had so happily and repeatedly posited, I looked at it all day and the day after that, and then some, and still didn't know if it was genuine or not? Having seen it, however, at least I knew we weren't being flummoxed with some preposterous fraud. If it was a fake, it was a dandy.

What I needed right then was a little peace to sort out my thoughts, but it was almost as crowded in the reception area as in the gallery. The bar along one wall was open, and by now people had had enough to drink so that the sound level was about where it is a couple of hours into a successful cocktail party. I peeked around a partition to look into the somewhat isolated bay just outside Vachey's study, with the paintings by Duchamp, Villon, et al. To my relief, only one person was in it, a woman in her sixties, who was slumped in one of two armchairs in the center, quietly sipping cognac and contemplating the Duchamp. Near her, on a butler's table, a waiter had set down and forgotten a tray with seven or eight glasses of cognac and a few empties.

By this time I'd decided I could use another glass myself, so I helped myself to one from the tray, offering my companion a perfunctory smile when she glanced at me. I got an uncordial nod in return, but sat in the other chair anyway. If she didn't bother me, I wasn't about to bother her.

The brandy tasted stale and heavy. All the same, I drank most of it down. My mind felt stale and heavy too. Maybe I didn't want to think; maybe I just needed a few minutes of passive contemplation on my own. The far wall of the bay was mostly made up of the glass doors that led into Vachey's antique study, now softly illuminated with indirect amber light, like an interior by Rubens. For a while I let my eyes rest on the furnishings in a mild, pointless, but somehow rewarding bout of covetousness. Then I turned toward the silvery blue Duchamp on the wall a few feet away. I could read the title on the placard: *jeune fille qui chante*. Singing girl.

"You think he's so wonderful, don't you?" The woman said in French, quite loudly.

"I beg your pardon?" I thought she might be calling to someone out in the reception area.

"I said," she replied, staring at the painting and not at me, "you all think he's so wonderful, don't you?"

"Uh . . . Duchamp?"

"No, not Duchamp." She jerked her head to the left, toward Vachey's study. "The upstanding, the virtuous, René Vachey. You all stand in line to kiss his ass, don't you? The great benefactor of society. Yes? Well, I say shit to that."

I began to see why she had the bay to herself.

I also realized that the tray of cognac had not been accidentally left by an absent-minded waiter. It was hers alone, and until I'd arrived to horn in, she'd been making solitary progress through it.

She turned to look at me, a blowzy woman with an awful coppery-red wig and copper-dyed eyebrows tweezed and teased into painfully thin, scanty arcs in which each separate filament of hair could be seen. Dry-eyed for the moment, her face was blotched and out-of-focus from crying, the mascara smeared, the lurid lipstick blurred and off-center. In her hair, on the left side, was a black velvet bow glittering with rhinestones, girlish and pathetic.

"You like him?" she said.

"Uh . . . Vachey?"

"Not Vachey, Duchamp."

The conversation was not improving.

"So?" she prompted. "Tell me. You like that painting?"

"Yes, it's fine," I said, putting down my glass and thinking about going. But to leave now would look too much as if I were fleeing (which I would be), and I didn't have the heart to be rude to this forlorn old woman. No doubt Louis would explain to me that it was me I was worried about, not her—that I was reacting to feelings of guilt generalized from the childhood suppression of aggressive impulses toward my mother, etc., etc.—and maybe he'd be right. Anyway, I supposed I could stand it a little longer.

She gave a little snort. "He likes it fine."

She stood up, a little rocky, and a little top-heavy too; one of those boxy, thin-legged women who put on weight above the waist, not below. Once reasonably steady, she went to the painting and stood beside it, lifting both arms, looking upward, her stretchy red lips parted in what I believe she thought was a carefree expression. When she realized she was still holding her glass, she stuck it in my hand and resumed her stance, expression and all.

"You see?" she said out of the corner of her mouth. I didn't see.

Slowly she lowered her arms. "This picture was made in 1929," she said with simple, slurred dignity. "I am the little girl, the model." Briefly, she struck the pose again. "You don't see it? The line of the arm? The tilt of the head? The expression of childish abandon?"

Now, I don't know how familiar you are with the works of Marcel Duchamp. *Nude Descending a Staircase?* We are talking about the prime mover of Dadaism here, one of the original Cubo-Futurists, the man we all have to thank for Conceptual Art, and this picture was right up there: a swirl of hard-edged overlapping forms like steel plates arranged in a complex spiral. You might be able to find the line of an arm or the tilt of a head if you were willing to be open-minded about it, but an *expression?* Of childish abandon, no less? Not bloody likely.

When I couldn't think of what to say, she gave a sigh of exasperation. "Naturally, monsieur, one changes with time. I am, ah, sixty-eight years of age, as it happens."

Oddly enough, I believed her—not about the sixty-eight, but about having posed for Duchamp. "You knew him then, madame? You were a model?"

"No, no," she said, gratified by the question. "I had an uncle who was Duchamp's chess partner for a time, and he recommended me to the artist as a sitter. Only that once. No, my life was given to music, not art. I was an opera singer. Somewhat before your time, I'm afraid. My name is—" She drew herself up. One of those hairline eyebrows rose as she peeked at me from under lowered lids. "—Gisèle Grémonde."

"Gisèle Grémonde," I repeated wonderingly. "Why, of course. You were famous for . . . wasn't it—"

"My Gilda—yes, that's right," she purred. "And my Violetta."

"Of course!" I exclaimed. No, of course I'd never heard of her, but it seemed like the right thing to do.

Madame Grémonde turned into a prima donna before my eyes, taking back her cognac and re-seating herself as if she were on stage, regal and straight-backed. She finished her glass, picked up another, and gestured graciously toward the tray. "Please help yourself, monsieur."

But it didn't last. As she drank from the new glass, looking over its rim at the Duchamp, her eyes overflowed. Tears slid down her cheeks, leaving two oily tracks. Her mascara, her chins, and her body in the chair all slumped at once. She put down the glass and rubbed at her nose with a damp, wadded handkerchief that had been in her hand all along.

"Do you want to know the truth?" she asked, snuffling back the tears. "Would you like to hear the entire, sad, miserable story?"

I may be a pushover, but I knew I definitely didn't want to hear the entire miserable story. I put my glass on the table. "Madame, I've taken up too much of your time already. I've enjoyed—"

"René has had that painting for over forty years, did you know that? He bought it in 1951, to please me. It hung in his Paris apartment for many years. We used to look at it from our chairs at breakfast."

"At breakfast?" I was caught in spite of myself. "Are you—were you and Vachey—?"

"We were not married, no. Of course, René would have left his wife at a word from me, that was common knowledge, but my operatic schedule would not permit it, you see, and always my art came first. But we were very great friends." Her loose, crimson mouth wobbled, then firmed. "Well. That was some years ago. I bear no malice. Passion runs its course. One moves on to the new."

She laid a heavy hand on my forearm. "But always it was to be mine, this painting, you understand? He promised it to me some day, to *me*. And now I learn he has conveniently forgotten. I learn

..." Her face was mottled with an angry flush. "Why should the Louvre have it? Does a freely given promise count for nothing once love is spent? Is the Louvre in such need of another picture?"

She still had hold of me. I patted her hand clumsily. "Madame—"

"So you see, he's not so wonderful as you think, is he? Oh, yes, and I could tell you a few other things too."

She used my arm to push herself ponderously up. Luckily, I saw it coming, or we both might have wound up on the floor. She leaned heavily against the glass doors to Vachey's study.

"Do you see that book, the blue one on its side, on the end of the shelf there? The fat one? Wouldn't you like to know what's in it?"

"Actually, madame, I think I'd better—"

"I'll tell you, monsieur. The private record of all his 'great discoveries,' nothing less. You follow me?" Her eyes had turned cunning now, and mean. "All of them. Where they *really* came from, what they *really* are. Yes, that's right." With a drunk's malevolent snigger she held up a key she'd dug out of her sequined purse. "You see what I have?"

The key scratched clumsily at the door plate and found the slot. The tumblers turned. The door opened slightly. "Come, I'll show you. Don't be afraid."

Rude or not, it was past time to get out of there. I put on an awkward dumb show of seeing someone I knew near the bar, excused myself, and fled.

* * *

The truth is that I had come within a hair of taking her up. . . . *his "great discoveries"* . . . *where they* really *came from, what they* really *are.* If Gisèle knew what she was talking about, which was hardly a sure thing, everything I needed to know might be right there in that book. All I'd had to do was walk through that door with her and find out. But that kind of unethical adventuring is out of my line. I don't believe in prying uninvited into other people's offices, however virtuous the ends, and, to be honest, I don't have the stomach for it.

I mean, what if I got caught?

As you can imagine, the conversation hadn't done much to ease my mind. I slipped back into the gallery to look at the Rembrandt again. The longer I looked, the fishier it got, but I attributed that to the effects of Madame Grémonde and the cognac. Still, it made me nervous, and I decided again to leave it for tomorrow when I would be both fresh and sober. For now, I wanted to see how Charpentier was doing with the Léger.

Violon et Cruch. A relatively straightforward painting, as Légers go, about two feet by three, of a violin and a jug on a small table against a gaudy background of geometric patterns; squares, diamonds, circles, rectangles. I didn't have a clue as to whether it was real or fake, or good or bad. My impression—and that's all it was in this case; not even a guess—was that it wasn't a bad picture, presuming, of course, that you liked Légers. The colors were bright, the lines clean, the perspective attractively screwy, and the objects entertainingly distorted.

It seemed to me, in fact, to be a rather happy, even comic, picture, but you could never tell that from the sober, expectant group standing in front of it and taking up almost the whole of the alcove in which it hung. They were, I gathered, hoping to be in on a further exchange between Vachey and Charpentier.

The two men stood in a cleared space in front of the painting, Charpentier studying it down his nose, his head thrown back, his arms behind him, hands clasping elbows. Vachey stood beside him, radiating confidence. When I came in, I got a little smile from him.

After a minute or two Charpentier let a long, noisy snort out through his nose, brought his arms from behind him, and reclasped them in front the same way, each hand on the opposite elbow.

"So," he said.

"So?" said Vachey.

Charpentier looked at him with surprise. "You want to hear now? Here, in public?"

"Why not? What do I have to be afraid of? I already know what it is."

"All right. Well, you happen to be correct. I congratulate you. Without doubt, it comes the hand of Fernand Léger."

No one said anything, but you could feel a spark crackle through the room. In a corner I saw Froger looking as if he didn't know whether to yip for joy or to weep.

Vachey smiled at Charpentier, so self-assured—or self-controlled—that not a glimmer showed through of the relief he must have felt. I was impressed. Nobody can be that sure of a painting.

"Not a very good one, however," Charpentier said.

Vachey caught his breath, as if he'd been punched in the chest, then responded hotly. "Not a—not a very good—how can you—"

"Well, what do you expect me to say?" Charpentier out-growled him. "Do you want the truth or don't you? The composition is unsure, the handling of the oils lacks his finest sensitivity, the whole is tentative and unemphatic. It is experimental. Surely, you can see that for yourself. I should say it was done shortly after the war, when Léger was, shall we way, feeling his way toward the more explicitly figurative tradition of his later years. I'd put it at about 1918, or perhaps as late as 1920. It may—"

"Unemphatic!" Vachey burst out. "*Tentative?* I can hardly believe you seriously . . . Just look at it. ... And you call yourself a—" He choked on his words.

"You commissioned my opinion, monsieur, and you have it," Charpentier said sharply. "I don't propose to argue with you about it."

Vachey glared bitterly at him, eyes glistening, mouth clamped shut.

"Now look, René," Charpentier said, unbending just a little, "what we have here cannot be considered a major work by any stretch of the imagination, but as an addition to Léger's known oeuvre, it's not without interest and not without value. If that isn't good enough for you, get someone else's opinion."

Vachey looked as if he wanted to fight it out, but apparently thought better of it.

"Thank you, Jean-Luc," he said stiffly. "Is there anything else you can tell me?"

"Certainly, but not now. I would need more time with it."

Vachey nodded, stone-faced, but after another moment the smile crept back into place, a little crooked now. "Well, the reputation of Jean-Luc Charpentier remains intact. No one can accuse him of hesitating to speak his mind."

"You have a reputation too," Charpentier shot back. "Don't forget my fee."

Vachey joined in the mild laughter that followed this. He was about to say something more when he was stopped by a commotion. Gisèle Grémonde stood near the entrance to the alcove, listing and slovenly, her wig askew.

"You all think he's so wonderful, don't you?" she said.

"Now, Gisèle," Vachey said.

"The generous René Vachey," she said, her voice swelling. "The virtuous René Vachey."

Before she got herself fully in gear I slipped out. Once had been enough.

I don't think I consciously meant to return to Vachey's study, but that's where I wound up; in the isolated bay that fronted it, before the glass doors. The metal bar that slid into the doorframe when the key was turned was still withdrawn. The doors were still unlocked.

Thirty feet away from me lay the thick blue book, seductive and attainable. I peered at it through the glass, irresolute and waffling. Believe me, I was telling the truth before. Skulking uninvited into someone else's office to pry into his private affairs is not something that comes naturally to me. The right course of action, I knew all too well, was to walk away from there and confront Vachey himself about the painting. But I honestly doubted whether I'd get a straight answer. And whatever he told me, could I believe him?

The more I thought about it, the more I realized that I had an obligation, to myself and to SAM, and maybe even to art itself, to see if that book had anything to say about the Rembrandt. Or so it seemed after the two cognacs and the four (five?) glasses of wine I'd had that evening.

I shot one quick look over my shoulder, turned the handle, and walked in. Skulked in.

* * *

This time I didn't worry about the Aubusson. I went directly to the pair of painted eighteenth-century bookcases that stood against the wall behind Vachey's chair. The book lay on its side, next to an intricately tooled set of volumes, on the second shelf of the case on the right, within arm's reach of the chair. It was the blue looseleaf book Vachey had had open when I'd come to see him that afternoon, and as Madame Grémonde had said, it was evidently a scrapbook of some kind, with tag ends of newspaper clippings poking out at the edges of pages made curly and stiff by glue.

Unlike the other books in the case, this was no fancy piece of bookbinder's art. The cover was plain, sturdy buckram, darkened at the corners from use. I glanced furtively over my shoulder again—I must have looked every bit as sneaky as I felt—snatched it up, and took it to a part of the room where an angle in the wall made a recess in front of a set of French windows. There I couldn't be seen from the other side of the door. I lifted the cover.

In the middle of the first page, written in a large, careful hand, was *Les peintures de René Vachey*. There was another line, but the ink was old, and the two parchment-shaded lamps that were turned on in Vachey's study were more for the golden, Rubenesque ambience than for seeing by. I didn't dare turn on the overhead lights, but I did quietly open the curtained French windows to let in some light from the outdoor spotlights that illuminated the courtyard. If Vachey wasn't worried about the effects of urban air pollution on his five-hundred-year-old paneling, I didn't think I had to be either.

I got up close to the windows to let the light fall directly on the page. An unexpected aroma wafted up from it, not of musty old paper, but of something fresh and citrusy. *Collection complète, à partir du 4 novembre, 1942.*

The Paintings of René Vachey. The Complete Collection, Beginning November 4, 1942. Ah, my skulking was justified; there was something here. If there was information about the Rembrandt, I reasoned, it would probably be toward the end, so I flipped quickly—

Something hit me hard between the shoulder blades. The breath burst from my lungs. The book flew from my hands. I shot headfirst through the open windows, tumbling wildly into the night and down toward the old cobblestone courtyard two stories below.

CHAPTER 8

A word about French windows. French windows are built on the order of French doors; that is, they come in pairs, opening on hinges at the sides. However, not being doors, there is no need for them to go all the way down to the floor, and in seventeenth-century buildings they commonly end a little below knee height, at a wide sill that is often used today to hide desirable but unsightly modern improvements such as radiators. On the outside, this sill often extends to make a decorative little balcony, too narrow to stand on, that is surrounded by a low stone or wrought-iron balustrade, also strictly for cosmetic purposes.

Now here's what happened. When the unexpected shove came, I had one foot up on the inner sill, with the book on my knee. This was bad for me, because I was already halfway up and out. It couldn't have taken much to propel me all the way, and out I went. If it's all the same to you, I think I won't dwell on the next half-second or so, when I found myself airborne, with nothing but twenty-plus feet of thin night air between my nose, with which I was leading at the time, and the rough cobblestones, angled cars, and rusty iron gratings below. Suffice it to say that the assertion that the ground seems to leap up at you is discouragingly accurate.

I'm not trying to keep you in suspense, I'm just trying to explain what happened.

Out went my head into the night, yes, and my upper body along with it. Everything, in fact, right down to my ankles, which is where that low balustrade came into play. My feet, you see—the insteps, that is—hooked on the iron railing as I shot over it. So instead of continuing on that long and ill-fated parabola, I pivoted sharply around the railing, swinging back toward the building, head down, with my feet still hung up in the railing above me. Somehow, I was able to ward off the oncoming wall with my left arm while at the same time reaching up with my other hand to grab a wrought-iron curlicue of the balustrade beside my right ankle. For someone who is not ordinarily the world's most coordinated person, it was a hell of a performance—reflex all the way, I assure you. When it got through to me that I was splattered neither on the cobblestones nor against the wall, I reached upward—that is, toward my feet—with a shaky left hand and got a firm grip on some more wrought-iron filigree next to my left ankle. And there I hung, dazed and giddy.

"Hey!" I said.

Don't ask me what I had in mind. I could hardly expect whoever had shoved me out the window to pull me back in, but I had to do something. The blood was pounding in my head, the pressure on my insteps was excruciating, and I didn't think I could hold on to the rough, narrow iron very long.

As expected, there was no response from the study, but at least the guy didn't lean out and start hacking at my grip. I shifted my weight a little and groaned. By some complicated twisting that very nearly dropped me straight on my head onto the stones I was able to rearrange one foot at a time to get the worst of the pressure off them, but my shoulders were starting to burn. I made a try at pulling myself back onto the balcony, but my first movement tipped me so much off balance that I almost toppled off altogether. I yelped, gulped, hung on for dear life, and decided not to try it again. I had never felt more helpless. I couldn't even see; the twin spotlights above the window were blinding.

I shouted again for help, more loudly, but let me tell you, the mind under stress is a peculiar thing. I dreaded being found almost as much as I did letting go. I felt like a complete idiot. I mean, there I was, in my tuxedo, hanging by my hands and feet outside Vachey's window like some bizarre, blind tree sloth, yelling *"Au secours! Au secours!"* It was going to take some considerable explaining.

As it was, the need didn't arise. No one came. I could hear the continuing babble in the gallery, but they couldn't hear me. I was going to fall, then, and I didn't want to do it on my head. While I still had some strength in my fingers I twisted some more and managed to extricate both feet from the balustrade, my arms shaking with the strain. Now I was dangling by my hands, feet down. I thought about trying to swing up and over the balustrade, but I knew I didn't have the strength left. All I could do was hang there, and I couldn't do very much more of that. When I let go it might mean a couple of broken legs, maybe a broken pelvis, but not a broken head. An improvement, but nothing to look forward to.

I tried to remember everything I'd heard about jumping from a height: Keep the muscles loose, bend the knees when you hit the ground . . .

There were footsteps, several sets of them, in the study, and excited voices.

"But there's no one here," someone said in French. "I thought—"

"I'm out here!" I croaked. "I'm—"

"It's coming from outside," another voice said. "Downstairs, the courtyard."

"Let's go," somebody said.

"No, wait!" I tried to call, but they were already running for the stairs, and I couldn't suck in enough air to do it anyway. I knew that I wasn't going to last until they got outside. I couldn't breathe, my arms felt as if they were being dragged out of their sockets, muscles were jumping everywhere, and I couldn't feel my fingers at all. Still, I managed to hang on for another few seconds, or rather my fingers did it on their own, and then, just as I heard my would-be rescuers burst through the doorway below, my grip came undone, and down I plummeted.

No, I didn't land on anyone, although I suppose I might have aimed for them if they'd been within reach. I don't know whether I remembered to stay relaxed (between you and me, I rather doubt it) or to flex my knees. What I do remember is a totally unexpected *whump* as my feet hit, followed by a ponderous, elastic bounce, along the lines of what a 747 does when it hits the runway. My knees flexed—without any instructions from me, thank you—my feet shot out from under me, and I wound up, with another, lesser *whump*, on my behind, there to rock gradually to a stop.

At this stage my mind was far from its most acute, but I was pretty sure that, whatever else might happen when you fell out of a second-story window, you weren't supposed to bounce. Under my thighs I could feel a smooth, cold surface—definitely not cobblestones, but what? I opened my eyes (when had I shut them?), and although still a little dazzled from the spotlights, I saw well enough to realize what had happened.

Those cars. Those two glossy, gray, beautiful Renaults parked in a corner of the courtyard. I'd actually landed on the hood of one— an admirable, wonderful automobile with lovely, well-maintained shock absorbers. No broken legs, no broken pelvis, nothing but a couple of still-quivering arms that felt like tapioca pudding. I started to laugh, not without a shrill tinge of hysterical relief, but pulled myself up short when I remembered the people who had run down to the courtyard to rescue me.

I gathered myself together and turned to look at them. They stood frozen, half-a-dozen of them, arranged along the steps as if in a tableau, all of them staring mutely at me. In the strong, shadowed light of the courtyard, their expressions were easy enough to read: Incredulity. Amazement. Stupefaction. Perplexity.

"Good evening," I said. I slid gingerly off the hood and onto my feet. More *distingué,* don't you know.

Several people blinked. "What the hell is going on here?" one of them asked gruffly, but for the most part they continued to regard me with bewilderment.

And no wonder. They had heard shouts for help from the courtyard. They had rushed downstairs and arrived just in time to hear a couple of resounding *whumps* and to find me sitting on the hood of a car, tittering away to myself while the vehicle rocked slowly to a halt.

I didn't think any of them could have seen the fall itself, because the two side wings of Vachey's house—his study was in the right one—were recessed, some ten feet behind the central part, where the entrance was. I would have been behind them when they burst out, and they would have had to get a few feet out onto the stoop, or even down one or two of the steps, before they could see around the corner and into the recess.

"I thought I heard someone shout for help," I told them. "I came downstairs, but no one was here."

You can imagine how believable that was, but it was all I could think of.

Fortunately, no one asked me why I was bouncing on the Renault. "Maybe it was someone on the street?" a woman suggested doubtfully after a moment. Someone went to the gatehouse, unlatched the wide door, and went out into the Rue de la Préfecture . He came back shaking his head, looking at me oddly. "No, nothing."

They milled around a while, then drifted back inside, muttering to each other and looking at me out of the corners of their eyes. Calvin had arrived with the last of them, and stayed behind, coming up to me when the others had gone in.

"Christ, what happened, Chris?"

"You didn't find my explanation convincing?"

He reached toward my shoulder and tugged on a loose suspender strap. I glanced down. Both clasps had come loose, and the straps were up around my neck. My jacket had popped its buttons, my shirttails hung loose, and my new patent leather shoes looked as if they'd been run over by a tractor. My bow tie was hanging from a shirt stud about halfway down my chest.

"Not real convincing, no," Calvin said. "What the hell happened to you?"

I gave him a brief account.

His eyes, always a bit protuberant, bugged out a little more. "Who pushed you, Vachey?"

"I wish I knew, Calvin."

He looked up at the balcony. "Out of *that* window?"

I looked up too, and cringed.

"Jeez, Chris, are you sure you're okay?"

"I think so. Sort of."

Gently, I tried out my moving parts. Everything worked, even my fingers, although they felt more like claws. I was far from tiptop; my arms were still trembling and flaccid, my shoulders ached and burned, my insteps felt as if they'd been flayed, and my palms had deep, painful, red grooves in them. There was a taste of blood in my mouth from when I'd bitten my cheek as I hit the Renault. Minor, all of it, considering the way it could have turned out, but I felt like hell.

"That book could still be up there," I said. "I'm—"

"You just stay there," Calvin said masterfully. "I'll go."

I didn't argue. "Big blue looseleaf, like a scrapbook," I called after him. "Old."

While he was gone I leaned against the car hood again. There weren't even any dents in it. I patted the metal affectionately. Nice cars, Renaults. Dependable. Trustworthy.

Calvin was back in a minute, shaking his head as he came down the stairs.

"Not there?" I said.

"Nothing. What now?"

"I guess the first thing is to talk to Vachey. Whether he pushed me or not, he knows what's in the book."

"Well, he's still up in the gallery."

I shook my head. "Not tonight. All I want to do right now is crawl into bed. Tomorrow morning I'll tackle Vachey first thing." Cautiously I rotated a shoulder, trying to work out the kinks. "Ow. Assuming I can get out of bed."

"What about the cops?"

"What about them?"

"Well, somebody just tried to murder you. I always thought you were supposed to mention it to the police when that happened."

"Murder me?" Strangely enough, I hadn't thought about it that way. Somebody had wanted either to keep me from seeing what was in that binder or to get it for himself. To do it, he—I didn't think it was a woman; I'd been pushed with a lot of force—had found it necessary to shove me through an open window. That was as far as I'd thought it out.

"You're right," I said after a moment, "but I don't think I will."

"No cops?" he said incredulously.

"Well, not until I have a chance to talk to Vachey first."

"You're crazy."

"Look, Calvin, how do I explain what I was doing in Vachey's study? Would they even believe me?" I tapped my curling shirt front. "I look like a joke version of a lush, and I must smell like a winery. Can you see me telling them about being shoved out the window by someone I didn't see, and hanging off the balcony by my feet, and then landing on the car?"

"Well, it does sound a little—"

"You know what they'd say: 'Hmm, you 'ave 'ad per'aps a leetle wine to drink zis evening, monsieur?' Accompanied by a friendly wink."

"You got a point. And think about what the papers would do with it if they got hold of it: 'Seattle museum official mysteriously flung from window while rifling art collector's office.'" The prospect clearly amused him.

"I'm going back to the hotel," I told him wearily, pushing away from the car.

"I'll walk you," Calvin said. "You look a little shaky."

"You don't have to walk me. I'm not shaky."

But I was. We had only gone a few yards down the Rue de la Préfecture when I realized seven blocks was going to be too much for me. Luckily, there was a taxi stand at the first corner.

"Hey, I just realized," Calvin said as we settled into the back seat. "It wasn't Vachey,"

"What do you mean?"

"Vachey didn't push you out any window. When I came down, he was still standing in front of the Léger, trying to calm down the crazy lady."

"Good," I said.

"What do you mean, good?"

"I don't know what I mean. I guess I'm glad it wasn't him, that's all."

"Yeah, he's a likable old coot. But there's something about him . . ."

"I know. Well, I still want to start with him tomorrow. I think the first thing is to find out what's in that scrapbook."

"I'll go with you."

"Calvin, you don't have to go with me."

"I know, but what else do I have to do? What time, eight o'clock?"

I shuddered. "God, no. I'll call you when I get up. Maybe ten."

The cab pulled up in front of the Hôtel du Nord. I got out somewhat creakily; I'd begun to stiffen up.

"Don't forget to call me," Calvin said.

I leaned on the doorframe. "Look, Calvin, nobody's going to try to kill me tomorrow morning, if that's what you're worried about. There's no reason to. And I think I'd do better talking to Vachey alone."

Calvin heard me out. "Just call me, okay? Better yet, I'll call you. Ten o'clock."

"Okay, all right." I straightened up. "Tell me something, will you? Did Tony ask you to watch out for me or something? To make sure I didn't do anything dumb?"

Calvin tilted his head to one side and gave me his most rabbity grin. "You got it," he said.

* * *

Ordinarily, I kept clear of the hotel elevator, a rickety birdcage high on charm but low on everything else. Tonight, however, I was grateful to clank falteringly up to the fourth floor in it. Once in my room, I took a couple of aspirin, checked myself over for cuts (none) and abrasions (some), and got into a hot bath in which I soaked dreamily for three-quarters of an hour, drifting in and out of a doze.

It was after 1:00 a.m. when I climbed out, soothed but utterly washed out. I left a wake-up call for 9:30, and sank into the pillows.

At 7:50 the telephone rang. I got one eye open and glowered at it. On the fourth ring I got my muscles working and reached for it, growling something into the mouthpiece.

"Hiya, Chris." It was Calvin. "Did I wake you up?"

"It's not ten o'clock," I said.

"Listen," he said, "there's something in the paper I want to show you."

"Show me at ten."

"I'll be there in fifteen minutes, okay?" I gave up.

"Okay, but bring some—"

"'Bye."

The telephone clicked. "—coffee," I finished lamely.

I took another couple of aspirin from the bottle on the nightstand, got into a hot shower to loosen up my creaky joints, and shaved and dressed. Physically, I was feeling better than expected; aside from the predictable stiffness, the only parts of me that were still really sore were my insteps, just in front of the ankles, where, pressed and scraped against the wrought-iron grillwork, they'd borne most of my weight. It felt as if the bones themselves were bruised, and no wonder. I was sitting on the sofa, babying them by slipping my feet into a pair of disreputable but roomy jogging shoes, when Calvin came in.

"Well, nobody's going to have any trouble telling you're an American," he said, eyeing the shoes. "As far as I know, Velcro straps have yet to make it to the French fashion scene."

"Nobody has any trouble anyway," I said sourly. "What's up? What am I doing awake at 8:15?"

"Here," Calvin said brightly. "I figured you'd need a fix." He handed me a huge cardboard cup, milk shake-sized, of *café au lait.* "Picked it up on the way." He'd brought a smaller one for himself.

I brightened immediately. "Calvin, I apologize for what I was thinking about you."

"No problem," he said, and sat in the single wooden side chair with his cup while I got the lid off mine, inhaled the aroma, and had a long, milky, rehabilitative swallow.

"Now," I said, restored to my usual good humor, "what did you want me to see in the paper?"

He handed me a copy of *Echos Quotidiens—The Daily Gossip—* one of the livelier French tabloids. "Page one, bottom right. You're going to love it."

From his tone, I had my doubts. I turned to the article.

"PEINTURE DE MON PÈRE VOLÉE PAR COLLECTIONNEUR!" the headline blared. *My Father's Painting Stolen by Collector!* Underneath, the subheading was: *René Vachey a Tool of the Nazis, Saint-Denis Man Claims.*

"Christ," I muttered. "What a hell of a time for this to happen."

"It gets better," Calvin assured me. "More pertinent, you might say."

My misgivings increased. I read on.

In an exclusive interview with *Les Echos Quotidiens,* Mr. Julien Mann, a Paris Metro worker, has made a series of sensational charges against controversial Dijon art dealer and philanthropist René Vachey. Chief among them is the allegation that a Rembrandt painting recently donated by Mr. Vachey to the Seattle Art Museum is in reality a painting by Govert Flinck, which Mr. Vachey appropriated from Mr. Mann's father under conditions of extreme duress, during the German Occupation of World War II.

"Aargh," I said.

Calvin shrugged. "Told you."

With a sigh I leaned back against the sofa, took another draught of the coffee, and continued.

According to Mr. Mann, Mr. Vachey was at that time the owner of the Galerie Royale, located in Paris's Place des Vosges. As such, he bought up Jewish art collections at forced, greatly depressed prices, then sold them to Nazi buyers for removal to Germany at substantial profits to himself.

I lowered the paper. A slow shudder slithered down between my shoulder blades. René Vachey a Nazi collaborator, and a particularly vile one at that? I could hardly make myself think about it. A rogue, sure; a con man, no doubt about it; a humbug, well, yes, a little of that—but a beast who would fatten on the horrible plight of the Jews under the Nazis? With all my heart I hoped it wasn't so. I turned back to the article.

Mr. Mann claims that the alleged Rembrandt painting now in the possession of the Seattle Art Museum was purchased in this way from his father in 1942 for a price of 20,000 Occupation francs, less than one-hundredth of its actual value. This is in sharp contrast to Mr. Vachey's assertion that he purchased the painting at a Paris antique shop in 1992.

"It was the same thing as stealing it," Mr. Mann told our reporter bitterly. "Like Jewish families throughout France, we were desperate and persecuted, our rights gone, our possessions stripped. What choice did we have? If we had not 'sold' the painting to Mr. Vachey, the Nazis would have taken it at will. It broke my father's heart to part with it. My father was not a rich man, not a collector. He was, like me, a government employee. The picture was the only thing of value we owned. It had been left to him in 1936 by an aunt in the Netherlands. It hung in our living room. I grew up with it."

The painting, according to Mr. Mann, who was a child of seven at the time, is a portrait of an old soldier known to be by the seventeenth-century minor painter Govert Flinck. When asked how it was that Mr. Vachey and the Seattle Art Museum were now ascribing it to Rembrandt van Rijn, he replied: "You would have to ask them that."

Mr. Mann says he believes that the painting rightfully belongs to his family, and that he plans to press charges against Mr. Vachey in criminal court and to vigorously pursue the recovery of his property. He says he will gladly refund Mr. Vachey the 20,000

Occupation francs. In today's currency this would amount to 125 francs.

Our investigators have confirmed that it is also true that Mr. Vachey managed the now-defunct Galerie Royale during the German Occupation. Rumors of his dealings with Nazi officials have been heard before, but *Les Echos Quotidiens* believes that this is the first time specific allegations by an aggrieved party have been made. Whether proof is forthcoming is yet to be seen.

Proof. I raised my head. "That scrapbook," I said slowly. "It would have covered the acquisitions he made during the Occupation. It would have covered this."

"Maybe, maybe not," Calvin said. "You're not going to know until you talk to Vachey."

"Maybe that's what somebody didn't want me to see."

Calvin spread his hands. I lifted the paper again.

Mr. Vachey, who was involved some years ago in a spectacular court case stemming from his admitted theft of paintings from the Musée Barillot in Dijon, has refused comment to our reporters. Seattle Art Museum officials in the United States have likewise been unavailable for comment.

Les Echos Quotidiens believes it is in the public interest to continue its investigation into this matter. Mr. Mann's accusations raise serious questions about Mr. Vachey's recent gift to the Louvre of 34 paintings purported to be by various French and Dutch masters from the seventeenth to the twentieth centuries.

We will remain on the job!

I put down the newspaper, went to the high window, leaned my elbows on the sill and my chin on my forearms, and stared out at the ancient, narrow towers of Saint-Bénigne, drenched in clear morning sunlight.

"Who in the hell," Calvin said to the back of my head, "is Govert Flinck?"

CHAPTER 9

G overt Flinck (aka Govaert Flink), b. Cleves, 1615; d. Amsterdam, 1660.

Or maybe it was 1670. Either way, I told Calvin, he was bad news. Flinck had been another of Rembrandt's students. Not as famous anymore as some of the others have become, but well-known in his day, and—this was the bad news—particularly gifted in imitating the style of his master, as anyone who has seen his portrait of Rembrandt in London's National Gallery can attest. So gifted, in fact, that long after he left the workshop, he was going around selling his own paintings as Rembrandts. And getting away with it.

Had he been capable of painting the portrait in question, Calvin wanted to know.

That was the question, all right. Flinck had been a fine artist, good enough to take commissions away from Rembrandt—on his own merits—in the 1640s. There were pictures of his not only in the National Gallery, but the Met, the Louvre, and the Hermitage. When he'd been on his form, not too many of his contemporaries could beat him.

"Well, I'll need to look at it again," I said, "but I'd say that, at his best—his absolute best—probably, he could."

And was I capable of telling if he had? Calvin persisted.

"I don't know. Maybe."

"Jeez," said Calvin, "this thing isn't getting any tidier, is it?"

"You know, Calvin," I said, still looking out the window, "this question of who did or didn't paint that picture doesn't seem quite so important anymore. We've got a bigger problem to worry about now."

He looked up, squinting against the sunlight. "Who owns it, you mean. Can this guy Mann prove his case?"

"Exactly."

A lot of claims like this one had been made in the fifty years since World War II. Some had been won, but many more had been lost. For one thing, the more time passed, the harder it was to prove anything about anything, particularly when it involved the Occupation, an era that everyone would like to forget. For another, not everybody who made a charge like this was honest. Crooks and poseurs had gotten in on it, as on anything else where big money was involved, and as a result the rules of evidence had gotten very strict. Moreover, French law made it extremely difficult to get anything done about a crime committed more than thirty years ago. For that matter, what crime had Vachey committed? Mann himself said the painting had been bought, not stolen, but on the other hand …

"No," I said, turning from the window with a sigh, "who am I supposed to be kidding? The question isn't how good a case he can make, the question is, do we—Tony, you, me, the SAM board—want to get into the middle of a disputed ownership contest, especially one like this?"

"I don't see that we're in the middle of it," Calvin said. "This is between this guy and Vachey. Where do we come into it?"

"We come into it because we have to decide whether to take the painting or not. If we do, then it's us he'll have to make a claim against to get it back."

"So? Let's say the courts say it's rightfully his. That's that, he gets it. There's no problem. Nobody at SAM is going to fight him on that, Chris. You know that."

"Sure, but say he loses. Maybe it's not 'technically' his. Maybe his story doesn't stand up to the rules of evidence. What difference would it make? Regardless of what the courts decided, would we want it as long as we thought there might be any truth at all in what he says?" I shook my head roughly. "I don't know, the whole thing has turned so … so ugly—I'm starting to think we don't want anything to do with it."

Calvin put his coffee down on the end table and came to stand with me at the window. "Now, listen to me for just a minute," he said firmly. "You're jumping to conclusions. Why don't you just do your job and wait and see what happens? Even if this guy thinks he's telling the truth, that doesn't mean that's the way it was, you know. He was, what, seven at the time? So the chances are he's repeating things he heard from his father, not things he really remembers for himself."

This was Calvin earning his keep, Calvin the realist, the hard-headed M.B.A. snapping the muzzy, oversensitive art historian out of his funk and putting him back on track. Or trying to.

"That doesn't mean they aren't true," I said stubbornly.

"Look, Chris, how could he even know what Vachey's picture looks like? Vachey kept it a secret from everybody. Hell, we were the ones he was giving it to, and he wouldn't even let *us* see it ahead of time. Unless Mann was one of those hundred people there last night, which he wasn't, there'd be no way for him to have any idea if this was his father's painting or not. I'm telling you, the guy could be inventing the whole thing. He's probably just another crook." He grinned. "Think positive."

I drained my coffee and smiled back, but thinking positively was more than I could do. There was a queasy sensation deep in my chest, as if my stomach had shifted up where it didn't belong. The Rembrandt—the Flinck?—had been fishy enough from the beginning, and getting myself shoved out of a window hadn't improved my attitude about it. But now it was tainted with something genuinely repugnant. As much as I didn't want to believe Mann's story, it sounded like the truth. I didn't want to be involved in it, and I didn't want my museum involved.

"I'm going to call Tony and recommend that we forget it," I said.

"Well, you're not going to call him now. It's the middle of the night in Seattle. Listen, we were going to see Vachey this morning anyway. Why not put this Nazi thing to him and see what he says?"

"Calvin, it doesn't make any difference what he says. There's too much. I just want out. I have a lousy feeling about the whole—"

"Christ, give the guy a chance to defend himself, Chris. What can it hurt?"

I shrugged. He was right, I supposed. "All right, you're—" The telephone rang.

"This is Monsieur Norgren?" the unfamiliar voice asked in French.

I said it was.

"Of the art museum in Seattle?" I said it was.

"Very good. I am Sergeant Huvet of the Police Nationale. It would be helpful if you could come to the Galerie Vachey on the Rue de la Préfecture at ten o'clock. Is this convenient?"

I frowned. "Does this have something to do with—with what happened last night?"

"Pardon?"

"What is this about, please?"

"It is concerned," the sergeant said with businesslike detachment, "with matters proceeding from the death of Monsieur René Vachey."

* * *

Vachey had been found dead early that morning, the sergeant explained, in the Place Darcy, a small park near the center of town. The cause of death appeared to be a gunshot wound.

"You don't mean—do you mean he was *murdered?*"

"So it would appear."

That was as much as the sergeant would tell me. "You will be there at ten o'clock, monsieur?"

I told him I would.

"Your associate, Monsieur Calvin Boyer—he doesn't answer his telephone. Perhaps you know where we could reach him?"

"I'll have him there for you," I said numbly.

"Very good."

I sat slowly down on the bed, my thoughts tumbling.

"*Who's* murdered?" Calvin asked.

"Vachey," I said. I told him what little I knew, and sat there staring at my clunky jogging shoes.

"We better get going," Calvin said when I'd finished. "It's nine-fifteen.

We talked about the murder on our walk to Vachey's house, of course. Not that I remember much of it. I seemed to be functioning in a near stupor; a sort of jumble-headed reverie. How could he be dead, I kept thinking. Hadn't I seen him only last night—what, nine, ten hours ago?—and hadn't he been sparkling with life, rascally and genial? How could he be dead this morning? I found myself mouthing the question without meaning to: How could he be dead, how could he be dead?

"Look, Chris," Calvin said with some exasperation, "that's the way it works. A guy's alive, and then he's dead."

"I know, but—yeah, I know."

We stopped at a cafe on the Rue Musette for another *café au lait* and some croissants, which helped to settle my thoughts, but still left me sick and empty, dreading having to talk to the police. I suppose some of my reluctance came from realizing that I was going to have to tell them about my ill-thought-out incursion into Vachey's study; mostly, though, I just hated to think about him dead. Shot. I didn't know where he'd been shot, or how many times, or anything else about it, and I didn't want to know. I hadn't thought to ask if an arrest had been made. I just didn't want to accept it.

I had finished eating before something dawned belatedly on me. It didn't matter what I recommended to Tony; the business with the Rembrandt was over. Vachey had died without our meeting his conditions, so the gift could be valid. The picture belonged to whoever would have gotten it on Vachey's death if he hadn't decided to give it to us. The same went for the Léger. If that meant his son, Christian, which I supposed it did, then somehow I didn't think they were ever going to wind up on the walls of the Barillot or SAM.

Calvin nodded his agreement. "I think you're right. Unaccepted offer dies with the offerer, that's the way it works. Let's hope the Louvre has something on paper for its share."

"I hope so."

Actually, at this point I didn't much give a damn. I felt rotten.

At my instigation we dawdled—well, procrastinated—over a moody second cup of coffee, and arrived at the gallery five minutes late.

CHAPTER 10

We had assumed we were coming in for interrogation, but that wasn't it at all. This was a group affair, held in a large, sparsely furnished room at the back of the daylight basement, below Vachey's living quarters. Part storage area, part office for Marius Pepin, Vachey's secretary, the room had several irregular recesses in which were objects ranging from mattresses on their sides and folded card tables to broken Roman statuary. In the central area seven people sat in assorted chairs that had been arranged in a rough semicircle to face a plain wooden desk. A spare, balding man sitting to one side and a little behind the others motioned us with an imperious little snap of his fingers toward the only available seats, two folding metal chairs on the far right.

I nodded to Clotilde Guyot, Vachey's gallery manager, who was sitting next to me clutching a balled handkerchief, her round face blotchy from weeping. Next to her was Froger, showing no signs of tears over the demise of his old adversary. He did look a little sickly, however; probably because he'd come to the same conclusion we had about the fate of the two paintings and was mourning his lost Léger. Beyond him was Vachey's son, Christian, looking like a man nursing a hangover. He had taken a bottle of mineral water from a side tray and was rolling it, unopened, against his temple. Pepin was next to him, jumpy and distracted, and after him was a man I didn't know but whom I'd seen at the head table the previous evening.

Gisèle Grémonde, without her wig, without her gaudy makeup, rounded out the half circle. She was vacantly twisting her fingers, looking utterly shaken. Of course, she had drunk enough cognac

to shake an elephant not so many hours before, but it went beyond
that. I barely recognized the former opera star. She sat like a heap
of old meat, boneless and shrunken. With her thin gray hair and
gray, collapsed face she looked a hundred years old.

"I think we can begin now," the balding man said in a cool, nasal
voice when we'd sat down. "Everyone speaks French? Good. I am
Chief Inspector Lefevre of the Office of Judicial Police. I shall be in
charge of conducting the investigation into the death of Monsieur
René Vachey, as most of you already know."

"I want to know why I was summoned here," Froger said.

Lefevre ignored him. "When I learned that Monsieur Sully
planned to meet with the legatees of Monsieur Vachey's will before
some of them—that is to say, some of you—found it necessary to
leave the area, I asked to attend. I apologize for the necessity of
intruding at this sad time."

He crossed his legs and settled back. "Monsieur Sully—if you
please?"

Monsieur Sully was seated behind the desk. Plump, capon-
breasted and silver-haired, he wore an expression suggestive of
feathers that had been severely ruffled.

"That is not quite accurate, Inspector," he said, irritably fingering
a few handwritten sheets of lined white paper in front of him. "I
would like it to be understood that this gathering was instigated
by you. I am complying with your instructions, but I wish it to be
known that I consider it premature and highly irregular."

Lefevre gazed impassively back at him. "As you like."

"I also wish you to make it clear that if anyone prefers to leave,
he is under no compulsion to remain. I will contact all concerned
persons in due time."

"Certainly," Lefevre said. "All who wish to go are free to do so."

No one moved.

Lefevre looked steadily at Sully. "You have done your duty,
monsieur. Proceed."

Sully cleared his throat. "As some of you are aware, I am Charles
Sully, Monsieur Vachey's attorney of many years. All of you are
here because you are concerned in one way or another with the
estate of René Vachey."

Calvin and I exchanged surprised glances. What did that

mean? Were we in Vachey's will? Was it possible that he had actually *bequeathed* the Rembrandt to us, something I hadn't even considered? From the corner of my eye I saw Froger perk up; apparently his thoughts were running along similar lines. To my surprise, I felt my own attention quicken. Despite everything that had happened, apparently I wasn't as disinterested in the Rembrandt as I'd been telling Calvin—and myself.

"I must tell you," Sully went on, "that at this point I can relate to you only certain of the more significant provisions of Monsieur Vachey's will. The document is complex, and I do not have a copy with me. The original is in a Credit Lyonnais safe deposit box in Paris, for which Monsieur Vachey and I are joint signatories. It was placed there upon its completion in January of this year—"

"January of last year," Christian Vachey said.

The younger Vachey wasn't as young as I'd thought at dinner the previous night, when I'd been fooled by a softly rounded chin, smooth baby-cheeks, and an adolescent smirk. Seen up close he was well into his forties, a husky, laid-back, Hollywood ish kind of man with dark, curly, blow-dried hair that came down almost to his shoulders in back and hung in a Superman forelock in front. He was wearing a sharp double-breasted gray suit with no tie, but with his white shirt buttoned up to the collar. A gold earring in the form of a cross with a loop for its upper arm—the Egyptian *ankh* sign—dangled from his left ear.

Sully paused. "No, this year."

"No, last year. I think I ought to know, don't you?"

"I think *I* ought to know, monsieur," Sully said, "and I assure you it was January of this year."

"Now look—" Christian began, then stopped abruptly, and flapped his hand. "The hell with it. It's not important enough to argue about." But a vivid, nickel-sized red spot had leaped out on each cheek.

What do you know, Inspector Lefevre had gathered his first piece of information, assuming that was what he was there for. René Vachey had redrafted his will and hadn't told his black-sheep son about it. More than that, the will was in a safe deposit box that his lawyer could get into, but not his son. Interesting.

I frowned. Now why the hell should I find that interesting?

Was Vachey's murder beginning to nag at me, now that the initial numbness had passed? Was I looking for conflicts, motives, sources of friction?

Yes, I supposed I was. René Vachey had quickly grown on me. The accusations of Julien Mann had been unsettling, but they hadn't changed the way I'd reacted to the man as a person. I'd genuinely liked Vachey; he'd been a one-of-a-kind. I was sorry he was dead, and I wanted to know who had killed him. What was so strange about that? It hadn't escaped me, either, that in some way— through the blue scrapbook, perhaps, or the gift of the painting—I might be indirectly involved.

I looked over at Lefevre, who watched the exchange between Christian and Sully, observant but noncommittal.

Sully smiled smugly at Christian and went on. "In it he designated a number of bequests to legatees not in this room. The largest such bequest is for equal shares of some two hundred fifty thousand francs for his deceased wife's grandniece Astrid, residing in Switzerland, and his deceased sister's son, Armand, who lives, I believe, in Lille."

He went on in this vein for a while. There were bequests to Vachey's barber, to a bird sanctuary, to various charities. Sounds of fidgeting increased. I was getting a little restless myself.

He moved the top sheet aside. "Now, let us come to those beneficiaries, or their representatives, who are present this morning."

That took care of the fidgeting.

"First, the collected art works. The bulk of René Vachey's personal collection, some thirty-four paintings in oil and tempera, are willed to the Louvre. These are the same paintings now on display in the gallery above us, and which Monsieur Vachey announced as an intended donation last night." He looked up at the man on the end, the one I didn't know. "Do you have any questions, Monsieur Masseline?"

Ah. Jacques Masseline, chief curator of paintings at the Louvre. Silently, he shook his head.

"Congratulations," Christian said. "I'm very happy to see my father's collection go to the nation."

I had my doubts about how delighted he was, but I got the

impression that at least he wasn't surprised—which suggested that it had been in the earlier version of Vachey's will too.

Sully fingered a smaller piece of paper that lay among the others. Torn from a spiral-bound pad, it had a few scrawled lines written diagonally across it. For a moment he looked indecisive, then gathered himself together and spoke.

"There is, however, something which I feel must be mentioned here. Last night, quite late, René—Monsieur Vachey—took me aside. He said to me that he had been reminded of an obligation to an old friend, one he should never have forgotten, and he wished to meet it, though it would mean reneging on a more recent one. I was to act on it when I returned to Paris.

Inasmuch as I am not as conversant as I might be with all his paintings, he wrote down the following."

He lifted the torn sheet, cleared his throat, and read aloud: "'Duchamp's *Jeune fille qui chante*—remove from Louvre bequest, present to Gisèle.'" He put the slip down. "He was referring, of course, to Madame Grémonde."

Everyone looked at her. She stared blankly back, still wringing her hands. I wondered if she knew where she was.

After a second, Christian spoke through a slack and unconvincing smile. "I don't think I'm hearing right. Are you actually saying we're supposed to treat that scrap of paper as a legal document? I don't mean to spoil the fun here, but can I call to your attention the fact that we're talking about a major work of art, not some sentimental little piece of bric-a-brac? Look, my father had about six drinks too many last night—"

"Pardon me, monsieur, but I don't see that it's your affair," Sully shot back at him. "However, I agree that this paper is not legally binding: It is unsigned and unwitnessed." He looked at Masseline. "But I can assure you, monsieur, and would be happy to so attest, that it was his intent that Madame Grémonde have the painting."

"Madame Grémonde?" Gisèle repeated dully.

"And the Louvre will honor that intent," Masseline said straightforwardly. From his chair he gave her a gallant half-bow. "With great pleasure, madame."

"I . . . the Duchamp?" Gisèle whispered, and when Sully said, "Yes, madame, the Duchamp," her eyes overflowed. Pepin, next to her, commendably extended his clean, folded handkerchief. When she took it and blew her nose into it, he winced.

I settled back in my chair with what is usually referred to as a warm glow, the last thing I'd expected to feel that morning. Well, good for you, René, I thought.

And good for you too, Masseline. And Sully. My feelings toward Christian were less benevolent, but I could understand his reaction. Not many children are generously inclined toward their fathers' paramours.

"Now then," Sully said crisply, getting us back on track. "My client has left the Galerie Vachey, including its inventory, receivables, and furnishings to Clotilde Guyot, in appreciation—"

Beside me, Madame Guyot put her balled handkerchief to her mouth. "No, are you serious? I had no idea—why, I can hardly believe—never once did he cause me to think ..."

"You are surprised?" Inspector Lefevre asked; rather unnecessarily, it seemed to me.

"Why, yes, I'm ... I knew nothing of a new will. I had always understood that the gallery would go to . . ." She blushed and faltered. "That is to say, it was understood from the beginning that Monsieur Vachey had intended the gallery to go to . . ."

Christian bailed her out, lifting his arms and bowing his head in a mocking imitation of someone accepting applause. There was about Vachey's son an unappetizing slickness, the glib smoothness of a Las Vegas lounge performer working the early-bird, senior-citizen show.

Sully picked up the thread again. "In addition, Monsieur Vachey has granted you the continuing use of the gallery's existing premises in this building for a period of up to one year. He also expressed in his will the hope that you would continue to employ Monsieur Marius Pepin in his current capacity. This is not to be construed as legally binding, but only as—"

"Employ Marius?" She laughed. "But of course I will. It's impossible to imagine the Galerie Vachey without dear Marius—" She seemed to realize that she was sounding a bit bubbly for the occasion, and toned things down. "I shall be happy to continue the association of the Galerie Vachey with Monsieur Pepin," she said gravely, but still glowing, "assuming this is agreeable to him."

"I would be honored to continue, madame," Pepin responded primly.

Inspector Lefevre addressed him. "You were Monsieur Vachey's secretary?"

"His secretary, yes. I was also responsible for—for the security of the collections."

A brief, nasty bark of laughter came from Froger. I looked at him, surprised.

So did Lefevre. "Something amuses you, monsieur?"

Froger shook his head and waved him off. Lefevre didn't press it, but I could see him make a mental note. He would press it in his own time, I thought. Pepin, looking resentful, kept his eyes on the floor.

"Let us continue," Sully said. "Except for the bequests mentioned earlier, the residue of Monsieur Vachey's estate is willed to his son, Christian. This includes the residences in Dijon and Paris, and personally owned works of art not otherwise designated."

So Christian was going to do all right, after all, if not quite as well as he'd hoped. I looked over at him. He was about as expressive as a slug.

Sully sat back. "And those are the provisions of the will insofar as they are pertinent to those present." He gathered up the papers and put them in an attache case.

"Why was I summoned here?" Froger demanded curtly. He had been looking more and more impatient as the session had gone on, sighing and huffing and twisting in his chair. I hadn't been sighing or huffing, but I was starting to wonder the same thing.

"I'm coming to it," Sully said, ruffled again. From his case he had gotten another set of papers, typed and legal-looking. "In the matter of the paintings by Fernand Léger and Rembrandt van Rijn, we are presented with a somewhat different situation. These are not mentioned in the will, but are the subjects of identical conditional donations, the first to the Musée Barillot and the second to the Art Museum of Seattle. In—"

"What conditions?" Froger said. "I know of no conditions."

Sully frowned at him. "These donations were drawn up—and signed by my client—in readiness for their acceptance by the donees. There are certain stipulations set forth—"

"Stipulations, what stipulations?" Froger asked.

Sully appealed to Lefevre. "Am I to be permitted to continue?"

"Try to control yourself, Monsieur Froger," Lefevre said mildly.

Sully read the conditions aloud. They were what I already knew: no scientific analysis was to be permitted; our decisions were to be made no later than Friday (Vachey, true to his word, had appended a rider extending the time limit), with the paintings remaining open to our visual inspection at any time during normal business hours; Vachey would pay for transportation to the Barillot and to SAM at the end of the two-week invitational showing in the Galerie Vachey, and would provide for their continuing conservation and insurance; the paintings were to be prominently displayed as a Rembrandt and a Léger, at SAM and the Barillot respectively, for a period of not less than five years.

Froger listened keenly. "These stipulations, they also apply to the Seattle Art Museum?"

"I told you," Sully told him, "they are identical."

Christian emitted a patronizing sigh. "Can I just make one point? My father's dead, right? The stipulations haven't been met—these people haven't signed anything, right? So how can the offers be binding on my father's estate?"

Sully looked at him for a long time. "But they are," he said. "These are not contracts, monsieur, they are conditional donations. In effect, they have already been made. If and when the donees accept the conditions, the matter is closed. The death of the donor is immaterial."

"Immaterial?" Christian repeated, then laughed. "He'd love hearing that. Look, Monsieur Sully, I don't accept what you're telling us, and I'm telling you right now that I'm going to be conferring with my own attorney about it."

Sully shrugged his unconcern. "Confer with twenty attorneys. The law is clear."

"In the meantime, I assume I can refuse entry to my own property if I feel like it?"

Sully looked impatiently at him. "Meaning?"

"Meaning I hereby refuse permission to Edmond Froger and to him"—he tilted his head toward me—" to examine the paintings."

"Wait one moment," Froger said, his voice taking on an edge of outrage. "That Léger happens to be in the Galerie Vachey, which is now owned by Madame Guyot, not—"

"But the Galerie Vachey happens to be in a house that *I* now own, and I refuse you entrance," Christian said with a triumphant smirk. "Him too." That was me again.

Froger started sputtering. "You . . . I . . ." He looked helplessly at Sully. "Can he do that?"

"No," the attorney said. "The will makes it quite clear—"

"No?" Christian said. "No? Listen, Sully, I know a little about the law myself, and as the executor of my father's estate, it's damn well my prerogative—"

Sully cut in. "You are not the executor of your father's estate. I am the executor of your father's estate."

Christian's astonishment was almost comical. His lips came together, then separated with a moist pop, to remain open. The fight had drained out of him as completely as if a plug had been pulled.

"And as executor," Sully continued, "I grant these people free access to the Galerie Vachey for the purpose of evaluating the paintings. You, however, are within your rights to refuse them entrance to the living quarters."

Froger had regained his composure. He looked sleek and confident again. "I would also like to have Monsieur Charpentier examine the painting further."

"You may have whomever you wish to assist you."

"And I may assume his fees will be paid by the estate? Last night René made it clear—"

"I was present," Sully said. "Yes, monsieur, the estate will pay them."

"I bring it up, you understand, because it seems only fair—"

"I have already said the estate will pay them. No further questions?" He looked toward Lefevre. "We are free to leave and to go about our business?"

"Of course. But Monsieur Vachey, Madame Guyot, Madame Grémonde—perhaps you would all remain behind for a little while? I would like to speak with you individually. Monsieur Vachey, is there a more convenient room where we might do this?"

"What?" Christian was still recovering from the last of his

several shocks. "Oh—yes, all right. My father's study." Then, as an afterthought: "Clotilde, tell Madame Gaillard to make some coffee."

Clotilde Guyot's sunny features clouded. "Who are you to give me orders? I don't work for you. And I'm a gallery owner, not a servant; why should I fetch coffee?"

No, she didn't say it out loud—she was hardly the type—but the French can put a lot into a quivering eyebrow, a lifted chin, and a frigid stare. I may not have gotten every bit of it right, but you couldn't miss the general message. And I didn't think it was a case of unbridled feminism either. I thought it was simply a case of her not being able to stand Christian's guts. I was starting to feel sorry for the guy. Nobody liked him. Even the good Lorenzo's face had soured when his name had come up.

Nevertheless, Clotilde nodded, raised her soft bulk from the chair, and went out to make arrangements. Lefevre got up too, said he would be back in five minutes, and left.

CHAPTER 11

I went after him. It was time to let him know about my adventure last night, and to take whatever lumps I had coming. He was on the steps outside, having a cigarette.

"Inspector?"

He turned, blew two thick streams of smoke out of his nostrils and looked down his nose at me. He was taller than I'd realized, about six-three, straight as a ramrod, and with a way of carrying himself that was somewhat austere, to put it kindly. Or embalmed-looking, to put it otherwise.

"Yes? Monsieur Norgren, do I know you?"

"I don't think so."

"Are you sure? Your name is familiar."

I considered asking him if possibly he'd read my recent monograph on Andrea del Sarto and the early Italian Mannerists, but thought he might take it the wrong way.

"Sorry," I said, "I don't know why it would be familiar."

He peered coolly at me. "Weren't you recently involved in an art theft affair in Bologna?"

"Well . . . yes . . . last year. Only incidentally, actually. I happened to be there at the time, you see. About something else entirely. I was able to, er, provide the *carabinieri* with a little help."

The reason for this abject sniveling was that my encounter with the minions of the law in Bologna had taught me that policemen were not likely to take kindly to amateurs who stuck their noses into police matters without being asked. Even with the best of intentions. Even, in fact, when you wound up solving their case for them.

And, although I hadn't stuck my nose anywhere yet, and didn't intend to, I was in no hurry to get on the wrong side of the steely Inspector Lefevre.

"That's not quite what I recall," he said stiffly. "If memory serves, you seemed to be at the center of a number of misadventures that rather complicated matters for the *carabinieri.*"

"Not on purpose," I said with a grin, hoping a little self-deprecating American humor might soften him. *"Colonello* Antuono's theory was that someone put an evil eye on me when I was still in the womb."

Lefevre was unsoftened. "Well, I can't speak for the Italian police, but we, here in France, are perfectly capable of solving our crimes without unsolicited assistance. If you have pertinent information, we would like to have it. If we have questions, we would appreciate honest answers. Beyond that, please be kind enough to leave matters to us."

"Absolutely," I said. "Definitely."

His glance shifted to a man in shirt sleeves and a loosened tie who came out of the house, a toothpick jiggling at the corner of his mouth. "Phone call from the public prosecutor, Inspector. Wants to see you right now."

"Moury wants to see me now? This minute? Doesn't he realize how much we have to do?"

The man shrugged. The toothpick wagged. "He has some instructions for you."

I have since learned a little about the French criminal justice system, in which police inspectors are subject to the wishes, not of police superiors, but of public prosecutors. The police, as might be expected, often resent these intrusions.

Lefevre was no exception. *"Mon dieu,"* he murmured fervently. (I leave it in French to provide the authentic Gallic flavor.) His eyes rolled skyward and stayed there for a long time before he brought them down. His cigarette was flung onto the cobblestones and viciously ground out.

"All right, Huvet," he said. "Go inside and tell them it will be half an hour before we start."

Huvet grinned. "You're going to get Moury to shut up in half an hour?"

Lefevre sighed. "I know, but tell them anyway." Huvet nodded, and went back in.

"I'm sorry," Lefevre said to me. "There was something you wanted to say to me? I have a moment."

"It's going to take more than a moment."

"Nevertheless."

"Well, it's, uh, about something that, uh, happened last night," I began. "Urn . . ."

Talk about misadventures. Lefevre was going to love this. I sighed, cleared my throat and went nervously ahead. "It concerns an occurrence that. . . that occurred last night. It may be pertinent to, ah, that is to say, relevant to the matter of which—"

"You can speak English if you prefer," he said bluntly. A perceptive man. No wonder he was a chief inspector.

"Someone pushed me out of Vachey's study window," I said. In English.

He looked at me without comment for a long moment, squeezing his nose between thumb and forefinger. Then he turned, squinting into the sunlight and looked up at the window.

"Someone tried to push you out of that window last night," he said as if he were trying out the words for himself and not much liking them.

"Someone *did* push me out of it."

He looked back up at the window. He looked at the rough cobblestone paving—there were no cars there now—then up again, taking his time. Then at me.

"I, uh, landed on a car," I said. "It's not there now."

"Ah. And am I to know who it was that pushed you out of that window and onto the car that is no longer there?"

He had, I was beginning to see, that distressing knack for making you feel—making me feel—that, whatever I said, I was in the wrong, or at least that my foot was in my mouth. Handy for dealing with miscreants, I supposed.

"Now look, Inspector—" I began through clenched teeth, but then thought better of it. I couldn't really blame the guy. As far as he was concerned, flushed with my recent success with the *carabinieri* I was now embarked on complicating matters for the Police Nationale.

I swallowed my irritation and told him the whole thing: about my discomfort with Vachey's conditions on the Rembrandt, about Gisèle Grémonde's pointing out the blue scrapbook, about my sneaking into Vachey's study later on to look at it, about my subsequent exit through the window, and about the book's disappearance.

By the time I finished, he seemed resigned, as if deep in his heart he'd known, from the moment he'd recognized my name, that I was going to screw things up for him too.

He took a pack of Gauloises from his pocket and lit another cigarette. "I would be interested in knowing," he said, "exactly what you hoped to find in that book."

"I'm not sure. A record of where that Rembrandt really came from. Some clues to its history."

"You don't believe his story about the flea market?"

"Junk shop. It was the Léger that came from a flea market. Let's say neither story is highly likely. The book would have had information on the rest of his affairs during the Occupation too—he started it in 1942. I'd like to ask Madame Grémonde—"

"I," he said, "will ask Madame Grémonde. *You* will be so kind—"

Huvet reappeared. "Sorry, Inspector. Moury called again. He's having one of his fits. I think it might be best if—"

"I'm going, dammit," Lefevre snapped. "Mr. Norgren, I'll want to talk with you again. I assume you'll be available for the next few days?"

My heart sank. Anne would be in Seattle tonight. I had started to hope that I might be there tomorrow. "Actually, I was hoping to get back to the States. There are some things ..." His look was hardening. "Well, of course," I said, "if I can help, I'll stay."

"Good," he said. "Tell Sergeant Huvet how to reach you. I must go now." He shook hands formally, as the French do at every opportunity, sighed deeply, squared his shoulders, and marched off for his meeting with the public prosecutor with all the joy of a man heading for the guillotine.

"Well, you know, he has a hard life," Huvet told me matter-of-factly, as we watched him go.

Huvet seemed like a more easygoing man than his boss, and I wondered if he might be less likely to bite if I dared to ask a question. "Sergeant," I said, "can you tell me anything at all about René Vachey's death? I don't know any of the details."

"Details? He was killed at approximately five-thirty this morning," he said. "A single, small-caliber bullet behind the right ear, not self-inflicted. His body was found in the pond of the Place Darcy at seven. Blood spatters and tissue fragments indicate that he was shot while sitting on a bench a few feet away. Is that what you wished to know?"

It was more than I wished to know. "What was he doing in the Place Darcy at five-thirty in the morning?"

"Walking. He was an insomniac. He walked most mornings at five if the weather was all right. At six-thirty he would have coffee in one of the *brasseries.*"

"But that must narrow things down for you," I said. "How many people would know he'd be out then?"

"No more than a few million," Huvet said, shifting the toothpick to the other side of his mouth. "He was the subject of several magazine pieces. These solitary before-dawn walks were featured. One had a photograph of him against a cloudy sunrise. Taken in the Place Darcy.   Sitting on the same bench."

"So much for that," I said.

"Indeed," he said sadly.

* * *

When I came back in, Calvin was waiting for me in the lower hallway, outside Pepin's office. "What now, chief?"

"Well, we ought to have the gallery all to ourselves right now. Let's go see if I can tell a Flinck from a Rembrandt."

He looked at me, head cocked. "What for? I thought you didn't want anything to do with it."

"That was then. It's different now."

"Yeah, how is it different?"

"Vachey's dead," I said.

"What's that got to do with anything? That guy in Saint-Denis is still claiming it's his."

"I know, Calvin, but . . . I'm not sure I can explain what I mean, but Vachey's being killed changes everything. He wanted us to have the painting, he went to a lot of trouble to see that we'd get it, and now somebody's killed him." I shrugged. "I don't want to drop it now; I feel as if I owe him more than that."

He nodded. "I understand what you're saying." Good, I thought; I wasn't sure *I* did.

"Let's go on up," he said. "Who knows, maybe I'll learn something."

I laughed. "So you can impress your new girlfriend some more, right?"

"Sure," Calvin said, "what else?"

We went up to the second floor, but the movable walls at the head of the stairs had been shoved together and locked, so we had to go back down and get Pepin to let us in. Convincing him took some doing; the time lock would have to be disengaged, he groused, the alarm systems would have to be disarmed, there were many other demands on his attention at this moment, etc., etc. But we insisted, and he finally went unwillingly along with the idea, probably figuring that it would take less time to just let us in, than it would to keep arguing with us about it.

A few minutes later, he slid the walls apart and stood doubtfully aside to let us pass. "Touch nothing, please. You'll tell me when you go? I must arm the systems again."

"Of course," I told him.

"Arm the systems, hell," Calvin said as Pepin reluctantly left us on our own. "He probably wants to count the paintings when we leave."

I laughed. "Forget it, it's just his manner. Nothing personal. Come on, let's have a look. Maybe I'll learn something too."

* * *

"Looks good to me," Calvin said helpfully.

We'd been at it for half-an-hour. Calvin had listened uncomplainingly, possibly even comprehendingly, to my muttered comments on the paints, the manner of application, the surface crackling, the canvas, the frame construction.

"Looks good to me too, Calvin."

"As good as a Rembrandt?"

It wasn't easy to say. The technical details all seemed to be as they should have been on a genuine Rembrandt. But what did it prove? All of them applied to Flinck too. Same time period, same place, same materials, same equipment. And the same techniques, patiently learned over several years, from the master himself.

I took a few steps back to get away from the minutiae, to try to take in the subtleties, nontechnical and intangible. And the more I studied it, the more I thought I could see signs of that mysterious, brooding power that would bloom later in Rembrandt's career, the singular ability to make the viewer feel that he was looking into the mind, even the character, of the subject. The longer I looked at that worn and dissipated face, the more I seemed to see in it. No doubt about it, that wistful old bum was getting to me.

"I think," I said slowly, "it might be the real thing."

Calvin looked at me with interest. "Yeah? That's terrific."

"On the other hand …" I said.

He shook his head. "I love you guys. There's always another hand."

"It's a judgment call, that's all. I *think* it's a Rembrandt, but I wouldn't bet my life on it." After a moment, to cheer him up, I added: "Yours, maybe."

"Thanks. Tell me this: So let's say it doesn't belong to Julien Mann—is it good enough to hang in SAM?"

I nodded. "Oh, yeah, it's Dutch Baroque at its finest. Whoever painted it."

"If that's the way you feel about it, then what's the problem? Sign the contract, and we can worry about where it came from later."

"I just told you. I'm not positive it's a Rembrandt."

"Big deal," Calvin said, "you're not positive. You also just told me it's a great piece of art in its own right. Why do we have to say what we think it is or isn't? Can't we just waffle a little, sign the papers, and say thank you? So what if it turns out to be by Flinck or somebody else? We still wind up with a great painting, right? Unless it's really Mann's, in which case we turn it over to him. What's to lose?"

"No good, Calvin. You're forgetting one thing."

"What am I—? Oh, yeah." He settled down. "The restrictions. We have to display it as a Rembrandt."

"So that if it turned out *not* to be, we'd look like goats no matter how we tried to explain it away—which is just what we've been worried about from the beginning, isn't it?"

"Yeah, but—"

"Look at what *Les Echos Quotidiens* has already done to us. Not only do they have us accepting the painting, they've got us agreeing that it's a Rembrandt. And we haven't said a word yet."

Over the partitions we heard the voices of Pepin and Jean-Luc Charpentier. Charpentier, it appeared, had come at Froger's request to look at the Léger, and Pepin was delivering the same prissy lecture he'd given us, about not touching anything.

"See?" I said to Calvin. "He picks on everybody."

A moment later, Pepin himself appeared in the alcove, pushing his fingers through his dark, thinning hair. "Is everything all right? You are done?"

"Not quite," I said. "Could we take it down, please?"

He stared at me. *"Down?"*

"Yes, I'd like to examine the back."

"The back?" He was peering at me as if I'd asked him to be so kind as to slice the picture into eight equal segments. "Why do you want to examine the back?"

"I need to see what's on it. The back of a painting is part of it."

Not really. Any canvas this old had almost certainly been relined, possibly more than once, so that the back that would now be visible wouldn't be the original one. All the same, one finds all kinds of things on it—stickers, numbers, notations, stamps— that can tell something of its history. And this one needed all the provenance it could get.

He scowled at me, then at his watch. "No, I can't, I would have to get a *tournevis.*"

It was a word I didn't know. "Pardon?"

He made a twisting gesture. A screwdriver.

"All right," I said.

"No, monsieur, not all right," he said irritably. "I would have to disconnect an additional alarm system as well. Do you realize how much is expected of me today? I have a great many important things to attend to. I'm extremely busy. *Extremely* busy," he added, in case I failed to grasp the point.

"Nevertheless," I said firmly.

I'm not really this pushy. Ordinarily, I'm the least assertive, the most accommodating, of men. Ask anyone. Tony likes to poke fun at me for being the only person in the art world without known enemies, something he apparently regards as indicative of a personality defect. My friend, the endlessly helpful Louis, once explained to me over an Italian dinner that my narcissistic, ego-ideal-driven need to be liked had created an unhealthy avoidance of confrontation, particularly of dyadic confrontation. This, he further informed me, had contributed greatly to the failure of my marriage and to several subsequent post-divorce, pre-Anne disasters.

Well, Louis and Tony would both have been proud of me today. I wasn't making any friend of Marius Pepin. But I couldn't help feeling that he was going out of his way to be obstructive, for no reason I could see.

He stared frigidly at me. "Very well, monsieur." He pivoted with military crispness and went off in a huff.

"No, it's you," Calvin observed. "He doesn't like you."

"I'm not too crazy about him either. Something tells me he's not going to put himself out to hurry back here with his *tournevis*. Why don't we go see how Charpentier's doing in the other room?"

We found him standing before the canvas just the way he had last night: his big head thrown back, his hands behind him, clasping his elbows. He was wearing a scruffy, yellowish-brown tweed jacket with leather elbow patches (to protect against all that elbow-clasping?), a baggy tan sweater, a dull brown shirt with curling collar points, and an ancient, mustard-colored tie. It was the dress of a man who didn't care how he dressed, and he looked a lot more at home than he had in a tuxedo.

He turned his head as we came in, nodding abstractedly when I introduced Calvin. "You heard about Vachey?" he asked, returning to the picture.

"Yes," I said, "it's hard to believe."

His purplish lips curled. "Let's be honest, Christopher. It's a miracle no one killed the old scoundrel years ago." Charpentier was never going to be known as a man who went around with his heart on his sleeve.

I couldn't think of anything to reply. I'd taken a quick liking to Vachey, but all the same I knew what Charpentier meant. René

Vachey had been a man with a knack—possibly with a relish—for making enemies, and he'd spent a great many years doing it. Inspector Lefevre, I thought, was not going to have any trouble finding likely suspects.

I changed the subject, gesturing at the Léger. "What do you think of it this morning?"

He shrugged. "The same thing as I thought last night, why should it be different?"

"It's authentic? There's no doubt in your mind?"

"Doubt?" Charpentier said. "Are you joking? None whatever, none at all. Everything cries out 'Léger.' Not merely the composition, which can of course be imitated successfully, but the particularities of execution, which cannot. Look, for example, at the shading on the inside of the pitcher, how it is applied more thinly than the white—you see how the ground shows through, and the texture of the open-weave canvas as well? How, in addition, the ground itself makes up the greater part of the white background? What could be more characteristic?"

He moved closer to the canvas to point carefully at some unidentifiable—to me, anyway—small objects depicted on the table. "Note how the grays are on close inspection a range of carefully blended cream washes. And see, throughout, how the paint is thickly applied—but no impasto—and with precious little brush marking? These are all unmistakable attributes of Léger, impossible to simulate so exactly."

If Charpentier said so, who was I to argue? He really was one of the world's most sought-after authorities on the Cubists, and this wasn't the first time he'd been faced with a previously unknown Léger. Five or six years earlier he had made minor headlines of his own as head of an international team that had authenticated, as a Léger, a painting that had been hanging in a Basel restaurant for thirty years, on the wall of the corridor between the telephones and the restrooms. Originally, it had been reluctantly accepted by the owner in lieu of a thirty-dollar tab. Three years after its rediscovery it was on the auction block in London, where it went for somewhere in excess of two million dollars.

So there wasn't much doubt about his knowing his stuff. Still, I couldn't help thinking that what he was describing didn't seem so impossible to simulate. Why *couldn't* a knowledgeable and competent forger do all that? I suppose I was doing some wishful thinking. Since my first enigmatic talk with Vachey, I'd never shaken the idea that there was some kind of forgery involved in his show. I knew it couldn't be any of the paintings that were going to the Louvre; they were all impeccably documented. So was the Duchamp that Gisèle was getting. That meant it had to be the Léger, or the Rembrandt, or both. I sure as hell didn't want it to be the Rembrandt, which left the Léger as my favorite candidate.

But Charpentier wasn't interested in helping my case. "You can see," he went on mercilessly, his wild eyebrows almost brushing the canvas, "the characteristic pencil markings that show through the ground. And see here, gentlemen, where this cadmium yellow band has clearly been repositioned two times—no, three. Always, Léger was making these changes in striving for the perfection of his effect."

He straightened up. "Not, unfortunately, to be achieved this time. As I trust I made clear last night, a Léger it is, but a third-rate work at best, of the sort that even the finest artist produces from time to time. Usually, he destroys it. I tell you frankly, I wish he had done so with this."

"Well, at least it'll fit in at the Barillot," I said.

"Yes, there's always that," he said with a near-smile. "Froger, that pompous elephant, will no doubt convince himself he has a masterpiece, whatever I say. Ah, that reminds me. I'm going to see him when I'm finished here. He asked me to invite you to join us, if I saw you. If you prefer, I'll say I didn't see you."

"No, that's fine. I'll go over with you."

Pepin poked his head into the alcove. "So here you are," he said to me, as friendly as ever. "Make up your mind, do you want to get it down or not?"

"Please." Then to Charpentier: "I'll need another few minutes with the Rembrandt, Jean-Luc," I said. "Want to join us?"

He shook his head. "The Baroque," he said turning again to the rehung Léger with its welter of clashing colors, jarring angles, and harsh perspective, "is not my cup of tea."

Back in the Dutch section, Calvin and I stood by while Pepin used his *tournevis* to unscrew the clamps that held two sturdy eyelets in the back of the picture's frame to a pair of hooks on metal rods coming down from a bar that ran along the ceiling. When he'd gotten them loosened, he got himself set and began to lift the painting from the wall, brushing off my help at first, but I got pushy again. Taking old pictures down is a two-man job. Together we lifted it carefully from the hooks and placed it upright, with its back to us, on a carpeted dolly he'd brought.

The result wasn't worth the effort. As I'd anticipated, the picture had been relined; that is, the age-weakened old canvas had been glued to a fresh piece of linen backing to strengthen it, and the whole thing reattached to a new stretcher. There wasn't a mark on it.

"Recently done," I said. "New lightweight bars, thermoplastic adhesive, all brand-new . . . Vachey probably had it done himself."

In itself, there was nothing wrong with that. It's the proper way to treat old pictures, and the relining had been done competently enough. On the other hand, it's also the first thing a crook does if there's something about the back of a canvas that he wants to hide. Not that I had found anything yet to suggest there was something—

"Pick up Nadia, quarter to one, for lunch at the Toison d'Or," Calvin said matter-of-factly from over my left shoulder.

I turned toward him, frowning. "What?"

"Not you, me," he said. "That was my pen."

It took a moment to register. "Your pen talks? Now why doesn't that surprise me?"

"Neat, huh? Well, if you don't need me anymore, I ought to get going."

"I'll get along," I said, "somehow."

"Anything I can do to, you know, help things along this afternoon?"

"Sure, maybe you could see if you could dig up something useful."

"Such as."

"Anything. The name of the junk shop Vachey's supposed to have bought this from would be nice."

"Where am I supposed to get that?"

I lowered my voice. "You could try Pepin. He seems pretty forthcoming."

"Right. Sure. Will do. Well, gotta go."

I nodded mutely to him as he left, his toothy, cocky grin in place. *Pick up Nadia.* Lithe, sexy, pretty Nadia. How did the guy do it, I wondered glumly. And where, while I was on the topic of lithe, sexy, pretty people, was Anne right now? Sleeping, no doubt; it was just 4:00 a.m. on the West Coast. In an hour the pale early-morning light would begin to filter through the curtains onto her face. She would stir.

"We are finished?" Pepin asked, having had enough of watching me staring into the middle distance.

"We are finished," I said. Together we got the painting back up. I had to admit that no one could have handled it any more tenderly than Pepin did.

I was hot from the mild effort, which struck me as odd. Picture galleries usually have rigid climate control systems, and the ideal temperature is generally agreed to be sixty-eight degrees. But it felt more like seventy-four or seventy-five to me. It had the previous night as well, but I'd attributed that to the crush. The air seemed dry too, below the conventional fifty to fifty-five percent humidity, but I was less sure about that.

"Monsieur Pepin, does it seem a little warm in here to you?"

Pepin took this, as he took just about everything, as a personal insult.

"Thank you. Are there other complaints you wish me to convey to Monsieur Va—to Madame Guyot?"

"I'm not complaining, I—never mind, forget it."

The hell with it, I thought. A few weeks at seventy-four degrees wasn't going to hurt my Rembrandt. Not when you considered that it had apparently gotten along without my expert advice, or anybody's expert advice, for 360-plus years. Junk shops and attics are not known for their exacting temperature controls.

Oops. Did I just call it a *Rembrandt*? No quotation marks, no "alleged"? Did I just call it *my* Rembrandt? Watch it there, Norgren, don't commit yourself before you have to. Even dead, Vachey was likely to have a trick or two up his sleeve.

I thanked Pepin for his help, and went and got Charpentier.

"Frankly, Christopher," he said as we departed *le maison Vachey,* "I'm glad you're coming with me. You can restrain me if Froger again brings out the savage beast in me."

I laughed. "We can restrain each other."

CHAPTER 12

Hunching grouchily along with a cigarette loosely wedged in the corner of his mouth, hands in the pockets of his baggy tweed jacket, chin tucked into a wool muffler, and black beret jammed down to his ears—all despite the mild fall weather—Charpentier reminded me of one of those black-and-white photos of postwar France, in which everybody was riding a bicycle, or carrying a baguette, or both, all the while looking Gallic as hell.

Everybody still carries baguettes here, but there aren't so many bicycles anymore, and berets are a thing of the past, worn only by Spaniards and Americans—and a few rare mavericks like Charpentier. Add those Neanderthal eyebrows and the rubbery red nose to the rest of it, and he seemed like a throwback, a workman heading back to the job after his midday tumbler of red wine, crusty bread, and cheese.

I was feeling a bit Neanderthal myself, surrounded as we were by hordes of good-looking, well-dressed university students on their way back to class. Twice a day—for morning coffee and at lunch—the students briefly overwhelmed the otherwise quiet Old City, streaming to and from the cafés and sandwich bars. They are very noticeable too, and not just because of their number. French university students are strikingly different-looking from their American counterparts—languid and trendy in expensive bomber jackets and oversized sweaters with pushed-up sleeves, and meticulously groomed and dressed so as to create the impression of being carelessly groomed and dressed. To my discerning American eye they looked more like walking advertisements for Arpels or Calvin Klein than like serious, legitimate students. Where were their ragged cut-offs, for God's sake, their combat boots, their nose rings? Where were their Frisbees?

"Jean-Luc," I said, "did you know Vachey very well?"

"Not very well, no."

"Really? I got the impression last night you were old friends." Old acquaintances, anyway.

"No, no, I reviewed some of his paintings many, many years ago when I wrote for *ActuelArt*. My remarks failed to please him, I'm afraid."

"Do you mean his show, The Turbulent Century?"

"No. As a matter of fact, I did review The Turbulent Century as well, but, no, I refer now to his own works."

"His own works?"

He glanced at me, scowling through cigarette smoke. "You didn't know he once painted?"

"I had no idea. What kind of thing did he do?"

When we stepped out of the narrow, shaded Rue des Forges and into the sunny, open space of the Place Francois Rude with its fountain and outdoor café tables, Charpentier seemed to realize the day was anything but wintry. The beret was snatched off his head with one hand and stuffed in a pocket of his tweed jacket, the muffler was tugged from his neck with the other hand and stuffed into the opposite pocket. It made him look a little less anachronistic, but it didn't do anything for the shape of his jacket. And even in the sunshine, he walked as if he were breasting an Antarctic gale.

"René Vachey was an *artiste* with a purpose," he said, leaving no doubt about his view of *"artistes"* with purposes. "He believed that the Abstractionists had all but killed art. He wanted painting to return to the figurative Cubism of Braque and Picasso—of Léger, for that matter. And that's the way he painted."

He took an immense pull on the cigarette without taking it from his mouth. A half-inch of it sizzled into ash, drooped, and landed on his lapel. "Well, he was right about Abstractionism, I'll give him that much." He paused to unleash a long gust of smoke. "Painting has been going steadily to hell ever since the 1920s—Mondrian and his damned neoplasticists. Sterile. Nothing but dead end after dead end. You agree, I imagine?"

I did, except that if you ask me, painting's been going to hell for a lot longer than that, ever since Daubigny and his Barbizon group came along, way back in the 1850s.

Sorry, Tony, it just slipped out.

"But of course," he went on, "these reactionary movements have no chance. They're nothing but self-indulgent fantasies, impossible of success. Look at the Pre-Raphaelites—and Vachey was no Rossetti, I can tell you."

"But he was actually good enough to have his own show?"

Charpentier snorted, or maybe it was a laugh. "How good must you be to have a show in your own gallery? It was an exhibition, with all his usual, tiresome fanfare, of works by the small cadre of neo-Cubists in his circle. I had the questionable privilege of reviewing them for *ActuelArt.*"

"Not favorably, I gather."

"They were rubbish. And the six or seven pieces by Vachey himself were laughable—derivative, shallow, pallid, clumsy, uninformed. That is what I wrote, and I was forced to write it again two years later, when he was misguided enough to participate in a second show. Apparently, *that* review—admittedly somewhat less generous—convinced him that his career lay in the selling of pictures, in which he was already well-established, and not in the painting of them."

He stopped to deposit his cigarette stub in a waste bin. "I have always looked upon it," he said, "as my single greatest contribution to the welfare of art."

* * *

We stopped at a student-ravaged sandwich bar for its last two ham-and-tomato sandwiches on not-so-crusty bread, then walked a block further down the Rue Dauphine toward the Musée Barillot, Charpentier lighting up again as we left the bar, and pulling in smoke as hungrily as if he'd been without a cigarette for weeks. In France, they still take their smoking seriously.

"Jean-Luc ..."

He turned toward me, sucking on his teeth. "Um?"

"I was just wondering something. I understand that everything points to that painting being a genuine Léger, and yet—well, with what you've told me about Vachey having painted in the Cubist style, well—is there any possibility—"

I was searching for a delicate way to put it to the prickly Charpentier, but couldn't think of any. "—*any* possibility that the painting is a fake after all?"

The tangled eyebrows drew ominously together. "Fake?"

"By Vachey."

The eyebrows sprang apart. *"Vachey?"* His jaw dropped. The cigarette, pasted to his lower lip, stayed put. "Haven't you heard one damned thing I've said?"

"Yes, of course, it's just that I can't help feeling—"

He waved me quiet. "I know, I feel it too. René was up to something, but what? He was playing a game of cat-and-mouse, how can we have any doubt about that? But with whom?" He walked along without saying anything for a few steps. "And in the end," he said with a meaningful sidewise glance, "did the mouse turn upon the cat and rend it?"

He took the cigarette out of his mouth long enough to use a finger to work at some food stuck between his molars. "All I can tell you is this: "Whatever he was up to, it did not involve a counterfeit Léger. The *Violon et Cruche* is authentic, Christopher, infinitely beyond the capacities of René Vachey. Besides, you must remember that he hasn't painted in more than fifteen years."

"But who's to say when this was painted?"

He shook his head tolerantly, marveling at my persistence. "Tell me, what would you say is the possibility that Vachey himself painted your Rembrandt?"

"Are you serious? None at all. One in a billion."

"Well, then, why is it so hard to believe me when I tell you the same thing about the other? Of course, I realize that you are not a great admirer of Léger's works—"

"I never said—"

"You hardly need to say it," he said, "but even you must admit that his technical command, even in an artistically unfulfilled work like *Violon et Cruche,* is staggering. The idea that any forger, let alone a sophomoric dauber like Vachey, would be capable of having fabricated it is simply . . . No, as amusing as your theory is, it's beyond the realm of possibility. I'm afraid we need another one."

We were at the entrance of the Barillot. Charpentier tossed away the cigarette stub and clapped me bearishly on the shoulder. "Come, into the lion's den."

* * *

The Barillot, as I've suggested before, was the kind of museum that gives museums a bad name, the kind whose main excuse for existing is that the original donor bequeathed the building—and the collection—to the city and left a modest fund to keep it afloat. There were perhaps three good pieces in the place (four, including the Goya charcoal Vachey had donated after his all-in-fun-no-hard-feelings theft), but it would have been too depressing to hunt for them in the tiny, badly lit rooms jammed with somber, dark paintings, sometimes literally from floor to ceiling.

Many of the pictures had placards like ATTRIBUÉ A ABRAHAM VAN DEN TEMPEL or D'APRÈS JEROME BOSCH beside them; less than emphatic, as labels go. We have some at SAM too—every museum does—but most of the ones here were very obviously no more than amateur efforts, or student exercises at best, some of them flat-out dreadful. The more boldly identified paintings, and there were some by bona fide Old Masters, were almost as bad. Every artist has off-days, of course, and the Barillot offered living proof. In a way, it was unmatched in that respect. It had a bad Murillo, a bad Steen, a bad Tintoretto, and a bad Fragonard, and how many museums can you say that about? There was even a bad Velázquez, and that might just be unique.

And now, it seemed, they would be getting a bad Léger for company.

The building itself, an eighteenth-century townhouse, was still impressive, but it hurt me to see the once-delicate decorative moldings on lintels, jambs, doors, and ceilings buried under so many layers of thick white paint that they were no more than lumpy globs. Fortunately, there wasn't too much anyone could do to the central staircase, an austerely handsome stone spiral that Charpentier and I took upstairs, to where Froger's office was.

At the top, Charpentier put a hand on my arm. "Would you care to make a wager?" he asked. "Froger's first words will be to the effect that the demise of his dear friend René Vachey has shocked him to his soul, and that he himself will go to any lengths to see that justice is done. He may even have tears in his eyes. In fact, I'll include that in the wager."

I smiled. "No bet."

Froger had plenty of warning that we were coming, because we had to walk through three tiny "galleries" with wooden floors so squeaky that we sounded like an army. And we were the only visitors, this being the off-season as far as tourists were concerned, and the people of Dijon having better sense.

Froger's office was larger than most of the gallery rooms. It had no paintings in it, but there was a pedestal bearing an early version of Houdon's marble bust of Mirabeau in one corner, three good Sèvres vases in a wall cupboard, and on one wall a large, faded Gobelin tapestry of hunting goddesses and deer, which hadn't been cleaned in two hundred years. Otherwise, there was just an elegant desk in the center of the room, actually a converted, drop-leaf gaming table from the early eighteenth century, and a couple of superb Empire chairs. Funny kind of a museum, I thought, where the classiest *objets d'art* in the place were in the director's office.

Seated behind the desk, facing us as we entered, was Froger himself, his hands folded on his belly, and his beefy face grave and composed.

"So somebody's finally killed the arrogant son of a bitch," he said.

I promised myself that the next time Charpentier offered me a bet, I'd take him up on it.

"Do they know who did it?" he asked me.

"How would I know that?"

"You went outside this morning. You had a talk with the inspector."

I'd forgotten he'd been there for the session on Vachey's will. "Well, if he knows, he didn't tell me," I said.

He waved us into the Empire chairs. "There shouldn't be any shortage of suspects, God knows."

There, at least, he, Charpentier, and I were all in agreement. I wondered if it had occurred to him that he was likely to be on the list himself. His feud with Vachey had been long and bitter, and last night's spiky, highly public encounter hadn't improved things.

"Beginning with me," he said with a rumbling laugh.

I was starting to have a bit more respect for Froger. He might be a horse's ass, but he wasn't a hundred percent horse's ass.

"Well, Jean-Luc," he said, "you've examined the painting again?"

"I have."

"And?"

"And it is still a Léger. Still an extremely poor one."

Froger's chin came off his chest. "Extremely poor? Last night it was merely not so good."

Charpentier pursed his lips. "I was being charitable. I may have been carried away."

Froger glowered momentarily, then rearranged his face and smiled. Clearly, he had resolved not to let Charpentier get his goat this time. "In any case," he said, moistening his lips, "you advise me to accept it?"

"I advise nothing. I'm not being paid to advise."

"But it *is* a Léger? You're sure of that?"

"It is a Léger," Charpentier said with truly amazing patience, given the fact that he had to be pretty tired of having his expertise questioned by now. "If that's all that matters to you, accept it."

Froger got his fingers into his collar, under the rolls of flesh, and tugged at it. "Look, Jean-Luc, no offense, but I'm very nervous about this. No one knows Léger better than you, I freely admit it, but even you can't be *sure* it's authentic."

"I am ready to stake my reputation on it," Charpentier said quietly.

But it was Froger's reputation that was worrying Froger. He hunched his massive shoulders uneasily. "It's just that I don't know what I'm getting into, and I don't want to be made a fool of."

Charpentier had finally had enough. He thumped the desk with a fist. "If you don't trust my judgment, damn it, go ahead and get someone else. They'll tell you exactly what I've told you."

Fat chance, I thought. Getting someone else would mean the Barillot, not Vachey's estate, would be footing the bill. Predictably, Froger started hemming and hawing. "Well, no, that is to say, of course I trust your judgment, Jean-Luc. Implicitly. That goes without saying. Er—Christopher, what about your Rembrandt? Are you going to accept it?"

"Probably, yes, if I can get some questions about its history settled. I think it's authentic."

How about that, I'd actually said it out loud. It was a bit of a shock hearing it.

"Gentlemen." Froger had summoned up his bottom-of-the-well baritone. He leaned forward, thick elbows on the satiny, billowing surface of the desk. "Gentlemen, if you're right, if this is an authentic painting by Léger, an authentic painting by Rembrandt—then what are we to make of Vachey's posturing and fooling about, of his absolute refusal to allow tests? What was he trying to do?"

That was a switch. Last night he'd been telling us what Vachey had in mind, not asking us.

"According to you," Charpentier said, not letting him forget it, "it's because they're forgeries. Well, they're not forgeries, and I would have thought that would be enough for you. As to Vachey, whatever he had in mind, no one is ever likely to know what it was now."

That didn't satisfy Froger. "All right, let me put it this way, Jean-Luc. Let's say I had independently commissioned you to help me decide whether to buy this painting, the very same painting. Let's say there were no restrictions about testing. Would you recommend that I send it to a laboratory to be absolutely certain it's authentic before purchasing it?"

Charpentier rubbed his nose. He got out his pack of Gitanes and lit up. Froger hurriedly produced an onyx ashtray and put it in front of him. "Only if you had money you were determined to waste," Charpentier said. "In the first place, every criterion reveals it as a Léger and nothing else; every single one. Second, remember that Léger is a twentieth-century master, not an artist of the Baroque or the Renaissance, so there is very little help that scientific tests can provide."

That seemed like an overstatement to me. True, even the most advanced dating techniques weren't going to be of much use on a painting less than a hundred years old, but what about infrared photography to highlight painting techniques, spectroscopy to analyze paint formulas, and all the rest of it? (Not that I could claim an overwhelmingly thorough grasp of all the rest of it.)

"Do you mean you never advise your clients to test modern paintings?" I asked him.

"Once in a great while I do, if there is some question that expert scrutiny cannot answer. But ordinarily, no. A scientific test is no better than the technician performing it. Technicians are people, and people make mistakes, Christopher."

"Experts are people too," I said.

Charpentier smiled thinly at me through a blue-tinged haze. "Let's consider the Rembrandt for a moment, and not the Léger. You would like to have it tested? Very good. But what if the technician innocently takes a paint sample from an area restored in the nineteenth century, what happens then to the dating? This has happened, my dear Christopher."

"I know that. You need informed judgment too. That's why I wouldn't have been any happier about it if Vachey had reversed it and said we could submit the paintings to all the tests we wanted, but we weren't allowed to look at them. You need both, not just—"

"And what about errors that are not so innocent? Fakers can add metallic salts to underpainting, and throw off X-ray analysis. This, too, has happened, and not so long ago. They can confound infrared photography by—"

"I just don't like to be made a fool of," Froger muttered again. "There's *something* wrong. Even dead, I don't trust the son of a bitch."

"No one's going to argue with you there, Edmond," Charpentier said.

"I remember that Turbulent Century fiasco of his," Froger went on. "I reviewed it for the *Revue,* you know. Now don't climb back on your high horse, Jean-Luc. I know you thought highly of it—"

"I did not think highly of it," Charpentier said irritably. "Get your facts straight. I thought highly of the figurative and Analytical Cubist portion of it. René had collected some remarkable works there. As for the rest of the exhibition, I wasn't qualified to make judgments, but I certainly had my doubts about the quality of some of the pieces."

"Yes, well, I can't speak for your Analytical Cubists, but, by God, I know Seurat and the Neoimpressionists; that's *my* specialty. And I tell you, that show was *filled* with trash that Vachey was trying to put over on us. It was shameful. I said it at the time—I don't hold my tongue when I have something to say, you know that—and I still say it. Well, naturally, I'm worried now. How could I help it?"

"Edmond, do you mean actual forgeries?" I asked. I'd never read his review of Vachey's notorious exhibition, or Charpen tier's, or anybody else's, but I'd certainly developed an interest.

The word made him skittish. His hand went to his collar again. "Forgeries? No, when did I use the word *forgeries?* Did you hear me use the word *forgeries?* We could fill this museum—your museum too, and the Louvre, and the Metropolitan—with disputed attributions without ever touching on forgeries, isn't that so?"

I had to admit it was so.

"No," he said, "I didn't say forgeries, I said only ... I meant only . . . inferior works."

"So what are you worried about?" Charpentier asked brusquely. "Haven't I just finished telling you that this Léger of yours is an inferior work? You already know it. What sinister surprise is to be feared?"

Froger shook his head darkly. He still didn't trust the son of a bitch.

Charpentier ground out his cigarette in the ashtray, and stood up. "I don't see what else there is for me to tell you. I'll give you a report in a few days, but there won't be anything startling in it. Are you going to accept the painting?"

"I—yes, I suppose so. Isn't that what you're advising me? Isn't that what it comes to? If it isn't too much to ask for your advice."

"I'm advising you to put it in one of the dark corners with which the Barillot is so richly supplied. If you're lucky, no one will notice it. Good day, Edmond."

CHAPTER 13

It was only two o'clock, but I was fatigued and still a little tottery from the previous night's episode, so I went back to the hotel to put my feet up, once again taking the chattering old elevator to the fourth floor instead of walking. Inside the room, I took off my shoes, plumped up the pillows, and lay back on the bed. It felt good too.

Charpentier's remarks had started me thinking about this business of the tests again. He'd overdone it, but he was essentially right about laboratory analysis not being as useful on forgeries of modern paintings as on forgeries of old ones. The best thing a test can do for you in pinpointing a fake is to show you that a purported 360-year-old Rembrandt is painted on a 50-year-old canvas, or uses pigments that weren't developed until the late nineteenth century, or is painted over a picture of a 1960 Ford Fairlane. The older a picture is supposed to be, the more a lab has to go on. From that standpoint, it would seem that, of the two—the Léger and the Rembrandt—the likelier candidate for fake was the Rembrandt. That was Charpentier's point.

But we weren't dealing with a *modern* forgery of a Rembrandt; of that I was sure. As a matter of fact, there weren't many modern forgeries of them around—precisely because there were so many Rembrandt-like paintings still available from Rembrandt's own time. At the worst, that's what *An Officer* was. And all the scientific wizardry in the world can't help you detect a 360-year-old fake of a 360-year-old painting.

So what was the point of the prohibition? I was right back at what Calvin had aptly enough called square one. Back at it? When had I ever been off it?

I settled in more comfortably to give it some deeper contemplation.

At 6:20 the telephone rang. I got it to my ear without opening my eyes.

"Hey, Chris—"

"Calvin, why are you always waking me up?"

"Why are you always asleep?"

I yawned and swung my feet over the side of the bed. "L'Atelier Saint-Jean," Calvin said, "89 Rue de Rivoli, *propriétaire* M. Gibeault."

I finished my yawn. "Hm. French, *nest-ce pas?*"

"It's the junk shop, Chris."

That opened my eyes. "The—you mean where he said he bought the Rembrandt? Pepin actually gave it to you?"

"Are you kidding me? Not that I didn't ask him, but he claims he doesn't know anything about the Rembrandt. Apparently, there were a lot of things that Vachey kept close to his vest, and this was one."

"So then, who told you—"

"I got it from Madame Guyot." He coughed modestly. "She sort of took a shine to me."

"Calvin, that's great," I said. "I can catch a train to Paris tomorrow—"

"I found out some other interesting stuff too. If you think this whole thing is already as weird as it's going to get, think again. You had your dinner yet?"

"I've been asleep. I'm not terrifically hungry."

"There's a *brasserie* at the foot of the Rue de la Liberté, practically across the street from you. We can get an omelet or something. Meet you there in five minutes."

* * *

"Guess," Calvin said, smugly watching me over his glass of white wine, "who Pepin is."

"What do you mean, who he is? Vachey's secretary, his security head, whatever."

"Ho-ho, there's more to it than that, my man."

I poured most of my tiny bottle of Badoit mineral water (I

wasn't feeling up to wine yet) into my glass. "Calvin, this is very entertaining, but how about just telling me?"

"Well, you know that heist that Vachey pulled off at the Barillot ten years ago?"

"It wasn't a 'heist,'" I said irritably. "He was making a point. They got their paintings back, and more."

Calvin's eyes widened. I was surprised myself. When had I gone so far over into Vachey's camp that I would defend the theft of art, whatever the reason behind it? I quickly corrected myself. "All right, yes, it was a heist. Sorry. But what about it?"

"And how Froger fired his security chief over the lapse in precautions? Well, you want to guess the name of that fired security chief?"

"You're telling me it was *Pepin?*"

"You got it. Vachey gave him a job the next week, and Pepin's been there ever since." He grinned. "You don't suppose that might explain why he's a teeny bit paranoid about anybody getting within arm's length of anything in the Galerie Vachey?"

I nodded. Once burned, twice shy. "You know, it also might ..."

The waiter set down our orders. A ham omelet for Calvin, a cheese omelet for me, each served alongside two minuscule tomato wedges on a miniature lettuce leaf. With them came a basket of rolls, a tray with bottles of vinegar and oil on it, and—as with almost everything else in this town—a pot of Dijon mustard.

"It also might what?" Calvin asked when my sentence died away.

Frowning, I broke open a roll. "I was just thinking . . . Let's say that happened to you. That Vachey hired you to work for him after Froger fired you. How would you feel?"

Calvin hunched his shoulders. "Relieved, I guess. There couldn't have been too many places that would have been willing to take a chance on him after that."

"How would you feel toward Vachey?"

"I don't know—grateful?"

"Even though he's the one that got you fired in the first place? Even though you'd never be able to get a job in the field with anybody else?"

"Oh, I see what you mean. You'd have sort of mixed feelings, wouldn't you? You'd be grateful—but you'd also hate his guts every time you looked at him."

"Exactly," I said. "I was just wondering if he might have hated him enough to kill him."

"But why right at this particular time? All that happened years ago."

"For one thing, to make it look as if it had something to do with the exhibition, or those charges in *Les Echos Quotidiens,* or any of the other things that are going on right now."

Calvin was shaking his head. "Maybe, but it sounds kind of far-out to me, Chris. A lot of people probably hated Vachey enough to kill him. Jeez, we know about twenty of them ourselves."

"Like who?"

"Like Gisèle Grémonde."

"You mean because of the Duchamp? But he gave it to her before he died."

"Yeah, but she didn't find that out until this morning, after he was already dead."

"Well, yes, but—"

"And what about that sleazeball son, Christian? You see how shocked he was to hear about the new will? Maybe he thought Vachey was only *planning* to change his will, and he murdered him to head him off. And then he finds out this morning he was too late by a year or so. Didn't you catch that oh-shit look on his face?"

"That's true, I guess—"

"Don't forget Mann either. Talk about an ax to grind. For all we know he's been hunting Vachey all these years and just found out where he lived."

I sighed. They didn't add up to twenty, but they were enough. "You're right. I guess I was just thinking out loud."

"And don't forget all the people we *don't* know who probably hated his guts."

I started on the omelet, and for a minute or two we ate in silence.

"Guess who Clotilde Guyot is," Calvin said. I looked up, fork in hand.

"You're full of surprises, aren't you? Who?"

"This is something you probably know more about than I do. You know what Aryanization was?"

Yes, I knew. During World War II, early in the Occupation, Jewish businesses had been declared ownerless. The Nazi logic was unassailable: Jews had been made technically stateless by German decree, and how could stateless people have property rights? Jewish firms were therefore commandeered by the authorities. The owners were trucked off to the death camps in the East, or interned in France, or if they were lucky, they bought their way out of Europe or otherwise managed to disappear from sight.

There was some local outrage over this, of course, but the French were in no position to pursue complaints with vigor; besides, a number of influential citizens were beneficiaries of the policy. Confiscated Jewish firms were turned over, lock, stock, and barrel, to local businessmen of indisputably Aryan descent. Once cleansed of non-Aryan pollution, the firms were soon back in business. The conversion process was referred to by the Germans as "Aryanization."

"Well, that's how Vachey got his first gallery," Calvin told me. "The Nazis handed it to him. It was the Galerie Royale in Paris— you know, the one Vachey owned in 1942. Well, before that, it'd belonged to Clotilde's uncle."

I put down my fork. My appetite, not very hearty to start with, was gone. "Oh, hell, Calvin," I said quietly.

He looked surprised. "Why oh hell? I mean, look, it was a lousy deal, but it's not as if Vachey personally *stole* it from the guy. He probably didn't have any choice in the matter either."

"No, Calvin, it wasn't like that. Who do you think the Nazis gave these businesses to? The people they already loved doing business with, that's who. The toadies, the stooges, the collaborators, the parasites." And whether I wanted to believe it or not, it was starting to look as if René Vachey had been one, or even all, of the above.

Calvin was shaking his head. "Well, that's not the way she remembers it. The way she sees it, Vachey walked on water." He put down his fork and leaned forward. "Let me tell you."

If the story she had told Calvin was even half-true, and I hoped it was, I could see why she felt that way. Far from being a despicable predator who had thrived on others' misery, he had been a genuine hero, according to Clotilde. Yes, he had taken over her Uncle Joachim Lippe's Galerie Royale under the Nazis' policy, but he had used his earnings and his influence to assist others less fortunate. He had spent 80,000 francs—real francs, not Occupation notes; a colossal sum to him in those days—and had undergone enormous personal risk besides, in trying to arrange the Lippe family's escape from Occupied Europe.

In Joachim's case, he had failed—the Gestapo arrested the elderly man three hours before he was to leave Paris, and he had frozen to death in a cattle car while en route to Auschwitz—but Vachey did succeed in getting Joachim's wife and two little girls to Vichy France, then to Portugal, and finally to Canada. Afterward, he had continued to send them money until the mid-1950s, when Mrs. Lippe married again.

Clotilde, then sixteen, wasn't Jewish herself, but as far as the Gestapo were concerned, having a Jewish uncle had been close enough. With her arrest and deportation to slave labor in Eastern Europe imminent, Vachey had hidden her, her mother, and Clotilde's six-year-old brother in his own basement for seven weeks—an act that would have resulted in his own death if it had been known—while he cajoled and bribed French and German officials into issuing the precious papers that certified the Guyots' non-Jewishness.

Once they were safe, he had given Clotilde a job in the gallery, and she had worked for him ever since.

"Fifty goddamn years, can you imagine?" Calvin said. "How'd you like to work for Tony for fifty years? I'm telling you, she thinks he was the greatest thing that ever walked around on two legs." He shook his head slowly. "And no wonder."

Still, I did wonder. Clotilde's relationship to Vachey was even more equivocal than Pepin's. Vachey had risked his own life to save her and her family—but he'd also been the man who'd profited from the death of her uncle and the confiscation of his gallery, the man who'd taken it over with the approval of, and perhaps on the instructions of, the Nazi authorities. Now, in the end, he'd given it back to her, but he had already made good use of it as a springboard to wealth, while she had remained a paid employee for half a century.

Did she hate him? Love him? Both? What would I have felt in her position, or in Pepin's? It was impossible to imagine. Here I'd known the man only a single day, and I couldn't seem to figure out whether I admired him or despised him.

"What else did she say?" I asked.

"Nothing much. Why, what else did you want her to say?"

"Possibly something about this Flinck thing. If she's been working for Vachey since 1942, she'd know whether there was anything to Mann's charges."

Calvin finished his omelet and slid the plate aside. "Yeah, but would she tell? She's really loyal to the guy, Chris. If you want, I could talk to her tomorrow and see."

"Let me do it, Calvin. I'll catch her in the morning, before I go to Paris and hunt down that junk shop. You know what you can do, though; you can get hold of *Les Echos Quotidiens* and set them straight on our actual position on the Rembrandt." I smiled. "Which is no position at all, of course."

He nodded. "Will do. Tony already asked me to talk to them. The rest of the press too. My instructions are to stonewall. I'm real good at that."

"Tony? When did you talk to him?"

"This afternoon. The *Echos Quotidiens* people tried to get a statement out of him, and he didn't know what they were talking about." He raised his eyebrows. "He knows now."

"You filled him in on everything?"

He nodded. "Oh, except about your getting sloshed, and sneaking into Vachey's study, and falling out the window. I forgot that part."

"Thank you, I owe you. What did he say?"

"Well, you know Tony; it's hard to fluster him. But he needs to talk to you."

"I need to talk to him. It's eight o'clock," I said, looking at a wall clock. "Eleven in Seattle. If I call him right now, I can probably get him before he goes to lunch." I signaled the waiter for our check.

"Go ahead," Calvin said, "I'll get the check. And if I were you, I'd hit the sack early. You look bushed."

I stood up. "I think I'll do that. Thanks, Calvin." I started for the door, then turned with a laugh. "And thanks again for forgetting the part about Vachey's study."

He grinned back at me. "Hell, he wouldn't have believed it anyway."

CHAPTER 14

I reached Tony at 11:20 a.m. Seattle time. The call was forwarded to him by his secretary.

"Well, well, Chris, how's everything in France?" he asked jovially. "Things going well?"

Tony Whitehead was a man of more than one telephone voice. I recognized this particular persona as the avuncular one that he used when speaking with staff members while important people—board members, donors, journalists—were within earshot. It was meant, I believe, to convey the impression (more or less accurate, give or take the occasional crisis) that we were one big, happy, problem-free family.

"Call me when you're free," I said. "I'll be in the rest of the night."

"I'll certainly do that," Tony boomed. "Wonderful hearing from you, Chris. Keep up the good work."

Sixty seconds later my phone chirped. "Calvin tells me you've run into some problems." He sounded like Tony again, not like Santa Claus. "Sorry to hear it."

"Well, you did tell me it'd be interesting."

"Do they know who killed Vachey?"

"I don't think so."

I heard a familiar *crik-crak* over the line; the sound that my office chair made when it was tipped back. Tony had gone down the hall to make the call from my office. I imagined him leaning back, looking out over Elliott Bay, watching the green-and-white ferries pull into Colman dock.

"Calvin says you like the picture."

"It's beautiful," I told him enthusiastically. "It's a portrait of the old man they used to call Rembrandt's father. It's just about as fine as the one in Malibu, Tony."

"That's saying a lot," he said, and I could hear the suppressed excitement. "So—is it by Rembrandt?"

"Maybe. Probably."

"Not by Govert Flinck?"

"I don't think so, but that's not the main issue anymore, Tony. Now there are Vachey's wartime activities to think about. Even if this isn't the painting Julien Mann's talking about, it's still possible Vachey got it the same way. If he did, I don't think we'd want to touch it . . . would we?"

"Absolutely not," Tony said without hesitation. "I'd want to see it back where it belongs. "However—" He let out a long sigh. "I want to ask a big favor of you, Chris."

He paused for an affirmative response, but I held my tongue. When Tony skips the flimflamming and tells you right up front that he's about to ask you for a big favor—you can count on it being a big one, all right.

"We don't have to sign for it until Friday, is that right?" he asked when I didn't reply. "Three more days?"

"That's right. Vachey extended the time limit."

"Now, I know you want to fly home tomorrow—no, don't stop me—and I know how long it's been since you've seen Anne, and that she's only going to be here until Saturday, but. . . well, I'd like you to stay on in France a few more days."

"Tony—"

"I know, and, believe me, I hate to ask it. But this could be the most significant acquisition—"

"If it's authentic. And if it hasn't been extorted from Mann's father or anyone else."

"Right. Exactly. And that's my point. We still have three days. I'd like you to see if you can dig up anything at all on its provenance, look into Mann's claim, find out if there's anything else in the woodwork we need to worry about. Maybe you can find the junk shop where Vachey says he bought it. Go to Paris if you have to . . . uh, Chris, are you there?"

I was there. I was just wondering whether I ought to mention to Tony that Inspector Lefevre had made it plain that I wasn't leaving

France for the next several days in any case, and that I had in fact already learned the name of the junk shop, and had made plans to go to Paris. Hearing this would certainly ease Tony's conscience. On the other hand, it would have been nice to have him thinking he owed me a favor.

It was an ethical dilemma, over which I agonized for almost two nanoseconds.

"Yes, I'm here, Tony," I said stoically. "All right, if you think it's for the best . . . I'll stick around."

"Thanks, Chris," he said warmly. "I knew you'd come through."

"Forget it." Now he was starting to make me feel guilty. "Anything else?"

"Just one suggestion. You might want to look up Ferdinand Oscar de Quincy and see what light he can throw on things."

I blinked stupidly at the receiver. "Ferdinand de Quincy is still alive?"

De Quincy was the man who had been the director of SAM in the early 1950s, the man who, a decade before that, had supposedly located and returned some of Vachey's paintings to him after they had disappeared eastward with the Nazis, the man because of whom Vachey was giving us the Rembrandt in the first place. It had never occurred to me that he might still be around.

"Yeah, I was surprised too. But it suddenly dawned on me that he was only about thirty in 1945, which would put him in his seventies now, so I asked Lloyd to see what he could find out. And it turns out he lives just outside of Paris."

"But—then why wasn't he at the reception? Surely Vachey would have invited him, surely he'd have wanted to come—"

"I have no idea. Why don't you go find out? He's bound to have information on Vachey. His number's—"

"Wait. Pen. Okay, go ahead."

"His number's 43-54-23-31."

I wrote it on the flyleaf of a Wallace Stegner paperback I'd brought with me to pass the time when things got dull. Needless to say, this was the first time I'd opened it.

* * *

After I hung up, I sat on the edge of the bed and stared moodily at the telephone. My mind was still in Seattle, but not on Tony or SAM. I was thinking about the house I rented in Magnolia, about two miles from the museum. Anne would be arriving tonight, and I wanted to talk to her. It looked as if I was going to be stuck here until Friday, which meant I couldn't be back in Seattle until Saturday, which would leave us just a single day together. One day— and no nights; a dismal yield after all those months of anticipation and planning.

But I had an idea for salvaging something. Anne's conference was a one-day affair. It would be over at the end of tomorrow, Wednesday. What if she arranged for a military flight back to Europe tomorrow night? There were plenty of them to England, Germany, and Holland. She could be here in Dijon late Thursday. That would give us Friday together, and Saturday, and even a bonus of Sunday, because Kaiserslautern was only three hours from Dijon, and she wouldn't have to leave until late afternoon. What's more, my time limit for coming to a decision on the painting was the close of business Friday, so one way or another my work would be done the day after she got here. We could go back up to Paris for a couple of days, or rent a car and drive through Provence, or do whatever she wanted.

The more I thought about it, the more sense it made. If she couldn't get on a military flight, we'd get her a commercial one. Maybe we'd do that anyway, and book her first class. It'd be my treat. What better way did I have to splurge?

But it was barely afternoon in Seattle, so she was still somewhere on the road, probably on the Olympic Peninsula near Kalaloch or Ruby Beach if she was taking the route we'd planned. It hurt to think of how much pleasure there would have been in showing her those wild, magical places. Still, something was better than nothing.

I sighed, punched in my own telephone number, and waited for my voice to come on. When she arrived, she would turn on the answering machine to see if I had left anything for her.

"Hello," said a sepulchral voice. "This is Chris Norgren." It paused to allow this complex message to be grasped, and proceeded somberly. "I'm sorry I can't come to the phone now, but if you will wait for the signal and leave a message, I will . . ."

I tapped my foot impatiently. Was that really what I sounded like, or was it some mysterious quirk of answering-machines that made everybody sound like a zombie?

Finally, the beep came. "Hi, Anne," I said, making an all-out effort to sound like a living person, "welcome to the Emerald City, and hope you had a wonderful drive. There are lots of good things in the freezer, and you know where the booze is. Everything in the fridge should be fresh, more or less. Listen, I just had a terrific idea. Call me when you get in. Don't worry about the time—"

Click. "Chris?"

It was a moment before I could reverse gears and get my voice going again. "Anne? What are you doing there?"

"I got in early. I swung over to Highway 5 at Portland. I wanted to save the Peninsula to see with you."

And bless you for it, I thought warmly. "Listen, I'm glad I caught you early. I'm going to have to stay over in France for another two or three days—"

"Three days! But that'd only leave us—Why do you have to stay three more days?

"Well, the police asked me to—"

"*Police?* What's going on there?"

And so I had to shift gears again and explain, which took some time; it had been an eventful couple of days. I even told her about getting pitched out the window, managing to minimize the more ludicrous aspects of it without playing down the dramatic, brush-with-death elements.

"My God, Chris," she said, gratifyingly shocked, "I'm just glad you're all right. You *are* all right?"

"I'm fine. And I have a great idea. I want you to come here to Dijon. Fly back to Europe early."

I told her about the marvelous fall weather northern Europe was having. I suggested driving to Languedoc and spending a night in one of the old inns in the walled city of Carcassonne, something she'd talked about wanting to do. I pointed out that the new plan would give us Sunday together, which we wouldn't get otherwise.

"Can't," she said.

"Why not?"

"If you knew the strings I had to pull to get my nights, you wouldn't ask me to change them."

"Well, don't change them. Come commercial. I'll arrange your tickets from here."

"Chris, I just can't. It would be too—well, too embarrassing to cancel, after the trouble I put them to. I just can't do it. They bumped people to get me on."

"Well, couldn't you—" But I didn't have anything to offer. "Oh, hell." I was feeling good and sorry for myself.

"Chris, it's not the end of the world. It's just a logistical snag, that's all. We've had them before."

I smiled. "That's what I was telling you last week." A snatch of that conversation came back to me. "Did you have a chance to do your thinking?" I asked.

She hesitated. "Did I tell you I wanted to do some thinking?"

"Yes." Now I hesitated. "You didn't say about what, though."

I heard her swallow some wine. "I think you know."

"Your commission," I said.

Anne was at a crossroads of her career. After ten years in the Air Force, she had been thinking about the possibility of resigning her commission and coming back to civilian life. But she was also up for early promotion to major, and I knew how much that meant to her.

"Yes, my commission."

"And?"

"And I came to a decision. Sort of." I heard her drink some more. I heard her put the glass down.

"And are you planning to let me in on it?"

"Well, it's still not completely made. I have to . . . there's more to it."

"Do I get a hint?"

"No, you don't get a hint," she said with sudden sharpness, "because if I discuss it with you, you get all self-sacrificing and reasonable, and then I start taking your needs into consideration, and I just think that this is one decision I ought to be making for myself."

"It's important to me, too, Anne, that's all I'm saying," I said. Reasonably, of course.

"Ah, Chris, I know that." I could tell that she was already sorry about the flare-up. "But let's drop it for now. I don't want to talk about it on the telephone."

"Of course," I said, "if that's what you want."

I was being so reasonable that I was starting to irritate *me*. But underneath, I wasn't feeling reasonable at all, and both of us knew it. I wanted her to resign. I wanted her to come back to the States and find a real job. I wanted her to live near me, where she belonged damnit. I wanted her to live *with* me.

But apparently it wasn't going to work out that way. Why would she worry about breaking that to me on the telephone? I didn't say anything more for a long time, for fear of saying something decidedly unreasonable and not in the least self-sacrificing.

Finally, she spoke, very quietly. "Well, then, I guess I'll see you Saturday?"

"Yes. I'll get back earlier if I possibly can. I—I love you."

"I love you, Chris."

There was a click and a hum, and I was sitting alone on a hotel bed in a room "lit" by three 25-watt bulbs, six thousand miles from home and from the only person who really mattered to me. I put the receiver back in its cradle.

All things considered, I didn't think it was going to go down as one of my better nights.

* * *

Clotilde Guyot's eyes were bright and brimming. "René Vachey was a saint."

I had brought this jolly, affable woman close to indignant tears with what I'd thought was a reasonably innocuous question: Could she tell me anything that might throw some light on Julien Mann's charges?

"Can you have any idea," she asked, "what it was for him to hide a family wanted by the Nazis? It wasn't only the risk of our being heard or seen, or of a surprise visit by the Gestapo, you see. It was the *number* of people whose goodness had to be relied on— the milkman who pretended to take no notice when a bachelor began buying three liters of milk a week, the doctor who asked no questions about a six-year-old 'nephew' never seen before, who had come down with whooping cough. We never knew when someone might take offense at a fancied slight and drop a vindictive word to some petty functionary. There was never a knock on the door when our hearts wouldn't stop."

She looked at me accusingly. "And he didn't have to do it, monsieur. He did it out of pity, out of kindness."

"I'm sorry, madame," I said sincerely. "I didn't mean to imply otherwise. I'm only trying to find out whatever I can about the Rembrandt and where it came from."

She shrugged. "I wouldn't know anything about his private purchases. I know where he bought it, that's all, as I told your friend."

"Yes," I said, careful not to tread too heavily, "but Julien Mann says it's actually a Flinck that—"

"I know what he says," she said tightly. She folded her hands on her desk. "I am quite sure he is mistaken."

"I think so, too, but I thought perhaps you might remember something about him—about his father, I mean—"

She jerked her head no. The tears were very close now. "It was fifty years ago, monsieur," she said through a throat that had all but closed up. "I don't recollect him at all."

"Well, then, anything at all that you can tell me about—about the way Monsieur Vachey conducted the business of the Galerie Royale, anything that might—"

The brilliant eyes finally overflowed, the tears running copiously down her cheeks and dripping from her soft chin. A crumpled handkerchief was pulled from somewhere to mop up, but the flood kept coming. She cried without sobs or snuffles, silently except for the accompaniment of long, hollow sighs. I began to apologize and get to my feet, but she waved me back into my chair, and after a while she was able to take a final dab at her reddened nose and tuck the handkerchief away again. A last, shaky sigh, and then came the flood of words.

What Julien Mann had told *Les Echos Quotidiens* was an unfounded distortion of a patriot's life. Yes, Vachey had worked with the Nazis, all right, but not *for* them, never *for* them. Yes, he had bought up Jewish collections that he'd known the Nazis would be interested in. No, he couldn't pay what they were worth, how could he? He paid what he could. And yes, he sold them to the Nazis, if you can call such transactions sales—sometimes he was paid a few francs more than he had paid himself. Just as often, not as much. And sometimes, if they felt like it, they would "pay" him with worthless modern paintings that even Hitler didn't want. One did not try to negotiate with the Nazis.

"I know these things for facts, monsieur. I was there."

"I'm sure you do," I said humbly.

"And if he hadn't done this, then what?" Madame Guyot went steadily on, her voice dignified and steady now. "Goering and Rosenberg and the rest of them would have seized the art directly from the Jews, simply walked in with their hooligans and taken it away, as they did in so many other cases, with no thought of paying anything at all for it. What René Vachey did in these matters, he did for the Jews, and for France, not for the Nazis. Because of him, many received the money they needed to flee, to save themselves. My own mother, my small brother ..." Her eyes shone.

"I know, madame," I said softly. "My friend told me about it." I was embarrassed: uncomfortably aware of the privileged, painless life I'd led; and aware, also, of how quickly I'd leaped to accuse Vachey, if only in my mind. It was good to hear another side of the story. I was starting to wonder how many more there were.

Madame Guyot, her face a shiny pink, seemed embarrassed too. Effusive and talkative she might be, but I didn't think that these deep, raw emotions had very often been put on public display. But she appeared to be relieved as well, purged by the deluge of memory and tears. A terminal sigh that lifted and dropped her shoulders was followed by a sweet, proud, almost playful smile, and a change of subject. "So, Monsieur Norgren, how do you like the office of the new proprietor of the Galerie Vachey?"

I looked around me, ready to change the subject myself. Clotilde Guyot's workspace made my office in SAM look like the grand ballroom at Fontainebleau. Located at the back of the house, behind the gallery, it was more like a utility room (which was probably what it had once been) than an office; a windowless, closetlike cubicle about twelve feet by twelve, with fuse boxes, fire extinguishers, and alarm system displays on the walls instead of artwork. There were metal file cabinets in two of the corners, and fiberboard storage boxes stacked up on the floor. A small table against one wall held a copier and a fax machine.

It was, in other words, still a utility room, except for the student-sized desk and two chairs that had been sandwiched between the copier and one of the cabinets.

I smiled back at her. "You must be looking forward to moving into Monsieur Vachey's office."

She goggled as if I'd made an indecent proposal. "Oh, I could *never* do that. I—no, that wouldn't be right at all."

But I could see that the idea simply hadn't occurred to her before, and that even while she was instinctively rejecting it, she was beginning to turn it over in her mind.

"Well, perhaps after a respectful interval," she allowed, trying the thought out on me. "Naturally, I wouldn't ask for the furnishings; they would be Christian's...." For a few seconds she floated off among bright images of Vachey's large and airy study. Then she blushed, distressed at the impropriety of such notions, and blurted: "Oh, monsieur, who would kill a man like that?"

"I don't know," I told her gently. "I know the police are doing their best to find out."

"Of course," she said without conviction.

"Madame, perhaps you can help. There are some things . . ."

Her eyes lit up again. "Yes?"

I leaned toward her over the cluttered desk. "There was a blue book in Monsieur Vachey's study, a scrapbook with clippings pasted into it. You know it?"

She nodded.

"You know what's in it?"

"Oh, yes."

I tried not to sound excited. "Yes? What?"

She smiled charmingly at me, her plump cheeks dimpling. "Oh, I couldn't possibly tell you that."

I stared at her. "But—is there anything about the Rembrandt?"
She shook her head.

"The Flinck, then?" I said after a moment. She shook her head.

"But it *is* a record of how he came by his collection, isn't that right?"
But she just went on wagging her head from side to side, sweetly

smiling all the while. She wasn't saying no, she was telling me I wasn't going to get an answer out of her.

My lips were dry. I licked them. "Madame, I *know* that's what it is. Perhaps I haven't been clear; I think it may have had something to do with his death."

"Oh, I think not. You must trust me, I'm afraid."

"But—" I paused to settle myself down. "I think it's pretty obvious to everyone," I said with a knowing, encouraging smile, "that Monsieur Vachey had some kind of plan in mind in connection with the gallery's current exhibition. Some kind of— of game. Everything about these two paintings—the Léger, the Rembrandt—has been peculiar, right from the beginning. You must see that."

"Certainly, I see it," she agreed.

"Well, that book might give us some clue as to what that game was."

"Ah, but I already know what it was."

"You do? What?"

"Oh, I couldn't possibly tell you that either." She was being positively coy now. I tried to think just where it was that I'd lost control of the conversation. Or had I ever had it?

"But he may have been killed over it," I said.

"Oh, I doubt that very much."

"If you won't tell me, you have to tell the police."

"I have to do no such thing, Monsieur Norgren."

"Madame Guyot," I said, doing what I thought was an excellent job of keeping my voice down, "surely you see that his murder could have been related to—to whatever he was planning."

"Well, I don't see how. It hasn't happened yet."

"All the same . . ." I stared at her. *Yet?* "Do you mean that it's still going to happen?"

Her smile was at its most grandmotherly and serene. "I certainly hope so, young man."

* * *

Good work, Norgren. Your skillful interrogation, disguised by a clever facade of bumbling incoherence, had pried from the elusive Madame Guyot a significant fact: "It" hadn't happened yet.

Whether "it" really had any connection with Vachey's death, I didn't know. Despite her supreme confidence that it didn't, I was reserving judgment. As to whether it had any bearing on the Rembrandt, I didn't see that there was much room for doubt. What else was there but the Rembrandt and the Léger?

There was, of course, one little thing I hadn't quite managed to find out: What was "it"? All I knew now that I hadn't known before was that the fireworks weren't over yet. Whatever kind of stink bomb Vachey had lit, there was a delayed-action fuse on it. But for the moment, there wasn't much to be done about it. All I could do, in effect, was wait for another shoe—dropped by a dead man—to hit the floor. And something told me it was going to make a hell of a noise.

On leaving the Galerie Vachey I went back to the Hôtel du Nord and called the prefecture of police to let them know that I would be in Paris overnight, staying at the Hôtel Saint-Louis. I left the message with a clerk, getting off the line before Lefevre could come on to hector me about keeping my nose out of official police matters. Not that my Paris plans had any direct relation to Vachey's death. I was going there to see what I could learn that might be relevant to the Rembrandt, and that was all. If I did happen to find out something that seemed pertinent to the murder, I would pass it right along to the inspector, braving the abuse I would no doubt receive for my trouble.

I threw a change of clothes and some toiletries into an overnight bag, stopped at the hotel desk to tell them I'd be back late the next day, and walked three blocks along the Avenue Maréchal-Foch to the railway station, where I was twenty-five minutes early for the 12:16 train for Paris. There wasn't time for lunch in the crowded buffet, but I went downstairs to where the coffee bar was, to get a quick double-espresso (I'd been away from Seattle too long; my blood was starting to thin) and a ham-and-cheese-stuffed croissant. Taking them to a circular stand-up counter with room for four, I glanced up at the tall, stooped, balding man across from me. We both spoke at the same time.

"Lorenzo! I thought you'd gone back to Florence."

"Christopher! I didn't know you were still here."

"Yes," I said, "I'm still trying to decide what to do about the Rembrandt. But what about you?"

"As long as I'm here in France—*ah, mi scusi, signora*—I thought I would visit some dealers. You know, I'm—*scusi, signore*—"

When Lorenzo Bolzano spoke, arms and elbows were likely to fly anywhere. The people on either side of him scowled at him, gathered up as much of their drinks as hadn't been spilled, and went elsewhere, muttering.

Lorenzo, grandly unaware of their withering glances, continued: "You know, I'm making some big changes in the collection, Christopher."

"Oh?" The "collection" was the great assemblage of paintings, rich in Old Masters, that had been begun by his father, Claudio, a man who made René Vachey seem almost like a penny-ante dabbler.

"Yes, I want to develop some real depth in the Synthetists. What do you think?"

What did I think? I thought it sounded like Lorenzo. The Synthetists—or Symbolists or Cloisonnistes—were a school of French artists who rejected naturalistic interpretation for a more "expressive" style in which objects were represented by areas of flat, brilliant color bounded by heavy swaths of black. Open-minded though I am, I've never been able to make much sense of them. They were Lorenzo's cup of tea, all right.

"Jean-Luc Charpentier is helping me. We're off to Lyon today to look at an Anquetin and a couple of Bernards." He poured the last of his Orangina into a paper cup, sipped from it, and smacked his lips. "It comes at a good time, you know. I finally managed to sell off those two Bronzinos, remember them?—brr, so cold, so formal—so I can afford to expand in other directions. When are you coming to Florence, Christopher? I want you to see."

The idea of finding Bronzino's elegant, exquisitely finished figures and limpid, enameled colors replaced by the turbid mush of Redon and company was enough to make me shudder. Lorenzo's discriminating father, I imagined, would be turning over in his grave about now. Of course, this is not to say that Claudio Bolzano had not been been lacking in certain respects. He had been a crook and a murderer, for example. Lorenzo, for all his nuttiness, was as honest and open as anyone could be.

"I'd like to do that, Lorenzo. Can I ask you about something else?"

"Sure, ask."

"It's about Vachey—"

His mobile face darkened. "Ah, Vachey. How terrible."

"You've bought a fair number of paintings from him, haven't you?"

He nodded, sipping the Orangina.

"Look, you're aware that I've got good reason to think there might be something fishy about this Rembrandt—it might not even *be a* Rembrandt. What I want to know is: Have you ever had any reason to doubt the authenticity of anything he sold you? Could you always rely on his attribution?"

Lorenzo's coffee-bean eyes gleamed; I had given him the kind of opening he loved. "But wherein does an attribution lie?" he asked in his rhetorical singsong. "Entirely in the perception of the attributer, no? Ah-ha-ha. Your question presupposes a simple dichotomy of possibilities that are inherent in the object—authentic or inauthentic, and nothing else, yes? And yet, surely you would not deny that the levels of attributional certainty are unlimited, and that they pertain more to the artificial and predetermined constructs of the attributer's perspective—"

I let him warm up long enough to allow me to swallow some of the croissant, then held up my hand. "Lorenzo, believe me, I'd like nothing better than to argue this out with you, but I have to catch a train in a minute. You know what I mean: Did he ever knowingly try to sell you a fake?" I drank some coffee. "Or unknowingly, for that matter."

The struggle was apparent in his face. Answering a yes-or-no question with a yes or a no didn't come naturally to Lorenzo. His Adam's apple bobbed up and down. "No," he said, practically sweating with the effort.

"Do you usually run your own tests on the objects you buy?"

"Certainly not. You don't need tests if you know what you're doing."

Maybe not, but did Lorenzo know what he was doing? In all the years I'd known him, I'd never resolved that question to my satisfaction. As a professor of art criticism and as a collector, he demonstrated formidable breadth. On the other hand, if you really believed that there wasn't any difference between fake and genuine, then how were you supposed to tell one from the other? Someday I'd have to pursue that with him.

"Once, years ago, my father began to have questions about a Ferdinand Hodler we'd gotten from Vachey," he admitted.

"They were unsubstantiated, as it turned out, but Vachey offered at once to take it back, without hesitation. This was five years after it had been purchased. So I think we can say he was a man of honor, in that regard at least."

Maybe yes, maybe no. A willingness to take back a dubious painting didn't say much one way or the other. Art dealers necessarily work hard to protect their reputations. They flinch from even the insinuation that a fake has ever passed through their hands. Rather than let the issue publicly arise, they will leap to refund money or make a quiet exchange at the first sign that a buyer is beginning to have doubts.

Naturally, that doesn't mean the next pigeon won't get stuck with it.

But at least I knew that Lorenzo and his father, who between them had been buying from Vachey for three decades, had never found anything, explicit or otherwise, to link Vachey with a fake, and that was something.

"However—" Lorenzo said, and I knew by the quickening of his voice that our descent into the concrete was over; we were off and running again, Lorenzo-style. "However, doesn't the very framing of your question assume, a priori, the existence of a unidimensional pole of reality entirely at odds with the precepts of Einstein's theory of the unified field—"

I was saved from the unimaginable consummation of this thought by the appearance of Jean-Luc Charpentier, who dragged Lorenzo off for the Lyon train. I waved them on their way, gulped the last of my croissant, and ran for the train to Paris.

CHAPTER 15

The Rue de Rivoli is one of Paris's great avenues, a broad and gracious thoroughfare bordering the Louvre and the Tuileries, designed under Napoleon and completed in the reign of Louis-Philippe. Elegant, block-long porticoes front massive, classical buildings crowned with striking mansard roofs. The arcades are crammed with smart shops, bookstores, and art galleries, and three of the world's most stately hotels—the Crillon, the Inter-Continental, and the Meurice—front it within three blocks of each other. Architectural historians generally describe this pleasing, harmonious boulevard as one of the triumphs of nineteenth-century urban design.

They are talking about the western half of it, from the Place de la Concorde to the Louvre. The other half doesn't get much play in the urban architecture journals. East of the Louvre, the Rue de Rivoli turns abruptly proletarian, becoming, in the space of a single block, a bustling, hustling center of gimcrackery and tourist schlock. Here is where you come when you want to purchase a scarf emblazoned with a map of the Paris Metro system, or when you've broken your gilt model of the Eiffel Tower and need to replace it, or, when you're looking for a good buy in Taiwanese Levi's.

Would you care to hazard a guess in which part of the Rue de Rivoli I found number 89—the address at which Vachey had supposedly purchased the Rembrandt? Correct, but why not, inasmuch as Vachey had never called the Atelier Saint-Jean anything but a junk shop?

The store shared a small, off-the-street arcade with a money exchange, a place that seemed to specialize in used issues of *Paris-*

Match, and a snack bar called Le Snack Bar. L'Atelier Saint-Jean itself had changed its name to Top Souvenirs, which I did not regard as an encouraging sign, and now seemed to specialize in plasticized place mats with pictures of Paris street scenes on them, and miniature, plastic-resin reproductions of the Winged Victory of Samothrace, the Venus de Milo, and other treasures of the Louvre. There wasn't a piece of original art in the place, old or new.

I asked the clerk if she knew where I could find Monsieur Gibeault.

"Alphonse!" she yelled at the top of her voice, and a moment later a bald, preoccupied man in a dirty yellow shirt came out of a side room, closing the door after himself. He peered at me, rotating a dead cigar stub in his mouth, then took me aside, a few feet from some browsers, and lifted his chin, watching me through narrowed eyes.

"You're Monsieur Gibeault, the proprietor?" I asked in French.

He nodded.

"I'm trying to find out about a painting you sold to a friend of mine a while ago."

"I don't sell paintings." He gestured at the shop. "You see any paintings?"

"I'm sure he bought it here—"

"Not from me. From my cousin."

"Your cousin?"

"He owned the place before me. He sold some paintings, stuff he picked up at auctions. Not me, they're a pain in the ass, not worth the trouble."

My confidence level continued to fall. "Could you tell me where I can get in touch with him?"

He laughed. "Sure, try the Montrouge Cemetery."

"He's dead?"

"As a baked codfish."

Somehow I got the impression they hadn't been close. "You wouldn't know where his sales records are?" Shrug.

"If I could see them, it might, er, be worth something to you."

It isn't the sort of line I'm very good at, and he just laughed some more. He spit some tobacco shreds onto the floor. "What kind of painting was this?"

"It may have been a Rembrandt."

He stared at me. "This guy—your friend—says he bought a Rembrandt *here?*"

I had to admit, it didn't seem very likely. "Well, it didn't look like a Rembrandt at the time. It was covered with grime—"

But he was laughing too hard to hear, real belly laughs of amusement. He clapped me on the shoulder. "Hey, I'll tell you what. If your friend's interested in some more Rembrandts, send him around. I'll give him a good price, he won't beat it anywhere. Van Goghs too, Michelangelos, you name it."

He laughed all the way back into the side room. "Unbelievable," I heard him splutter as he shut the door. He was wiping tears from his eyes.

If nothing else, I had certainly enlivened his day.

* * *

This unproductive encounter had been my first enterprise in Paris. I'd taken a taxi directly from the Gare de Lyon to the Rue de Rivoli. Now I hoisted my shoulder bag, found another taxi, and went to my hotel on the Île Saint-Louis to check in and drop off my things, telling the cab driver to come back in twenty minutes.

The Hôtel Saint-Louis is another one of those quiet, homey, unassuming little places—*sans prétensions,* as they like to say—at which I've been staying since my college days, but which Tony grumbles are no longer commensurate with my distinguished status as the representative of an important museum. Maybe not, but how many decent hotels are there in Paris, where you are a stone's throw—a literal stone's throw—from Notre-Dame, and yet able to sleep with your windows open for fresh air without getting a whiff of exhaust or hearing a single car all night long? Not many, I can tell you.

I got a top-floor room again (there is something about me that makes hotel clerks send me straight to the attic), unpacked the next day's clothes, and hung them in the closet. Actually, I like garret rooms. There is something about being under the eaves and looking out from dormer windows over the rooftops and chimney pots of an old city like Paris that puts you back a century or so. The shop windows four or five stories below have changed a lot over the years, and the people on the narrow streets are inescapably twentieth century, but the rooftops are right out of Daumier. I could have been looking from a nineteenth-century window onto a nineteenth-century roofscape. Well, I was, but you know what I mean.

But today my mind was firmly in the twentieth century; not the 1990s but the darker time of the 1940s. At four o'clock, in a little over half an hour, I was due at the apartment of Julien Mann, the Saint-Denis man who was claiming that the Rembrandt was no Rembrandt, and that René Vachey, Nazi stooge and profiteer, had virtually stolen it from his father fifty years before.

The efficient Calvin had gotten his telephone number for me, and I'd called him the previous evening after talking to Anne.

Getting him to speak with me, even on the telephone, hadn't been easy. I'd had to work hard to convince his wife, first that I wasn't a reporter, and second that, museum curator or not, I had no wish to do him out of a painting if it was rightfully his.

He'd picked up the telephone with undisguised reluctance. I had hoped, of course, that he would come across as an oily shyster who had seen a good thing and jumped at the chance to make a killing. Instead, he had been testy and curt, replying with crabby monosyllables to my long explanation of who I was and what I wanted to talk about. It had been all I could do to get him to agree to see me today, after he got home from his job at the payroll office of the Paris Metro.

Sad to say, he hadn't seemed remotely like a shyster.

The taxi took me north from the island over the Pont de Sully, past the blankly modernistic new opera house at the Place de la Bastille—state-of-the-art, they tell me, but about as cozy-looking as the infamous old prison that once stood there—and then up the Boulevard Beaumarchais, one of those lively streets that is everyone's idea of a Paris boulevard. Green-awninged cafes, *brasseries,* and restaurants follow one after another, most with calendar-scene tables and chairs out on the pavement. There are hordes of people who seem to have nothing more urgent to do than sit with a newspaper and a cup of coffee or an apéritif and watch the world go by. Even on a murky afternoon like this one, it was captivating.

But a little farther on, the character changes. The awnings thin out. The people do too. The buildings become more stark and functional, and by the time you pass the Gare du Nord and the railroad yards, you are in a crushingly bleak, low-rise zone of light-industry plants—window glass, mattress covers, food processing, electronics—with isolated ten- or twelve-story apartment buildings rising meagerly among them like skeleton fingers. On top of every apartment house is a huge neon advertisement lit in blue or red, even at 4:00 p.m. MINOLTA, the signs say, or MITA, or VOLVO, or SANYO; one towering word per rooftop, creating a weird, sparse forest of twisting neon. They are there to catch the eyes of train passengers coming into Paris. Thus, when you approach *from* Paris, they're backward: OVLOV, ATIM, ATLONIM. You begin to wonder whether you're in the outskirts of Paris or Smolensk.

Julien Mann lived in this charmless area, on the fourth floor of the OVLOV building. His wife, a self-effacing, slightly crosseyed woman in a simple, floral-printed dress—what used to be called a housedress in the United States before it went out of fashion forty years ago—let me into a foyer, then took me through an old-fashioned kitchen with a faint, greasy smell of lamb, and into a living room filled with heavy, dark furniture from the fifties. Everything was spotless, dustless, and in its place. I wondered if she had spent the day cleaning on my account.

Mann was sitting in one of a pair of overstuffed armchairs, waiting for me. According to the newspaper article he had been seven in 1942, so he was now fifty-seven. He looked seventy, and an old seventy at that—a frail, severe, schoolmasterish man in suit and tie, with a pinched nose, a long, narrow mouth, and fierce, squinting eyes behind thick lenses. His gray hair had retreated halfway up his scalp, but what was left stood up in two stiff waves reminiscent of the "horns"—rays, actually—on Michelangelo's *Moses*.

He rose halfway and shook hands perfunctorily. "Good day," he said in clipped French. His nose was faintly blue at the tip. He gestured me into the corner of the massive couch opposite him and resumed his seat, inspecting me from under drawn-together brows.

"So he's dead," he said.

Mrs. Mann murmured something and left us alone, closing the door behind her and going out—into the kitchen? The foyer? Silence followed. I had thought Mann was waiting for her to leave before continuing, but he just sat there, hunched alertly forward, elbows on the arms of his chair, squeezing the fingertips of one hand with the fingers of the other, scrutinizing me with unsettling directness. "So he's dead," it appeared, was all he meant to say.

"About the painting," I said.

His attention was acute but he didn't move, didn't speak. This was going to be up to me.

"First," I said, "I want you to know that I'm not against you. If the painting is rightfully yours—if Vachey got it the way you say he did—then my museum would never stand in the way of your getting it back."

He responded the way he had when I'd told him pretty much the same thing the night before, which is to say he didn't.

"On the other hand," I went on, "you can understand that since his story is so different from yours, I have to do my best to find out as much as I can for myself."

Silence. His fingers continued to pinch each other.

"May I ask you a few questions, Monsieur Mann? About René Vachey, to begin with?"

A dip of the chin, wary and reserved. It was more than I'd gotten till then.

"According to the *Echos Quotidiens* article, you said Vachey bought up Jewish art collections at desperation prices, then sold them to the Nazis at a profit."

Another minuscule nod.

"Aside from your own case, do you have any evidence for that?" I winced the moment the words were out. It sounded like an interrogation.

He stiffened. "It was no secret. Everyone knew it was so," he said sharply.

"But you were only seven," I said, trying to seem less like a cross-examiner. "I'm surprised that a child would be aware of such things."

I didn't like pressing him, but I had to find out what I could about Vachey's wartime activities. If he had really built his collection on what he'd made as a Nazi middleman and profiteer, then—even if the Rembrandt turned out not to be Mann's Flinck—Christian Vachey was welcome to it.

"I know," Mann said through clamped jaws, "because my father told me. Later ... in the camp."

"Did you know Vachey yourself? Were you ever in his gallery?"

"I saw him when he came for the painting. A cold man, with a cruel smile. He frightened me; I clung to my father's hand." He shook his thin shoulders, like a horse ridding itself of a biting fly. "My father pleaded for a reasonable amount, but Vachey laughed in his face and told him he was lucky to get anything. I recall this with perfect clarity, monsieur."

Did he? Or was it what Calvin had suggested—that he couldn't distinguish between what he remembered, what his father had told him, and what he had built up in his mind over the years? And what hope was there of my finding out after all this time?

"Maybe we ought to talk about the painting itself," I suggested. "You haven't actually seen it—that's right, isn't it?"

This was another important question Calvin had raised. Vachey's reception and showing were invitational affairs, not open to the general public. And no photos had been allowed. So how could Mann know what the picture looked like, let alone that it was the same one that had hung in his father's house?

"Not since 1942," he said.

"No, I'm talking specifically about the picture that's now on display in the Galerie Vachey."

His mouth set. "Not . . . since . . . 1942."

Time for another tack. "What I'm trying to find out, monsieur, is what makes you think that the Rembrandt that's now in Dijon is the same one—"

"Flinck," he said aggressively, "not Rembrandt."

"Well, either way, how do you know—"

"How do I know?" he said sharply. "I'll tell you how I know." He pushed himself forward a little more, chin thrust out. Perched on the edge of his seat, with those hunched shoulders and that pointy nose, he was like a belligerent little sparrow hawk.

"I never forgot that painting, monsieur. How could I? And I didn't forget Vachey either, but I didn't know what had happened to him. A few years ago I learned he was still alive, in Dijon, but what could I do? I assumed the painting was long gone. Then, a few weeks ago, there were stories of a mysterious Rembrandt he was giving away—a picture of an old soldier, it was said. Well, that gave the game away, because my father's painting was of an old soldier, and it was once thought that it might be by Rembrandt. But he had it looked into, you see."

"He had it appraised?"

"Yes, by some expert he'd heard of; from the Sorbonne, I think. It's definitely by Flinck. He was Rembrandt's student, you know."

"Ah. Even so, mightn't—"

"Let me finish. As it happens, my wife's cousin's son knows an *Echos Quotidiens* reporter who is familiar with the story. She was invited to the reception on Monday, and called me at once to describe it." His chin was thrust pugnaciously out; the tendons in his neck looked as if they might snap. "It is the same painting in every detail, monsieur!" he said triumphantly. "The old soldier, the hat, the plume!"

"Still," I said, "if you haven't seen it for yourself, you can't be sure—"

"And how am I to do that?" he said angrily. "My brother-in-law—ah, that is to say, my attorney—has demanded that I be given an opportunity to view it, and the Vachey people refuse. How then am I supposed to identify it? I ask you, is this just?"

Actually, yes. The thing was, the burden of proof was on Mann, and Sully had the right to refuse to let him see the picture. In a case like this, so the reasoning ran, it would be too easy for a spurious claimant to look at the object in question and say: "Yes, definitely, that is the very same painting stolen from my family fifty years ago. Now I remember this fly speck, that fleck of glue on the frame, this repair." Who could argue? On the other hand, keeping the painting hidden from view left precious little in the way of ammunition for a legitimate claimant who had no independent proof—no photographs, no insurance records—that it was his.

It was just, all right. What it wasn't, was fair.

"My apologies, monsieur," Mann said abruptly. "Would you care for an apéritif?"

I nodded gratefully. I cared for anything that might loosen things up.

The side table next to him held a tray with a freshly opened bottle of Chablis, a cut-glass decanter of *cassis,* the blood-red blackcurrant syrup the French love so much, and two silver-rimmed, ornately etched glasses that would have been right at home in my Norwegian grandmother's cupboard. He mixed us two *Kirs*—wine and *cassis*—and handed one to me. "To your health, monsieur." He swallowed.

The stuff is a bit sweet for my taste, but I raised my glass to him and took a sip. "Have you gone to the authorities about this, Monsieur Mann?"

He nodded. "The Ministry of Culture, the Ministry of Justice. They gave me a form to fill out. You know what they want to know?" He laughed bitterly. "'Describe any identifying marks on the back. Describe the type of frame.' Can you believe this? A seven-year-old child is expected to know such things, and then remember fifty years later?"

I was glad I hadn't gotten started on the list of questions I'd thought up for him: Which way was the subject facing? What color was the plume? Could you see one hand, two hands, no hands? For one thing, Mann would have taken offense and possibly thrown me out on my ear. For another, he was right: you couldn't expect a kid to be accurate about details half a century later. If he got the answers wrong, that didn't prove his story wasn't true. And if he got them right, that wouldn't prove he hadn't been coached.

"I have no such proof to offer, monsieur; just my own memory of the painting hanging in our living room."

"No papers at all? What about the attribution? Wasn't it documented?"

He shrugged. "Gone."

"Well, do you know anything about its provenance, about who owned it before?"

"It had been my Aunt Marthe's. She had it a long time. I think it was in her husband's family. They're all dead now." He spread his palms. "That's all I know. I wish I knew more."

So did I. "There aren't any relatives who could testify that they'd seen the picture in your house?"

He lifted his glass to his mouth with both hands and drank. His face was hidden. "From those days," he said, "I have no more relatives."

"What about—what about friends, neighbors? People who'd been in your house in the old days?"

He smiled. "I'll tell you a little story, monsieur." He stood up and went to the window, looking down on the railroad yards.

"In those days we lived in a pleasant apartment in the thirteenth *arrondisement*. Very nice neighbors. My father was a supervisor in the Post Office; a valuable employee, the Nazis let him stay on. But on December 28, 1942—just a few weeks after Vachey came and bought the picture—they came for him. For my mother, too, and my brother, Alfred. And me. We went to Birkenau, you know where that is?"

"Poland," I said softly. It was one of the camps at Auschwitz.

"Yes, Poland. Well, three years later I came back, without a family now, and went to live in Strasbourg with the family of an older boy I met in the camp. Then, in 1948, I returned to Paris. I was fourteen. I went back to see our apartment building. It was on the Avenue D'lvry. Some of our old neighbors still lived there, a very kind old couple named Odillard, just below our old apartment. They were happy to see me, and terribly distressed to hear about the deaths of my father and mother and brother, and they made me stay for dinner. They gave me *boeuf à la mode,* not so easy to find in those days."

He was leaning on the windowsill, staring into the haze but not seeing it. "They gave it to me on my parents' dinnerware," he said tightly. "The willow-pattern plates my mother had bought when my brother, Alfred, was born, the silver that had been a wedding gift from her sister in Toulouse. In the corner was the buffet that we had kept them in. They didn't even realize it." He turned toward me, as if curious as to what my response would be.

I didn't know what to say. "They'd stolen them?"

I think he smiled, but it was hard to tell. "Not stolen, no. These were good, kind-hearted people, not thieves or monsters. Still, after the Nazis took us away, they just walked upstairs and took what they wanted. So did our other neighbors. We were Jews, after all, and what ever they might say now, they didn't expect ever to see us again. And then, somehow, these good, kind-hearted people managed to forget where they'd gotten these fine, new possessions, managed to forget the times my mother had served *them* coffee and cake on those same cups and plates. And they really *did* forget, you see."

He came back and sat wearily down. "And so, Monsieur Norgren," he said, picking up his *Kir* again, "do you really expect that I could find friends and neighbors who would remember the beautiful portrait that hung in our home, and vouch for my claim?"

Again, there wasn't much I could say. I sipped some more from my drink.

Mann had finished his, and the alcohol appeared to have mellowed him. I suspected he didn't often drink; both bottles had been full to start with. "You seem like a nice young man," he said—making that twice in one day that someone had called me "young man." "But I must warn you that I will not rest until this painting is returned. What's right is right."

Underneath the resolution there was a kind of subdued despair. He was fighting the good fight, I thought, but in his heart he didn't believe he could win it. Not against the famous René Vachey. Not against a big American museum.

"I understand," I said. "We're not against you, Monsieur Mann. We want the painting to go where it rightfully belongs. If it's your father's painting, I will do what I can to help you get it back. I mean that sincerely."

Behind the bottle-bottom glasses Mann's small, fierce eyes reappraised me. He'd begun with the idea that he was receiving an enemy. Now he wondered if I was—maybe not an enemy.

"Thank you," he said gruffly. "I would like you to know that my motive is not profit. I would never sell it. It's all that's left of my father's. Everything else—everything from my childhood—is gone."

"I understand," I said again. I was almost starting to wish it *would* turn out to be his.

He leaned dreamily against the back of his chair. "It's a wonderful painting, isn't it? As a boy, I—another drink, monsieur?"

I shook my head. The talk was winding down, and I sensed that I'd be going soon. Chalk up one more conversation that had answered no questions, resolved no ambiguities.

"As a boy, my older brother and I—Alfred was his name—would play at soldiers. The old man in the picture was our captain; *Capitaine Le Nez,* we called him. Because of the nose, you see. We would line up before him and salute ..." An unreadable expression rolled over his face. His hand moved up to rest, trembling, on his domed forehead. "My God . . ."

My interest quickened. "What is it?"

"It's broken," he said wonderingly. "I forgot completely. We broke it."

"You broke the painting?"

"The frame—we broke the frame. I can describe it perfectly." Agitated, he reached out to touch my wrist with dry, spidery fingers. "That would be proof, wouldn't it?"

He and his brother, he said, had been reporting to *Capitaine Le Nez* one morning, when the play had gotten a little rough. They had accidentally knocked the picture from the wall and chipped a piece from the lower right corner. Terrified, they had glued it back on and apparently gotten away with it; their father had never noticed the repair.

"I'm afraid I don't remember noticing it either," I said.

"Well, we did a good job gluing it!" He was squirming with excitement. "Look for it, you'll see; the lower right corner! A piece—so big." He used his fingers to make a triangular shape about an inch on a side.

"What kind of frame was it?"

He gestured impatiently. "I don't remember the frame—no wait, I think it had fancy carving—but the break—look for it!"

"I'll look," I said. "You'd better mention this to your attorney too."

He jerked his head no. "I don't trust him. I trust you, monsieur. *You* look, please." He was out of his chair and practically pulling me out of mine, as if the sooner he got me up and walking, the sooner I'd be back in Dijon.

"I'll look," I promised again as I stood up, "but—I'm sorry, Monsieur Mann—I think I would already have seen it if it was there."

CHAPTER 16

I not only didn't think it was there, I *knew* it wasn't there. I'd examined every millimeter of that painting, and there weren't any repaired cracks in the lower right corner or anywhere else. Somewhere along the line, the frame (which did have carving on it, but how hard would it have been to guess that?) had been stripped down to bare wood and lightly stained, so even an expertly done job would have been visible, let alone the work of a couple of scared kids.

But that proved nothing, one way or the other. The picture had recently been relined; who was to say it hadn't been reframed as well?

How about the rest of Mann's story? Well, in general, I believed it; that is, I believed that his father had sold *some* painting to Vachey in *some* circumstance, that it was probably a picture of an old man who had a hat with a plume, and that *somebody* had identified its creator as Govert Flinck. I also believed that Mann was telling the truth as he remembered it; why would he invent the tale about breaking the frame if it hadn't really happened?

He had nothing to gain from urging me to look for a crack that wasn't there.

Beyond that, I didn't know how much to take at face value. Mann's perceptions were too old, too thoroughly pickled in bitterness. A well-justified bitterness, to be sure, but did Vachey—Vachey, personally—deserve it? How could I reconcile Mann's cruel, smiling profiteer with Clotilde Guyot's compassionate patriot? I knew which one I wanted to believe in, but I didn't know which one was true.

And what about the painting itself, the one Mann and his dead brother had played in front of—could it really have been painted by Govert Flinck? Sure, but if so, it wasn't the same painting Vachey had donated to SAM. The more I thought about that picture—and I'd been thinking about it a lot—the more convinced I'd become that that subtle, marvelous old soldier had been beyond anything Flinck could have done. It was a Rembrandt, all right; Mann was wrong about that. If I had to, I was ready to stand up to the Rembrandt Police and defend it.

But that didn't mean I was out of the woods. It was still possible that *Un Officier* was indeed the picture Vachey had bought from Mann's father, but that it had been incorrectly ascribed to Flinck instead of to Rembrandt at the time, and Mann had been talking about a Rembrandt all along; he just didn't know it.

Under ordinary circumstances, I wouldn't have given that a lot of credence—there are quite a few similar pictures out there, of quite a few similar old men, by quite a few competent but lesser Dutch artists (such as Govert Flinck), and Mann's picture was most likely to be one of them. If so, it was probably somewhere in Russia or eastern Germany, and he didn't stand a chance of ever seeing it again. But Vachey's prankish conditions and whimsical behavior—and above all, his murder—had made the circumstances anything but ordinary. All bets were off.

I was so muddled and dithery by this time that I was half-rooting for Julien Mann—maybe more than half—to prove his case, which was a pretty strange state of affairs, considering where I stood if he did.

Such were my disordered reflections when the taxi I'd taken from Mann's apartment building in Saint-Denis let me off at 27 Rue Jean-Mermoz, the snazzy Right Bank condominium that Calvin the Resourceful had learned was the address of Gisèle Grémonde, ex-diva, ex-lover of René Vachey . . . and the woman who had been so eager to tell me just what was in that mysterious, missing blue book that had gotten me pitched out of a window—and perhaps gotten René Vachey pitched out of this life.

* * *

She wasn't so eager anymore. "I am entertaining," she told me imperiously, standing in her doorway and squarely blocking my way. "And I am about to go out. One would do better to telephone before calling, monsieur."

She was light years removed from the stricken hag who had sat numbly through the presentation of Vachey's will—and from that blowzy and malicious drunk who'd cornered me at the reception as well. Her coppery wig was back in place—not in the least askew this time—her vivid makeup had been recently and emphatically plastered on, and she was manifestly in control of her faculties.

Behind her was a small foyer, a very different thing from Julien Mann's, with a parquet floor, and a compact Mazarin writing desk and Louis XIV chair against one wall, beneath a collection of signed photographs. I recognized Toscanini, Pinza, and Callas. From the room beyond came the raspy sound of an old recording; a soprano singing a lilting, Verdi-like aria. I thought I could make out, in the middle tones, a hauntingly sweet, youthful version of Madame Grémonde's time-coarsened voice.

I apologized for the second time (I'd had to do some fast talking at the downstairs speaker-phone to get her to let me into the building). "Perhaps you don't remember speaking with me at the reception the other night," I said now, "but—"

"You are correct, Monsieur Norgren, I don't."

"You were telling me about a book of Monsieur Vachey's; a blue scrapbook . . . ."

She watched me impatiently, one plucked eyebrow slightly raised. "I do not recall it," she said coldly. "I have no idea what you're talking about."

"Madame, are you telling me the police haven't been in touch with you about this?"

Her mouth tightened. "So I have you to thank for that. Well, I'll tell you what I told them. If I indeed said what you said I did, I'm afraid I have no idea at all what was in my mind. I may have had something more to drink than was good for me. When that happens I have been known to become a little, shall we say, fanciful."

No, I thought, that wasn't it. The difference between now and Monday night wasn't in her blood-alcohol level, it was in her feelings toward Vachey. Last Monday she had thought he was giving her treasured Duchamp to someone else, and she had burned to destroy him for it. Now she knew that in almost his last act he had lived up to his old promise, and like Clotilde Guyot she was determined to protect his memory.

"I'll tell you what I think, madame," I said bluntly. "I think there are records in it of his purchases during the Occupation. I think you're trying to keep them from coming out to preserve his reputation, and I think you're making a mistake. It was fifty years ago, a lifetime away."

"You may think as you please, monsieur," she said. "And now, if that is all . . . ?"

I made a last try at keeping her from shutting the door in my face. "The music—it's beautiful."

She warmed slightly. "Thank you. You like grand opera?"

"Very much," I said, wondering why I hadn't started this way. I tilted my head, the better to hear the music. "I've always loved Verdi, and that soprano is wonderful—" I let a slow smile come to my face. "Why, that's you, isn't it?"

Contemptible, I admit it, but it was a desperate stab. Who else was there who could fill me in on that damn scrapbook?

Madame Grémonde's face iced up again. "The composer is not Verdi but Bellini. And the singer is not me, it is Lily Pons." She pursed her crimson lips, lifted her several powdered chins, and swung the door closed. A second later she opened it a crack. "*I* had no trouble with my lower registers. Good evening, monsieur."

* * *

So, after almost a full day in Paris, after hustling in and out of taxis to hunt down Julien Mann, Gisèle Grémonde, and M. Gibeault of Top Souvenirs, I had come away with next to nothing. Well, with nothing.

There was still one person left on my Paris agenda: Ferdinand Oscar de Quincy, former director of the Seattle Art Museum, former captain with MFA & A, the U.S. Army's art recovery squad, and the man who had once found and returned a dozen of Vachey's own paintings, thereby sowing the seed—so Vachey had claimed—for his eventual donation of the Rembrandt to SAM. I was hoping de Quincy could help me get straight in my mind just who René

Vachey was. But that wouldn't be until tomorrow morning, when we were to meet at the Louvre. For the moment, I was at liberty, alone and with nothing to do in the City of Lights. Nothing I felt like doing, anyway.

There comes a time in most foreign trips, especially when things are not going as well as they might, when one craves the solace of one's native food, and this felt like it. From Madame Grémonde's condominium I walked a block to the Champs Elysées, then turned right for two more blocks until I came to the huge, multifloored Burger King. There, surrounded by black- and-white photographs of American movie actors looking curiously Gallic—a tousled Clark Gable with a woebegone and philosophical half smile, a sleepy-eyed Gary Cooper in three-quarter profile, cigarette dangling from the corner of his mouth as if he were doing an Yves Montand imitation—I made a solitary, satisfying dinner of *le chicken deluxe* (a double-order), *le milkshake au chocolat,* and *les frites,* earning a pitying look from the server when I asked him to hold the mayo and give me some ketchup to go along with the fries.

Afterward, I walked a few steps to a movie theater and watched Kevin Costner emote in dubbed French as *Robin de Bois, Prince des Voleurs.*

* * *

By the next morning a fresh breeze had blown away the murk that had been hanging over Paris. The city looked glorious, and I was full of Yankee optimism and energy, the result, no doubt, of all that fried chicken in my bloodstream. At the hotel I had the standard Parisian breakfast of coffee, rolls, and croissants, and started off on foot for the Louvre, a distance of a mile and a half.

Walking in Paris these days is easier than it used to be, mostly because you no longer have to keep an apprehensive eye on your feet; the notoriously messy dog-droppings (Parisian dogs must be fed a richer diet than those anywhere else) are largely a thing of the past. Seemingly, this is due to the painted white signs on the sidewalks showing an alert-looking dachshund in profile, its nose pointed intelligently toward the curbside gutters down which a cleansing tide of water is flushed several times a day. Beneath the dachshunds, white arrows point in the same direction for good measure, so that even the dumbest dog should get the message.

Apparently they do, because *les dejections canines,* as the French so delicately put it, are no longer the problem they were. You can safely raise your eyes to look at Paris now.

And on a crisp, sparkling fall morning, Paris really is the most gorgeous city in the world. It has everything: trees, parks, a handsome river, historic bridges, breathtaking architecture. And surely no great city is less overwhelming. Along the Quai du Louvre—along the entire length of the Champs Elysées, for that matter—there isn't a building over nine stories high, and most are the same pleasing, uniform seven floors. Aside from the Eiffel Tower, only a single tall structure is visible, and that is a relatively modest skyscraper off in the distance to the south, beyond the Luxembourg Gardens. In the heart of Paris, unlike the heart of London or Tokyo or New York, you get plenty of sky.

It was a good morning for a brisk pace, and I reached the Louvre in under twenty minutes, but it took me almost another ten to walk the length of the south facade and around the east wing to the new entrance (before it was the world's biggest museum, which it still is, it was the world's biggest palace). Still, I arrived ten minutes early at the place de Quincy and I had arranged to meet: the gleaming, columnar base of the science-fictionish elevator in the new subterranean lobby. There was no sign of anyone who might be de Quincy. The only person who looked as if he were waiting for someone was a gnarly, jug-eared, close-cropped, wide-eyed old codger in a knit sport shirt, double-knit trousers, and Day-Glo orange-and-purple jogging shoes; American, all right, but with Boise, Idaho, or Billings, Montana, written all over him, along with "first goldanged trip to Europe."

I wandered around the big new shop on the mezzanine, peeking over the railing every few minutes for a sign of de Quincy. We had picked the Louvre to meet because de Quincy, who lived on the outskirts of Paris in the picture-postcard village of Sceaux, had said he had errands to run in the city, and why not meet in a museum, and what was my favorite museum in Paris?

He'd been in a hurry to get off the telephone, and I had instinctively said the Louvre, which isn't what you're supposed to say, not if you're a visiting *cognoscente*. You're supposed to name some charming little museum that ordinary people have never heard of: the Musée Cognacq-Jay, for example, or the Nissim de Camondo. Just as in New York it's bad form to tell anyone your favorite museum is the Met on Fifth Avenue. You're supposed to say the Cloisters, or the Cooper-Hewitt.

But the Louvre *is* my favorite museum in Paris, and I said so, and de Quincy had been agreeable, and here I was. And there, unless I was mistaken, was de Quincy, a tall, patrician-looking old man in a well-cut double-breasted suit, who was glancing around him— looking for me, I supposed—with some impatience. I know quite a few Americans who've lived abroad for a long time, and there is a certain look they get, an expatriate manner, proud, defiant, and forlorn all at once. And however Italianized or Frenchified they become, there is always an indefinable kernel of something that gives them away as displaced Yanks.

I went downstairs and walked up to him. "Mr. de Quincy? I'm Chris Norgren. It's a—"

"*Pardon, monsieur,*" he said politely, "*je ne parle pas anglais.*" He edged away to do his waiting somewhere else.

A few yards away the other old gentlemen still stood there, tugging reflectively on an oversized earlobe and eyeing me.

Could it be? I approached tentatively. "Er, Mr. de Quincy?"

He grinned and stuck out his hand. "Call me Fuzzy."

* * *

Well, it had been a natural mistake. With a name like Ferdinand Oscar de Quincy, the image that comes to mind does not include Day-Glo jogging shoes and double-knits. But, it turned out, they suited him perfectly. At a time when it was almost a given that the directors of art museums would come from the cosmopolitan East Coast, be scions of art-collecting families, and have Ivy League degrees, de Quincy had been born on a wheat farm along the Idaho-Washington border (so I hadn't been so far off), and gotten his education at Gonzaga University in Spokane.

He had come to the Seattle Art Museum as a part-time bookkeeper and business manager, developed an interest in art, and gone to the University of Washington in his spare time for a master's degree in art history. He'd enlisted in the Army in 1941, fought his way through France and Belgium in the infantry, and then been transferred to MFA & A, where he'd worked for three years, in the thick of the most exciting and successful art recovery operation in history. Afterward, he'd returned to SAM, and when the directorship became vacant, he'd been a shoo-in.

All this I learned inside of ten minutes, in the mezzanine cafe, where de Quincy ordered a *croque-monsieur*—a toasted ham-and-cheese sandwich—and I had a plain omelet with fried potatoes. (The French breakfast croissant, tasty as it is, is not long on staying power.)

Ferdinand Oscar "Fuzzy" de Quincy was a friendly, lively chatterbox of a man. All I had to do was raise an interested eyebrow or murmur an encouraging monosyllable, and he would happily take the ball and run with it. After the day I'd spent yesterday trying to pry information out of one suspicious, close-mouthed individual after another, he was a pleasure.

He'd read with sadness about Vachey's death, he'd heard about Julien Mann's claims, he even knew that I was looking into Vachey's background, and he was delighted—" just tickled pink"—that I'd sought him out. I'd come to the right man, he assured me.

He explained that he'd been part of the MFA & A team that had been assigned to Neuschwanstein, the fairyland Bavarian castle in which the Germans had stored the bulk of their French loot. While there, he'd identified and supervised the return of twelve eighteenth-century French paintings taken from Vachey's personal collection. He'd met Vachey for the first time shortly afterward, and the overjoyed Vachey had talked about repaying him. De Quincy had suggested that he give something to the Seattle Art Museum some time when he—

"Could we just hold up a minute, Mr. de Quincy?"

"Fuzzy."

"Fuzzy. You're saying the Nazis *took* these paintings from him, right?"

"Sure did. Confiscated most of his collection. Trumped up some charge or other. Consorting with Jews, something like that." Voluble though he was, de Quincy didn't believe in wasting words just to make complete sentences.

"If that's so, it suggests that he wasn't working *for* them at all, that Mann's story isn't accurate."

He snorted. "Story's piffle. Vachey was trying to help those Hebrew folk, not hurt 'em. Couldn't stand the Nazis. Fella's all mixed up, take it from me."

I put down my fork. This was what I'd hoped to hear. And it came from a man who had no ax to grind. I felt a tingling in the muscles of my shoulders, as if a weight that had sat on them for a long time had begun to lift.

"So what Clotilde told me is true," I said, more to myself than to him.

De Quincy, chewing, watched me with interest. "Gallery manager? Depends on what she told you."

I told him what she'd said: that Vachey had bought pictures during the Occupation and re-sold them to the Nazis—out of compassion, not avarice—that he'd made no profit and had meant to make no profit, that often the Germans had "paid" him not in money but in worthless paintings they'd forced him to take, or in almost equally worthless Occupation francs.

De Quincy waved a corner of his sandwich until he got his mouthful down. "Story's piffle too," he said.

My shoulders stopped tingling. "But—"

"You happen to know a Swiss dealer named Gessner?"

"I don't think so."

"Zurich. You ought to talk to him sometime. If he's still alive. Bought a bunch of those worthless paintings from Vachey in forty-four. Nice little odalisque by Matisse, couple of Vlaminck still lifes . . . let's see, Dufy, Rouault, Pierre Bonnard—"

"I don't understand."

De Quincy smiled. "Well, what do you mean by 'worthless'? Depends on who's doing the valuing, wouldn't you say?"

I almost asked him if he'd been talking to Lorenzo, but he quickly explained what he meant. Hitler had detested modern French art so much that he had forbidden the shipment of it into Germany. Thus, when the Nazi "collection agencies" in France found pieces of twentieth-century French art in their hauls, they were unable to do anything with them but try to sell them in a virtually nonexistent French market—or, as in Vachey's case, trade them for art that met the Führer's aesthetic standards. So Vachey was able to buy up, say, a Flinck at negligible cost, trade it for, say, a Matisse from the Germans, and then make a huge profit in the Swiss market, which had remained active through the war. This he did more than once, and according to de Quincy, the proceeds had provided the nest egg from which he'd built his fortune.

"In Switzerland, you see," De Quincy said, "he could get some real money, not the play money they had here during the Occupation."

"Yes, I see," I said woodenly. I saw that Vachey, after all was said and done, had been what Mann had said he was: a parasite who'd fed on his countrymen's helplessness in the most terrible of times.

"Now don't go off all half-cocked," de Quincy said. "My opinion, Vachey was an honest-to-Jesus hero, Chris. Took some real risks—I mean stand-him-in-front-of-the-firing-squad risks—to help people get away before the Nazis got them. Helped them get rid of their collections, helped them get out of the country—"

"And made a killing doing it."

"Sure he did, why shouldn't he? Guy wasn't a professional hero, he was a businessman, what do you expect? I'm telling you, he did a lot of good. More than you know. Lot of sides to the man. Come on, you want to walk through the museum or not?"

I had a final, half-hearted bite of the cooling omelet. "Sure, let's."

But the Louvre is not a museum you walk "through," not unless you have three days to do it. You have to pick your area, and I chose the first floor of the Denon wing, where the main European painting collection was. As we slowly climbed the broad staircase past *Winged Victory*—the full-size marble version—de Quincy told me about an aspect of Vachey's endlessly varied life of which I'd known nothing.

In the early eighties, it seemed, he had acted as a middleman for the French government, successfully negotiating with shadowy figures in East Germany for the return of a famous ceramics collection that had been looted from a museum in Nancy during the war. This patriotic mission he took on without any payment and without any public recognition. His part in it came out only when the French government minister involved retired and published his memoirs. More recently there had been governmental leaks suggesting that it had been only one of several such delicate assignments Vachey had performed for his country.

"So you see," de Quincy said, pausing to catch his breath at the top of the stairs, "more to the man than meets the eye."

"Amen to that," I said. "Did you stay in contact with him all these years?"

"Not really. Followed his career, of course. Ran into him now and again. Always liked the fella. Something to him."

"Fuzzy, why didn't he invite you to the reception the other night? That gift was really in your honor."

He smiled, pleased. "Did invite me. Fact is, I don't go much of anyplace if it involves sleeping out." He patted his hip. "Ligament troubles. Need to sleep in my own bed. Tell me, what's the Rembrandt look like?"

"It looks good. I think it's authentic; a lot like the one in the Getty, but with a huge plume and a greenish cast in the background. I'm sure it's not listed in Bredius. Does it sound like anything you've ever run into with Vachey?"

He shook his head. "Nope. Wasn't in his collection when I saw it way back when."

"I don't suppose you'd have any idea where he might have gotten it?"

"Nope. All I know is what he said. Junk shop. Knowing him, it could be true."

We walked through the Apollo Gallery, where groups of avid schoolchildren were clustered three deep around cases holding the crown jewels, turned right, and found ourselves at one end of what used to be called the Grande Galerie, and with good reason. Now blandly referred to as Denon Rooms 4 to 8 for touristic ease, these adjacent spaces form a single glorious gallery 1,000 feet long (I know because I paced it once and counted 332 steps), the longest, greatest gallery of art that ever existed, densely lined on both sides with masterpieces of French painting—Watteau, Poussin, La Tour, Fragonard—and a few dozen assorted Italians—Botticelli, Giotto, Giovanni Bellini, for starters—thrown in to avoid too parochial a flavor. The elegant, arched ceiling is punctuated every 250 feet or so by an ornate, marble-columned cupola. At the far end, you go around a crick in the floor plan, and there you are, looking down an additional 300 feet of Flemish, Dutch, and Spanish masterworks.

All this is one half of one floor of one wing. And there are three wings. Some museum.

While we walked slowly through it, pausing occasionally to look at a particular painting, I told de Quincy about the puzzling restrictions that Vachey had placed on both the Barillot and SAM, and about the generally queer goings-on that had followed them.

By the time I'd finished, we'd walked the entire floor—the lengths of four football fields, as an American guidebook predictably puts it—and were sitting on a stone bench at the head of the east staircase, surrounded by El Grecos, Murillos, and Riberas.

"Interesting," de Quincy said when I was done. "What do you make of it?"

"That's what I was going to ask you. What do you suppose he could have been up to?"

He shook his head slowly back and forth. "Got me."

"Look, Fuzzy, I have to come to a decision tomorrow. If you were in my place, would you take the painting?"

"If what's holding you back is worrying about what he did or didn't do in the forties, I'd say yes, for damn sure, take it."

"That's the main thing, but those weird conditions of his make me nervous too. You knew him pretty well—"

"Not so well."

"But you liked him, you admired him." He nodded. "Fair statement."

"Well, would you say you could take him at his word?"

"Well—"

"If he told you what he told me—that there was nothing tricky behind the restriction on testing, or behind the time limits he set up, or behind anything else, would you trust him?"

De Quincy pulled thoughtfully at his earlobe. "About as far as I could throw him."

CHAPTER 17

I got back to Dijon at 3:00 p.m., which left me just twenty-seven hours to make up my mind about the Rembrandt. If I didn't sign off on Vachey's conditions by the close of business Friday, the offer would be void, and the painting, presumably, would revert with the rest of Vachey's "residue" to his son, Christian.

Christian, who had tried to keep me away from the Rembrandt, and Froger away from the Léger. Christian, who had tried to wrest the Duchamp from Gisèle Grémonde. Christian, who was so little trusted by his father that the older man had kept his new will secret from him, and in it had aced him out of the ownership of the Galerie Vachey and removed him as executor besides.

However, Christian had also been living in the same house with his father for the last six months. Disappointed in his son or not, it seemed probable that Vachey would have let him in on whatever game he was playing with the paintings, and even more likely that Christian would know something about that scrapbook. Until now, however, I hadn't even tried to talk to him. I didn't think he'd see me, for one thing (he had done his best to keep me out of the house altogether), and for another, how could I trust anything told to me by a man who was in line to get the Rembrandt if I turned it down? So I had started with likelier sources, and struck out. Pepin claimed he knew nothing about anything; Gisèle knew about the book but wasn't telling. And Clotilde knew about the book *and* about Vachey's intentions, but she wasn't telling either. That left Christian.

* * *

"Okay, I'll say it one more time," Christian said with a sort of nonchalant irritation. "One: I don't know anything about any blue scrapbook, I never heard of any blue scrapbook, I never saw any blue scrapbook. Two: I was born in 1956, so do you want to tell me how I'm supposed to know anything about my father's activities in the war? Three: I don't know what my father had in mind when he offered you the Rembrandt, why should I? Okay?"

He went back to what he'd been doing: arranging a carton of dog-eared papers and index cards into neat little stacks on the surface of an aged rolltop desk. His English was idiomatic and barely accented, the pronunciation American rather than British, with a slangy, choppy flavor that gave credence to the stories of mob connections in Miami.

"That's hard to believe," I said. "You're his son. You were living in the same house."

He shrugged and stood up, stretching. There was a faint whiff of expensive cologne, dry and lemony. "Well, I can't help what you want to believe. Look, I'm sorry, but I have a million things to do, you know?"

This was the way it had gone from the beginning. We were on the first floor of Vachey's house, at the end of a blind corridor that served as a small study. Christian, in a pin-striped gray suit, again with no tie, hadn't been out-and-out rude, but he hadn't bothered to stop his paper-arranging when I'd arrived either, and he hadn't offered me a seat. I wasn't sure if I'd ever quite gotten his full attention.

Now he smiled and held out his hand. "Sorry, my friend. I wish I could have helped." I could see that his mind was already back on his cards.

There wasn't much I could do but go. "Well, thanks for your time," I said. "If you happen to think—"

And right then, as suddenly as that, one feature of the gluey, murky swamp I'd been sloshing around in for days popped into sharp, clean focus. I recognized his cologne. I remembered the last time I'd smelled it—a second or so before I went flying out the window of Vachey's study. At the time I'd had the impression that a faint, citrusy, distinctive smell had come from the opened pages of the scrapbook, but it hadn't come from the pages at all.

"You pushed me out that window," I said.

I finally had his attention. He jerked his hand out of mine and took a step back, eyes startled. I had laughed when I said it—a sort of delighted cackle—because it felt so good to finally *know* something, and Christian probably thought I'd gone around the bend.

"Don't be dumb," he said. "What window? What are you talking about? Why the hell would I want to push you out of a window?"

"To keep me from seeing the book."

"*What* book?" Finding that I didn't intend to strangle him after all, he'd managed to put some self-assurance back into his voice. He raised his eyes to the ceiling and tried an indignant laugh. "I can't believe it. This guy has the nerve to walk in here—"

"The hell with it," I said. "I'm not going to stand here and fight about it. You tried to kill me, and I can damn well prove it, and as far as I'm concerned, I'm just as happy letting Lefevre get it out of you."

I turned smartly and strode down the long corridor, the old wooden floor groaning at each step. I had made it all the way to the door that led to the public part of the house and gotten it open before he called out.

"Wait a minute, will you . . . Chris?"

I turned, still holding the handle. For a moment there, I thought I'd overplayed my hand.

"All right, okay, you're right," he said. He came down the long hallway with his rolling, cocky stride, letting a sheepish, oily half-smile form on his face, confident that no one could fail to be charmed by his unassuming candor.

"You're right," he said again when he reached me, "what can I say? But believe me, doing you any harm was the last thing I was thinking of. I mean, I don't bear you any personal animosity, Chris. Far from it."

"Well, that's a load off my mind."

He laughed. "Let me explain, okay? When I heard that damn woman start—"

"Gisèle Grémonde?"

He nodded. "—start in with that stuff about the upstanding René Vachey, the great René Vachey, and she actually started talking about that scrapbook of his, I took off for the study to make sure the door was locked and the damn thing was out of sight." He shrugged. "Well, you beat me to it, and I saw you disappearing behind a corner with the damn thing, so I followed you in and ... I guess I just acted without thinking. I'd had a few too many, you know?"

He flashed his friendly, between-us-guys smile to show that he knew I understood that it had all been in good fun. "Look, I wasn't thinking about pushing you out the window. All I was after was the book. I'm not a violent guy, Chris. Hell, I'm a pacifist, believe me."

"I believe you." I wasn't sure if I did or not, but I wasn't interested in arguing with him. It was information I was after.

"Thanks, Chris. So—you going to go to the cops?"

"That depends. I need to know what's in the book."

This was a bald-faced attempt to mislead him. Of course I would go to the police. But before I did, I wanted to see that scrapbook for myself. With the matter left in Lefevre's hands, who knew when, or if, I would ever see it? Not by six o'clock tomorrow, anyway.

"Sorry." He shook his head sadly. The dangling earring swayed, the Superman forelock stirred.

"Look, Christian," I said, "let's get something straight. All I'm trying to do is find out if there's anything in there that might make me think twice about accepting the painting. Otherwise, I'll just have to take a chance and go ahead and sign off on it."

He could hardly mistake the implication of this wily ploy: If I rejected the painting, he'd get it. So, if anything, it was to his advantage to let me see the scrapbook. It made sense to me; I hoped it made sense to him.

Apparently, it did. He stepped back into the hallway. "Okay, come on in."

Once inside, he closed the door. "I guess you know what's in it, then."

I nodded. "I think so. Notes and clippings your father kept of his art purchases—starting during the Occupation."

"That's it. Why he kept them all these years—why he kept them in the first place—I don't know. I suppose he figured that some day Julien Mann or someone like him would crawl out from under a rock and start whining about being robbed, and my father wanted to be able to prove he didn't do anything illegal."

No, there had to be more to it than that in Christian's mind. "Then why push me out the window to keep me from seeing it?"

He gazed sincerely at me, man to man. "Look, Chris, I'm not ashamed of anything my father did. But times change, you know? And what people had to do to survive in 1942—it's the easiest thing in the world to ... to make it look lousy today. People don't know the way it was. Well, my father had a hell of a lot of enemies, I think you know that, and they'd just love to haul his name through the mud if the stuff in that book ever got to be public knowledge. And that's something I can't let happen. My father's name is the most important thing he left me."

It sounded good, and Christian delivered it in manly fashion, with just the right amount of eyeball-glistening. But it all seemed a little too high-minded to me for the would-be kingpin of Tanzanian cement and New Caledonian seaweed. What Christian had really been trying to do, I thought, was simply to keep Vachey's records to himself, so as not to provoke other claims like Mann's against the estate. And I was betting there was more to it than that; that some of the paintings that Vachey had bought in the forties were still on the walls of this house, or in a vault somewhere, and Christian had plans to sell them. If so, he'd certainly want to hang tightly on to the records of those old transactions.

I told him as much.

He listened, head down, and looked up at the end with his crooked grin back in place. "Well, yes, okay, I admit it, a few of those old pictures are still in the basement, and, sure, I just might decide to put them up for sale. But between you and me, they're junk—seventeenth-, eighteenth-century apprentice stuff. My father gave up trying to peddle them twenty years ago and forgot all about them. I haven't looked at them myself in years. But things are different now, the art market's gone nuts—maybe I'll haul them out and see what I can get."

"I'm sure you will," I said.

"Look, Chris—no offense—but I don't really see where this is any of your business."

"Maybe not. But the Rembrandt is my business—"

"Sure, but there's nothing about it in that book, take my word for it."

"I'd have to see that for myself." When he hesitated, I added: "Otherwise, I go to the police right now."

"Well..." He adjusted his slightly disarranged forelock with a cupped hand. "The fact is, I don't have it, you know?"

"You don't *have* it?"

"No. Don't get excited, give me a chance to explain."

When I'd tumbled out the window, he told me, he had snatched the volume up from the floor, meaning to take it someplace safer. But I'd started such a racket from outside that he knew others would momentarily be bursting into the study, so he had hurriedly stuck it in the first place that came to hand, a crowded, waist-high bookcase across the room, thirty feet from where Gisèle had been telling everyone it was. Then he'd ducked out of the room just in time to keep my would-be rescuers from finding him there.

Five minutes later, when he'd come back, the book had been gone. Someone had identified it despite its location, and had taken advantage of the uproar to remove it. He had no idea who.

He shook his head. "I should have put it in a drawer or something, but there wasn't any time, and I was a little rattled. I mean, you were yelling out there—I didn't know whether you were dying or what."

I fell back against the wall. "Damn." Whether he was telling the truth or not, it was plain that I wasn't going to get to see the book. Another dead end, after all.

"Then I want to see those paintings in the basement," I said.

"Why? The Rembrandt's upstairs in the gallery where it always was."

"I just want to. Let's go, please."

He shrugged. "Whatever you say. I just want to cooperate."

He gestured me ahead of him down the hallway, but first I picked up the telephone in the vestibule and dialed Calvin's hotel. I may, as Tony says, not be the world's swiftest study when it comes to perceiving ulterior motives, but even I knew enough not to head off to the cellar, alone with a guy who'd shoved me out of a second-story window three days before. I wasn't going to give him another shot at me, with or without personal animosity.

"Calvin?" I said, when the hotel clerk had switched me to his room. "It's four-thirty right now, and I'm with Christian Vachey at his house. Just wanted you to know. I'll see you in an hour."

To make sure Christian didn't miss a word, I said it in French. As far as Calvin was concerned, I could have delivered it in New Caledonian, because he wasn't there. But this was for Christian's benefit, and I could see that he got the message.

We took the back stairs to the basement. At the rear of the house downstairs was a cheerless kitchen that hadn't changed much since the seventeenth century: flagstone floors, warped, scarred wooden tables, a huge, stone cooking fireplace, a few rusted, giant-sized cooking implements that looked like torture devices hanging on the soot-blackened walls. It was used for storage now, full of packing materials, paper, and disassembled picture crates. Next to it was Pepin's office, where we'd met for the presentation of the will. Pepin looked up from his desk in surprise, and was motioned by Christian to come along.

The three of us walked through to the front half of the house, past a small alcove set up as a studio with an easel and painting supplies, and then up to a steel door, which Christian unlocked. Behind it was a windowless room with insulated walls, in which thirty or forty glassine-wrapped paintings were neatly lined up in a two-layer wooden framework of carpeted bins.

Christian pointed to a group of ten or twelve wrapped pictures in the upper rack. "You want to unwrap those, Pepin?" To me, he said: "Those are the ones you wanted to see."

"No, I think I'd better see them all, please."

He didn't like it, but he spread his hands submissively and nodded to Pepin. "Do what the man says."

Pepin, predictably, didn't like it either, but he got to work taking off the wrappers and propping the paintings on the floor against the walls of the corridor.

He started with the ones in the lower rack. All were modern— early twentieth century. I thought I recognized some of the artists.

"Isn't that a Gris?" I asked. "And a Delaunay?"

"Sure are," Christian said. "And this one here is a Derain."

Could these be some of the "worthless" paintings de Quincy

told me about? But why would René Vachey have kept them here in the cellar all these years?

"They must be worth a fair amount of money," I said.

Christian grinned. "I sure hope so."

By now Pepin, working quickly, had come to the paintings in the upper rack—the pictures that the young René Vachey had bought in the forties, according to Christian—and begun to lay them out. They were what Christian had said they were: seventeenth- and eighteenth-century paintings of little value, some Dutch, some French, all age-darkened. Most of them appeared to be apprentice studies, many unfinished, the best of them no better than competent. They would have been right at home on the walls of the Barillot, if that tells you anything. They weren't worth the time it took to give them a second glance.

Except one.

I lifted it, examined it, checked the frame, and finally propped it back against the wall. Another piece of the puzzle had dropped into place. If this kept up, I might eventually figure out what was going on.

"Look familiar to you?" I asked Christian.

"What? No. Well, in a way. It looks a little like that Rembrandt."

"It looks a lot like that Rembrandt," I said.

Christian gave it a quintessential double take, eyes boggling, jaw dropping. "Rembrandt!" He stared hungrily at it, then at me, a laugh gurgling in his chest. "You're not telling me that this is actually a . . . that all this time, down here in the cellar, there's been a—a—"

"A Flinck," I said.

"A *flink!*" he shouted back at me. "What the fuck is a flink?"

Pepin, who was standing quietly behind us, said thoughtfully to me: "You may be right, monsieur."

"You've never seen this before?" I asked him.

"I have never seen any of these before."

"Who the fuck ..." Christian began again, and Pepin explained who Govert Flinck was.

It took a few seconds to penetrate. "You mean *this* is the painting this guy Mann wants back?" he said to me. "Not the Rembrandt upstairs?"

"That's exactly what I mean. Look at it. Picture of an old soldier—obviously the same model, same costume, same pose. He probably copied it directly from the Rembrandt picture—or more likely from some other student's copy."

Christian leaned over from the waist to examine it, hands on his knees. "Show me where it says 'Flinck.'"

"It doesn't. Nobody would sign a picture like this; it was just an exercise. Look, it isn't even properly finished. But I don't see how there can be much question that it's Mann's painting. How many pictures of this particular model, posed this particular way, could your father own? And you've already said he got these in the forties."

But there was more than that to back up Mann's claim. A small part of the lower right corner of the frame had been broken off and been glued back on. Some of the gilt around the break had flaked off, and the repair was plainly visible. It even looked like a job done by a couple of frightened kids, with a dried spurt of glue protruding from the back. We were looking at *Capitaine Le Nez*, all right.

I held back from mentioning the crack to Christian, however. It would have been too easy for him to get rid of the frame and put a new one on.

"What's it worth?" he asked.

"Just what you said—not much. It's nowhere near as good as the one upstairs and wasn't meant to be. It's a student exercise, a long way from Flinck at his best. And I doubt if there's any way to prove it *is* by Flinck." I turned from the picture to look directly at him. "Why don't you give it to him, Christian? Nobody's going to give you much money for it."

"*Give* it to him? What for? His father sold it, didn't he?"

"Come on, you know what the situation was. It would be a generous gesture on your part."

But his loose-lipped mouth had firmed. "If he thinks he has a case," he said sullenly, "let him go ahead and prove it in court."

And there I had to let it rest, not very hopefully. Even with that repair on the frame, I didn't give Julien Mann and his lawyer brother-in-law much chance of convincing a court of law that he had a legal right to it. A moral right, maybe, but courts didn't deal in moral rights.

We left Pepin rewrapping the paintings and came upstairs, back to the front door.

Christian had his easy, male-bonding smile in place again, and even went so far as to drape an arm over my shoulder. This was not a good move on his part; I could smell that now-familiar, citrusy cologne again. Back came distinct and unwelcome memories of pitching nose-first into the night.

"Well, what do you say, friend?" he said. "I've been as honest as I know how. Everything I know, you know. What now?"

"What do you mean, what now?" I got out from under his arm.

"You know what I mean. What are you going to do now?"

"What am I going to do now? I'm going to talk to Lefevre. Everything I know, he knows."

I opened the door and stepped out into the public vestibule. Several people were coming down from viewing the show. Christian, still smiling, waited for them to pass.

"Look, I see what you're trying to do. You're trying to get me to tell you what my father had cooked up, but I honest-to-God don't—"

"No, I'm telling you what I'm going to do."

"What the hell good will it do you? And what do you do if I deny everything? I don't believe you have any proof. What proof do you have?"

"So long, Christian." I went out and down the outside steps.

He followed me to the head of the staircase. The smile had disappeared. "Now wait," he shouted after me. "I thought . . . you led me to believe . . . Now look, Norgren, you can't . . . you can't . . ."

CHAPTER 18

I could, but I didn't. He was right about the proof. What was I supposed to tell Lefevre, that I recognized Christian's cologne? So what? How many other men in France wore the same scent? Besides, I believed his story, at least in its general outlines. He hadn't set out to murder me; it had been the book, the record, he was after, and I didn't think there was any connection between his hapless attempt to get it and his father's death. Even the business about somebody else making off with it rang true to me. As for Mann's portrait, that hadn't been a police matter to begin with, and it wasn't now.

I supposed I'd ultimately have to tell Lefevre all about it, but I knew he'd classify it under the heading of Unsolicited Assistance, and I wasn't up to his reaction yet. It could wait one more day. Right now, I was ready for a drink and something to eat.

When I got to the Hôtel du Nord, Gerard, the clerk behind the counter, called out to someone as I entered the small lobby. "Here he is now."

There was a movement on my left, in the corner where a group of easy chairs were arranged around a table. I turned toward it.

"Hi, Chris," Anne said.

* * *

The waiter laid out our breakfast, *café complet* for two: a big pitcher of hot coffee, a jug of hot milk, two six-inch chunks of baguette, croissants, hard rolls, butter, and foil-packed jams.

Anne did the pouring into the big cups. We tore off pieces of our croissants, littering the white tablecloth with flakes. We buttered our croissants. We took our first bites, our first sips. We looked at each other.

"Well," Anne said.

"Well," I said.

There is a way of saying "well" that means the small talk is over, and very pleasant it may have been, but now let's get down to serious business, if you please.

In our case it had been more than small talk, and it had been extremely pleasant. Once I'd come down off the ceiling the previous evening, Anne explained that she'd decided that my idea of a weekend in France was too good to pass up, and that maybe she could pull just a few more strings. She'd lined up a military flight to Rhein-Main Air Base in Germany. From the nearby Frankfurt Airport she'd caught a commercial plane to Paris, and then another flight on to Dijon. She'd arrived only an hour earlier, and she was starving.

We'd gone out for a simple, wonderful dinner of *moules marinière*, bread, and the house Chablis at a plain little restaurant on the Rue Dr. Maret, two blocks from the hotel. I hardly remember what we talked about, but it wasn't anything important. Mostly, I just basked in the knowledge that I was going to have three days to be with her after all. I think I didn't so much listen to her talk as watch her talk, happily taking in everything about her: those lovely, near-violet eyes, the wide, friendly mouth, the ghost of a tic that came and went in the soft skin below her eyes when she was nervous or excited, and which never failed to move me.

Somewhere toward the end of the meal I began edging toward the question of her commission, but the time hadn't been right for it, and we veered back to less threatening topics. She told me about her conference, I told her about what had been happening in Dijon and Paris. We laughed about the dachshunds painted on the Parisian sidewalks.

Afterward, when we went back to the hotel, we didn't talk about much of anything; there was a lot of lost time to make up for. Then this morning I'd awakened with my face against her smooth, honey-colored hair, and there hadn't been a lot of talk then either. We'd taken particular pains to stay well clear of the topic of her commission. Right up until that pair of *wells*.

I forced down a hunk of croissant.

"So," I said.

"So," she said.

This was serious stuff, all right. Bull-by-the-horns time. "What's it going to be, Anne?" I said. "Are you resigning or not?"

She tore off a tiny piece of croissant and rolled it in her fingers. "Which do you want first, the good news or the bad?" I'd been hoping it was all going to be good. "Bad," I said.

"All right. I'm staying in, Chris."

"I see."

"Don't look like that, Chris. Can't you be happy for me? I'll be heading up my own training unit." She smiled, proud and shy at the same time. "I got my line number for major. I'm right up at the top."

"Of course I'm happy for you." I leaned forward, put my hand on top of hers. "You deserve it. Congratulations, Anne, it's wonderful news."

It was the lousiest news I'd heard all year.

I couldn't have been too convincing, because she went into a long explanation of how the new assignment would tap her potential in ways that the old one hadn't, and what a wonderful career opportunity it was for her, and how the old notions of a sexual dichotomy of labor no longer applied in today's world.

I sat there doing my best to look liberated, but all I could think of was the dreary routine of seeing her only three or four times a year, and all the logistical coordination it took to make even that much work out. My face must have fallen enough for her to take pity on me, because she broke off her spiel and laughed.

"Are you about ready for the good news?"

"Good news?" I'd thought her promotion to major was the good news.

She nodded. "I haven't told you where I'm being assigned." I frowned. "Not Kaiserslautern?

She shook her head, her eyes sparkling. She looked like a kid with a secret she couldn't hang on to for another second. "I'll be at the Air Force Academy. I just got it all worked out yesterday, at the conference. I still can't believe it."

"You mean in Colorado?"

"Colorado Springs, yes. Chris, we'll practically be next-door neighbors."

"Next door? Anne, Colorado's a thousand miles from Seattle."

"That's a whole lot better than six thousand. Denver's only three hours from Seattle by air, and less than another hour to Colorado Springs. It's practically commuting distance. We could have lots of whole weekends together—with no jet lag. We'd only be one time zone apart, Chris!"

Oddly enough, it was the time zone that got through to me. There is something about living nine time zones away from your significant other that brings home the fact that you are rather a long way apart. A single time zone sounded like just around the corner.

"I could get on a plane on Friday after work," I said slowly, "and be there the same evening."

"Now you're getting the idea." She smiled tentatively. The faint tic appeared below her eyes. "It *is* good news, isn't it? It's going to work for us, isn't it? At least for now?"

"It's terrific," I said softly. I put my hand on her cheek, just under her eye, and felt the tender, trembling flesh quiet down. "It'll be great. Just think of those frequent-flyer bonuses we're going to earn."

She laughed and went happily back to eating. "Well, then, let's finish up. I want to see the famous Rembrandt I've been hearing so much about."

* * *

Pepin welcomed us at the door of the Galerie Vachey with his customary bonhomie. "I cannot understand why you are unable to make your visits in the afternoons, when the exhibition is open. And you cannot see Monsieur Vachey—Monsieur Christian Vachey. Inspector Lefevre is with him."

"Take heart, Monsieur Pepin," I said. "It's Madame Guyot I want, and it's the last time I'll bother you." I lifted my head and sniffed the air. "Do I smell something burning?"

"Madame Guyot has asked me to get rid of some old packing material. I'm burning it in the kitchen fireplace downstairs. You needn't concern yourself; every precaution is being taken."

"I never doubted it," I said with a comradely smile. Now that I had Anne beside me, was I going to let Marius Pepin get under my skin?

Ten minutes later, with the necessary locks unlocked and alarms disarmed, Anne and I stood alone in front of the Rembrandt. I resisted the temptation to deliver an explanatory lecture and let her look at the painting in peace, which she did for a couple of minutes.

"It's wonderful, Chris," she said simply. "It's as if you're looking into that old man's soul. And he's looking into yours." She turned to me. "Are you going to accept it?"

"Yes, I think so. It's not the painting Mann was talking about. Now that I've seen the Flinck for myself, I can stop worrying about that."

"And you think this is really painted by Rembrandt?"

"I do, yes. Where Vachey *did* get it, I don't have a clue. I'm starting to wonder if he didn't actually pick it up in that junk shop."

"Is that possible? Do things like that really happen?"

"If they happened to anybody, they'd happen to Vachey."

She wanted to see the other pictures, too, so we walked around the gallery for a while. Her tastes being a bit more modern than mine, we spent most of the time in the French section, where the twentieth-century works were.

"And this is the Léger?"

I nodded. *"Violon et Cruche"*

"It's quite handsome, isn't it?"

"Yes," I said. She'd been gratifyingly appreciative of the Rembrandt. I figured I could afford to be generous about the Léger.

She stepped closer to it. "It's not in very good condition, though, is it? Look here, where the paint's come away, and you can see signs of another picture underneath. I think I can see part of an ear or something ..."

I smiled indulgently. "No, you just think you see what's underneath," I explained. "The juxtapositions and perspectives can be a little startling if you're not familiar with his techniques, and sometimes you get the illusion that you're looking at more than one layer."

"How interesting," she said. "And do his techniques include peeling paint?"

"Peeling—" I took a hard look at the painting and let out a long breath. "You're right."

Except that it wasn't the paint that was peeling, it was the gesso underneath; the smooth white undercoat that provided the actual surface to which the oil paints were applied. An inch-wide curl stood out from near the center of the canvas like a wood paring, with another crack just erupting a few inches away.

There were some blisters in the surface as well, and in two places along the edges the gesso, along with its film of paint, had begun to pull away from the frame. On the wooden floor at my feet there were flecks of sloughed-off pigment. It was as if the surface of the painting were molting. Underneath it, as Anne had said, another painting peeked through.

"I think the other shoe just hit," I said quietly, my eyes on the picture. "This is the stink bomb. It has to be."

"Vachey's stink bomb? Do you mean he knew this would happen? I don't understand."

I didn't either, not entirely, but I was getting close. Gingerly, I touched the curl of paint. It came away and spiraled to the floor.

Anne caught her breath. "Chris, be careful! It's so fragile!"

"Trust me," I said. "But tell me if you hear Pepin coming. I wouldn't want him to have a fit." I picked away a little more.

"Chris—"

"You're right, that's an ear, all right." A bit more judicious scratching and a few more square centimeters of the underpainting emerged. "And an eye."

Anne watched closely over my shoulder. "It's another Léger, isn't it? Or am I wrong?"

"You're wrong," I said. I shook my head slowly back and forth. "My God, have I been dense."

She looked in confusion from the painting to me. "You wouldn't care to tell me what's going on?"

"In a minute. I still need another couple of pieces." I grabbed her hand. "Come on, let's go find Clotilde Guyot."

* * *

Madame Guyot hadn't wasted any time in following my suggestion about taking over Vachey's study. We found her there behind a large but nondescript desk. (Christian, true to form, had removed all the furnishings of value.) She was in conference with

Lorenzo Bolzano and Jean-Luc Charpentier. Madame Guyot, it seemed, thought that she might be able to arrange the purchase of a painting by Odilon Redon to add to Lorenzo's expanding Synthetist collection, and Charpentier was along to provide counsel.

Lorenzo, an old friend of Anne's as well as mine, leaped sprawling out of his chair to embrace her, then made her take his seat. "Don't worry, don't worry, we were getting ready to leave anyway."

"Is something the matter?" Clotilde asked, clearly puzzled by our barging in.

"There's seems to be a problem with the Léger," I said. Her friendly eyes became more alert, more expectant. "Oh?"

"The gesso's beginning to slip."

Lorenzo's jaw dropped. "Inherent vice!" he exclaimed.

This was not a mere Lorenzoism. "Inherent vice" is conservator-talk for the deterioration of a work due to the use of inferior materials.

"I don't think so," I said. "Not exactly."

"Well, I wouldn't worry too much," Charpentier said, looking at his watch. "These things can be remedied. Léger was not always the most painstaking of preparers, you know." He stood up, joining Lorenzo. "I think our business here is concluded. Madame, you'll let us know if Monsieur Boisson will consider our offer?"

"Of course," she said. "I have every hope." The two men bowed. "We'll find our own way out," Charpentier said.

Clotilde waited until they were gone. "So it's happened," she said. She was bubbling with excitement, her pink face glossy.

I took Charpentier's seat. "It's no accident, is it? That gesso was meant to crumble."

She beamed happily at me. I took it as a "yes."

"That's why the temperature in the gallery was kept so high, isn't it? To destabilize it. That was what Vachey wanted to happen, right?"

"Well, of course."

"What was he doing, settling some old scores?"

She continued to smile radiantly at me. "Tell me, Monsieur Norgren, do you intend to accept the Rembrandt?"

"What? Yes, why?"

"We'd like to have a small ceremony at the signing," she said. "Would five o'clock be convenient?"

I wondered if everyone had as much trouble as I did keeping to the subject with Madame Guyot. "Fine, but right now it's the Léger—"

"You will come, too, my dear," she said to Anne, who replied with a smiling nod, although I wasn't sure how well her rudimentary French was tracking the conversation.

"Madame—" I began, but Clotilde had picked up the desk telephone.

"Marius, will you—ah, Marie. Please tell Monsieur Pepin that the little gala that we have been planning will be held tonight at five. Will you ask him to prepare accordingly? I'm sure he'll need your help."

She hung up and smiled at me. "Now, monsieur, you were saying . . . ?"

"I was saying that I'm beginning to understand what's been going on here. The scrapbook—it had nothing to do with Vachey's purchases during the Occupation or any other time, did it? That wasn't what was in it at all. Christian lied to me about it, you lied to me about it—"

"I beg your pardon," Clotilde said. "I did not lie to you about it. I didn't say anything at all to you about it."

"No, but you knew I was on the wrong track, you knew I'd completely misunderstood—"

There was a tap at the glass door, and Pepin put his head in.

"I wanted you to know, madame, that security has been turned off in the northeast wing for a few minutes."

"Why, please?" Clotilde asked.

"It's that damned Charpentier. *Now* he decides he's interested in looking at the back. I left him with—"

I was out of my chair so explosively it flew over backward. Pepin, startled into immobility, had to be lifted out of the way by the elbows so I could get past him. I ran through the deserted reception area and into the wing with the French paintings. There was no Charpentier. There was no Léger either. The wall where it had hung was bare, the metal supporting bars naked and forlorn.

I stood there agitatedly, trying to think. Charpentier—of *course*, Charpentier! How could I have failed to see it? I had walked into Clotilde's office and practically handed him the painting. But where was he? What had he done with it? He couldn't have had more than a minute or two alone with it, and he hadn't taken it down the front stairs or I would have seen him. And the back stairs led only to the living quarters and the basement, so there was no—

Christ, the basement! The basement with its capacious old cooking fireplace blazing merrily away, fueled by all that volatile packing material. I tore open the back door and raced noisily down the two flights, nearly pitching headlong down the lower one in my rush. The heavy oak door to the kitchen was closed. I pulled it open.

"Charpentier!"

He was standing with his back to me before the massive stone fireplace, his arms raised, poised to throw the painting into the fire. When I called his name, he twisted his head to glower ferociously at me over his shoulder. Backlit by dancing orange flames, with the painting in his lifted hands, he was like some titanic figure from the Old Testament, like Charlton Heston himself, about to hurl down the tablets from the Mount.

For what seemed an eerily drawn-out time we stared at each other, mute and unmoving. Then, with a grunt, and with more speed than I would have given him credit for, he skimmed thepicture at me, Frisbee-style, but with both hands. All I could do was fling myself to the side and down, like a batter dropping out of the way of a ninety-mile-an-hour fastball.

The painting skimmed over me and through the open doorway with an ugly, whizzing sound, slammed heavily into the wall of the corridor, and clattered to the flagstone floor.

By the time I got to my feet, Charpentier was advancing with a rusty old kitchen tool he'd pulled down from the wall, probably something made to help turn a spit-roasting ox in the fireplace, but looking distressingly like a medieval foot soldier's pike; a five-foot-long pole tipped with a metal head consisting of a spike and an evil-looking hook. He was a big man, not athletic, but hulking and thick-boned, with a Mephistophelian cast at the best of times, and at this moment he was scaring the hell out of me.

I backed into the corridor, warding him off with upraised palms. "Jean-Luc, don't be ridiculous. You don't want to kill me."

"Yes," he said, "I do."

He did, too. He jabbed the spike at my eyes twice, first a feint and then a sudden, vicious thrust that was all business. I jumped back, managing to deflect the pike with my forearm, and stumbled into the corner of the corridor, floundering against some lengths of wood standing on end. Most of them went rattling to the floor, but clawing behind me with my other hand I got hold of one and brought it out in front of me.

Compared to that pike it wasn't much: about three feet long and the thickness of a piece of one-by-two lumber, probably part of the bracing for a picture crate. I brandished it in Charpentier's face like a cop's baton to keep him off, but he swept it angrily aside with the pike and closed in. I feinted at his face, then jabbed him in the abdomen with the wood, just below the end of his breastbone, but it was a tentative thrust, and mistimed besides. It occurred almost off-handedly to me that this was the first time I had ever used a weapon on a fellow human being—on any living thing bigger than a housefly—and it wasn't my kind of thing. The savage exultation of combat was not raging in my veins. I didn't want to hurt Charpentier, I didn't want to fight him. All I wanted was out.

Charpentier bellowed, more surprised than hurt, and with an almost casual flick of the pike caught the wood in the hook and jerked it out of my hands and over his shoulder.

Stunned, I watched it go flying end over end down the corridor. Did he actually know how to handle that thing, or had he been lucky?

Fortunately, he'd been lucky. His next thrust was clumsy and badly aimed. The rusty point grated against the stone wall a foot from my head. I even managed to grab hold of it as he pulled it back, but only got a couple of fingers on it, and he dragged it back out of my grasp. His clumsiness I saw as no particular cause for optimism. How many more times could he miss?

I was wedged into the corner with no way around him, and not much room for maneuvering. As for reasoning with him, the look in his eyes made the issue moot. I was groping blindly in back of me, trying to find another upright piece of wood when he feinted again, this time at my midsection. I flinched sideways and he came sharply around with the butt end of the pike, clubbing me alongside the right eye. I saw a pinpoint shower of sparks and at the edges of my vision a sudden, queer, wavering blackness like the fluttering specks and smudges in an old movie. For a horrible instant the darkness closed in entirely, but by the time my shoulders sagged against the rough wall I could more or less see again, but I was queasy and weak.

Charpentier was peering at me, as if to see how bad off I was. My appearance must have been satisfactorily dismal, because he raised the pike, tightened his grip, and set himself for a final thrust. When I'd gotten hold of another one of those one by twos I didn't remember, but it was in my hand, and almost automatically I swung it up and around, as hard as I could, cracking him on the side of the head just over the left ear.

I must have been improving with experience because he froze this time, then growled and shook himself—not just his head, but all over, like a bear. And he fell back—a single uncertain step to keep his balance. If I was going to get myself out of this alive, now was the time to do it. I dropped what was left of the one-by-two— it had broken when I hit him—and made a grab for the pike. This time I managed to wrench it out of his hands and had already started to bring the butt end around for another whack at his head when I sensed a change in him.

The heart had gone out of him. His shoulders drooped, his eyes had lost their crazy brilliance and turned opaque. I couldn't begin to read his expression except to know he had given up the fight. There was blood welling from his ear, where the skin had split. He touched it abstractedly but never bothered to look at his fingers, then turned his back on me and walked into the kitchen, heading for a back door that opened onto a row of off-the-street vegetable and flower gardens running the length of the block.

No, I didn't try to stop him. What was I supposed to do, yell at him to halt? And if he didn't (and he wouldn't have), what then? Run up and club him unconscious with the butt of the damn pike? Impale him with the point, perhaps transfixing him to one of the heavy wooden tables for safekeeping? Sorry, not my metier. Besides, the fight had gone out of me, too. I was woozy and nauseated, and my head had started hammering, and I'd had enough.

When he disappeared through the back door, leaving it open

behind him, I sank back against the stone wall of the corridor and closed my eyes. I realized that I'd been hearing the sounds of pounding feet for the last few seconds—people running down the stairs—and opened my eyes to see Inspector Lefevre, accompanied by Sergeant Huvet and another man, burst into the corridor and practically skid to a standstill when they saw me.

I gestured toward the kitchen. "Jean-Luc Charpentier," I said, surprised to find myself short of breath. "He just went . . . out the back. He's your murderer."

Lefevre and Huvet looked at each other.

". . . tried to burn the painting," I said, or rather panted. ". . . caught him . . . tried to kill me with this . . . this . . ."

But I couldn't think of the word for it, and besides, the blackness had begun to dance at the edges of my sight again, and with it came another sickly wave of dizziness. I tipped my head back against the wall, closed my eyes, and tried to steady myself. I would have put my head between my knees but I didn't want to do it in front of Lefevre.

"All right, have a look out there for him," I heard him tell his subordinates.

". . . gone by now," I said.

"If he's not there," Lefevre told them, "go to his hotel."

After a few more seconds the queasiness passed. I opened my eyes to find Lefevre silently studying the litter of wood strewn across the floor. Then he looked at the painting lying on its face, its frame knocked awry. Finally, he looked at me, clutching my medieval pike and leaning, bruised and battle-weary, against the stone wall.

He sighed. "Some things don't change, do they, Mr. Norgren?"

CHAPTER 19

L efevre led me a few steps down the corridor into Pepin's office, sat me down in Pepin's padded, high-backed chair behind the desk, and took a wooden armchair for himself. He telephoned upstairs to ask Madame Guyot to see that we weren't disturbed, and to request a cup of coffee laced with cognac for me, then waited for it to come before starting in on the inevitable grilling. He'd been upstairs himself, talking to the domestic staff, when he'd heard the commotion down below, he said. Now, if it wouldn't be too much trouble, perhaps I would tell him what all this was about?

"And I think you can put your pikestaff down now. You're safe with me."

I wasn't so sure about that, but I put it down anyway, surprised to find that I'd hung on to it all this time.

"Are you all right?" he asked when I took another sip without speaking.

I was all right—the brandied coffee was helping considerably—I was just trying to figure out where to begin. It had been no more than fifteen minutes since I'd put all the pieces together myself, and I didn't know yet what kind of a fit they made.

"Let's start with the painting," I said.

"The Léger?"

"It's not a Léger. It's two paintings, one on top of the other, and neither one of them is a Léger."

"Not a Léger?" Frowning, he went out to the corridor and brought the picture back, laying it on the desk and leaning over to study it. In addition to its being twisted from the rough treatment, some more of the overpainting had flecked away, and much of it had slipped an inch or two, crinkling up like the skin on a pan of scalded milk. The *violon* could have passed for an *accordéon*.

Gingerly, Lefevre pushed at the film of paint. "Let us hope you're right," he said. "No one could repair this." He looked up. "It's a forgery, then?"

"An extremely good forgery—painted on top of another extremely good forgery."

He leaned back in his chair, pulled a pack of Gauloises from his pocket, and lit up. "I feel confident that there is a reason for this, and that you are going to tell me what it is."

"I can tell you what I think it is." I had another swig of the fortifying liquid and told him what I believed had happened. The underlying painting had been covered with a coat of gesso to create a satisfactory working surface for the *Violon et Cruche* that would be painted on top, a common enough procedure in overpainting. The difference was that this particular gesso had been purposely *made* to slough off. My guess was that a thin coating of linseed oil had been put on the surface of the original painting before brushing on the gesso, which would tend to make the gesso slip. Then, the gesso itself had been applied as a single, thick layer instead of building it up in several thin coats, which would make it tend to split and curl—especially in a warm environment, as many a fledgling artist has discovered to his grief.

Lefevre listened skeptically. "And Vachey knew this?"

"Vachey *planned* it. That's why he ordered the gallery kept so warm. Otherwise it could have taken months for the gesso to start breaking up. But he didn't want it to happen later, he wanted it to happen right when it was getting the most publicity—during the two weeks of the exhibition. And the way to do that was to turn the heat up. The warmer it was, the faster it would deteriorate." I shook my head ruefully. "I noticed right away that the temperature was too high. Damn, I should have figured out what was going on."

Actually, I didn't really believe that *anybody* could have figured out what was going on, but I thought Lefevre would appreciate thinking that I'd missed something obvious.

"And to what end," he said, "would Vachey go to so much trouble?"

"To make a fool of Charpentier. The gesso would come off in

the middle of the show, followed by consternation and disbelief, and accompanied by loads of publicity. And when the experts got a look at the painting underneath, they would see beyond a doubt that it had been made in the last few years—which would mean that the overpainting couldn't possibly be from Léger's time. After the way Charpentier had come on about its being genuine, he'd be finished; his name would be a joke."

Through a shifting veil of cigarette smoke, Lefevre appraised me. "And all this is your own rendering of the way it is? Or is there perhaps some factual corroboration?"

"Factual—?" I laughed. "Well, there's the fact that Charpentier ran down here and tried to burn the thing the minute he heard about the gesso slipping. And there's the fact that he did his damnedest to do me in when I caught him at it."

He picked a shred of tobacco from his lip. "No, no, Mr. Norgren, these things support the hypothesis that Charpentier wished to keep the underpainting from being seen, yes; they are hardly proof that he murdered René Vachey."

"Well, no, but there are other things—"

The telephone on Pepin's desk chirped. Lefevre picked it up. "Yes, put him through."

He was on the telephone for two or three minutes, saying little, but issuing brief, inspectorish queries: "How? Where, exactly? When? What procedure have you followed?"

In the meantime I was trying to arrange my thoughts. Lefevre was right; I didn't have any proof that Charpentier had killed Vachey, but I had enough collateral evidence to sink a battleship. What I needed to do was to put it in cogent form. With my head still pounding, that was proving hard.

Lefevre gave a few brief commands over the telephone and hung up. "Charpentier is dead."

"Suicide?" I said automatically, less a question than a statement. It was odd. I hadn't given a moment's speculation to where Charpentier had been going or what he'd intended to do, and yet the news was so unsurprising it was almost as if I'd already heard it. I guess I'd been able to read that private, cloudy expression better than I'd thought.

"Yes," Lefevre said. "He was in his room. They knocked, they demanded entrance. And they heard a shot." He shrugged. "No more Charpentier." He was looking very thoughtful.

"Ah," I said. I wasn't feeling thoughtful. I was waiting to see what was coming next.

"The weapon with which he killed himself is a 6.35mm Mauser, the kind of thing that is called a pocket pistol in America, I believe?"

He was asking the wrong person about handgun terminology, but I thought I knew what he was driving at. "The same one that killed Vachey?" I asked.

"I have no doubt it will prove so. It's not a weapon one sees very often any longer." His Gauloises were lying on the desk, and he started to slip one out, but changed his mind and put them in his pocket instead, then cleared his throat and stood up abruptly.

"So, Mr. Norgren, it seems that once again you've been the inadvertent agent of justice." He tucked in his chin and made some more gargly noises. "Thank you for your efforts."

I didn't know about the "inadvertent," but I wasn't going to do any better than that from Lefevre. He'd had enough trouble getting that much out.

"You're welcome, but there's more I'd better tell you."

He nodded. "Better to do it at the préfecture, I think, unless you don't feel well enough. ..."

"No, I'm perfectly fine," I said, getting up too. I felt more fluttery than sick, and the pounding had almost subsided. "Let's go."

But Lefevre's attention had been caught by the painting again. "A forgery on top of a forgery," he mused, bending over it. "The one underneath—it's a portrait of some sort, abstract but not quite abstract, no? Isn't this an eye? Ah, and here's the corner of the mouth ..."

"It's a portrait, all right." I reached over and used my fingers to pull away a little more of the overpainting so that both eyes were visible, an arresting, smoky gray dappled with hazel.

After a second, Lefevre barked a brief note of laughter. "Vachey! It's a portrait of René Vachey."

"A *self-portrait,*" I said, and laughed a little myself. "Beautifully done ... in the unmistakable style of Fernand Léger."

CHAPTER 20

"Vachey was a *forger?*" Anne said, looking up from unwrapping a hunk of goat cheese.

"An extraordinary forger," I said. "He could do all the Cubists—Léger, Gris, Braque, Picasso. Not for a livelihood, you understand; more as an avocation, something he played away at once in a while as a matter of—well, of pride, I suppose."

"An avenue of self-actualization, you might say," Anne said dryly.

"Lorenzo might say," I said with a laugh, helping myself to cheese and bread.

We were in a little park a block from the hotel, one I'd often looked down on from the room; a square of prettily regimented greenery, with a formally laid out pond, and terraces and balustrades done in the ornate Italianate manner that had been popular in the time of Napoleon III. I'd come back from police headquarters looking, according to Anne, like something the cat dragged in, and although I hadn't felt like going anywhere, she had insisted on some fresh air and a *pique-nique*. Now I was glad she had; I'd been eating nonstop, not even waiting for her to get everything laid out between us on the bench.

"That's what the scrapbook was all about," I said, chewing. "His own record of all the fakes he painted, described in loving detail: pigments, techniques, materials. Right up to and including 'Léger's' *Violon et Cruche*."

"I don't understand. I thought it was a record of the paintings he'd *bought*." She frowned. "'*Les peintures de René Vachey*' ..."

"Right, 'The Paintings of René Vachey.' Well, think about it. If you're talking about a collector, it means the paintings he owns.

But if you're talking about an *artist,* it means the paintings he's created. It's the same in English; 'The Paintings of J. Paul Getty II' and 'The Paintings of Pablo Picasso' are two different things. I guess Vachey thought of himself more along the lines of Picasso. I misread it completely."

"Well ... all right, but how do you know you've got it right, now? Did they find the book?"

"No, it looks like Charpentier got rid of it somewhere. But Lefevre called in Clotilde Guyot while I was there, and she verified it all."

The book, Clotilde had said, contained comprehensive material on counterfeits by Vachey dating back to 1942; his own notes, plus newspaper clippings and magazine articles. Like many self-admiring forgers before him, he'd wanted to be sure that in the end he could prove the paintings had indeed come from his own hand.

I'd asked her rather pointedly why she hadn't told me that when I'd asked the day before. "Because," she said just as pointedly, "you neglected to mention the small fact that the book had been stolen." Indeed I had, and so Clotilde had understandably assumed that it was still in its usual place in Vachey's office, that no outsiders had any idea of what was in it, and how then could it have had any relevance to Vachey's death? I absorbed a sidewise, stinging look from Lefevre and let the matter drop.

"But how did *you* know what was in it?" Anne asked. "Before she verified it, I mean?"

"Oh, hell," I grumbled. "I should have figured that much out a long time ago."

Yesterday afternoon, anyway, when I was looking right at those Cubist paintings in Vachey's basement, the ones Christian had so obligingly unwrapped for me. Why, I should have asked myself a little harder, would anyone have kept authentic paintings by Gris, Derain, and the rest of them, a collection worth a fortune, stowed away in dusty wrappings in the cellar? And only a minute earlier I'd walked blithely by that alcove set up with paints and easel, and never had it occurred to me to wonder what it was doing there and who'd been using it.

But by that time, as I explained to Anne, I was no longer *thinking* forgery, not even about the Léger—not so much because of Charpentier's seeming confidence in it, but because of Vachey's. He had been so transparently shocked, so startled, at Charpentier's suggesting that it was anything but an absolutely first-rate Léger, that it had seemed impossible that he was perpetrating a fake. Now, of course, I understood: he hadn't been shocked, he'd been offended. Who the devil was Jean-Luc Charpentier to assert that a Léger by Vachey wasn't every bit as good as a Léger by Léger?

Anne had continued to lay out food while I spoke: two cheeses, a couple of baguettes, a slice of smooth liver pate with truffles, a plastic tub of green olives and another of string beans and peppers in vinaigrette, a split of red wine with two stemmed plastic wine glasses. And I had continued to gobble it down. She began to pour the wine.

"Not for me," I said. "I was drinking brandy at eleven o'clock this morning."

She stuffed the cork back in. "Me neither. I just thought maybe you could use it. Chris, how could Vachey have done the Léger so beautifully? Didn't you tell me he hadn't painted in twenty years?"

"Sure, and who told me? Charpentier. That's what he'd thought himself for twenty years, and he wanted me to keep thinking it. He'd just misattributed an outright forgery by Vachey, he'd killed Vachey over it, and he didn't want even the thought of a Vachey forgery to cross my mind." I found a bottle of mineral water in the paper sack and poured us some. "And it didn't."

"Mm." She chewed thoughtfully on an olive. "But how did *you* know it was Charpentier who killed him? I mean, I know how you know now, but how did you know before? When Pepin stuck his head in the door to say Charpentier had the painting off the wall, you were out of there so fast—"

"That's what gave it away. Until that minute I didn't have a clue. But why would Charpentier dash off and take the painting down the minute he heard about the gesso? The only reason I could think of was to somehow keep the evidence that it was a fake from coming out." I gestured with a bread slice. "And there you are."

"I am? Where?" Anne said with a tinge of annoyance. "I hate to sound dim-witted, but do remember, yesterday morning I was still in Tacoma with my mind full of job-reentry problems."

I accepted the rebuke. My mind had been on René Vachey for

a week, I'd been right here in France, I'd been aware of a hundred details she knew nothing about, and still I hadn't been able to put them together until they'd been handed to me on a platter. No wonder she was a little confused.

I put down the string beans I'd been working on and gathered my thoughts. "All right. Charpentier made a beeline for the painting the second he heard there was a problem with it. Why? Because he knew it was a fake. But he *hadn't* known it was a fake on Monday night or he'd never have gone into his speech about its being a Léger, but not a very good Léger, etcetera, etcetera. Question: When and how had he found out it was a fake? Answer: When—"

"When he stole the scrapbook."

"Right. Apparently, when Gisèle started ranting about it at the reception, and throwing around those innuendos about Vachey's 'great discoveries,' Charpentier started wondering if he'd been had, after all, the same way I had. So while she was still raving, he got away from the crowd and snuck off to Vachey's study—"

"To which you had snuck off only minutes before—"

"Me and Christian, only I suppose he wasn't sneaking, strictly speaking, since he lives there. Well, Christian found me with the book, heaved me through the window, stuck the book in another case, and got out. Whereupon—"

"Charpentier came in, snatched the book, and also got out?"

"Yes. You're doubtful?"

"Well, yes. It's just that it has the feel of—I mean, it sounds like The Three Stooges, Chris—everybody following everybody else."

"I don't think anybody was following anybody. We were all after the book. We were probably the only ones who had what you'd call a pressing interest in it."

She tore a slice of bread into pieces and offered them to a pair of small, softly honking white swans, handsome birds with black throats and red bills, that had paddled hopefully up to us on the pond we sat beside. When they wouldn't come near her outstretched hand, she tossed them some, and turned back to me.

"How did Charpentier know where to look for it? He could only have had a second before the crowd got there."

"Probably the same way Christian knew I had it. By looking through the glass door of the study while Christian was hiding it."

"You're guessing, though, aren't you?"

"Sure, I'm guessing. Charpentier's dead. Vachey's dead. What else is there to do but guess? I'm also guessing—but Lefevre agrees—that when Charpentier found out from the book that the Léger was a fake, he caught Vachey on his predawn walk the next morning. Maybe he tried to find out what Vachey had planned—remember, it was pretty obvious the guy had something tricky up his sleeve—maybe he tried to reason with him, maybe—who knows? Anyway, he wound up shooting him. With his little pocket pistol."

She was shaking her head. "No, I'm sorry, it still doesn't make sense. What good did it do to kill Vachey? That wouldn't stop the gesso from slipping."

"Ah, but Charpentier didn't know the gesso was going to slip."

"But he had the book—"

"All he knew was that it was a fake. There wasn't anything in it about the gesso. I have that straight from Clotilde. The entry wasn't complete. Vachey was waiting for the newspaper clippings that were sure to follow. So, as far as Charpentier knew, if he could just keep the picture from being scientifically tested—which was what Vachey wanted anyway—he'd be safe."

That was another little clue that I'd missed—how vehemently Charpentier had been against testing when we were talking to Froger at the Barillot. And how he'd been so much more negative about the painting than he'd been the evening before, advising Froger to stick it out of sight—and, he hoped, out of mind—in one of the Barillot's darkest corners.

"Attaboy," Anne said. One of the swans had waddled a few steps out of the water, made a tentative peck at the bread on her palm, and run back with it. The other had remained where it was, gobbling nervously.

She tossed it a chunk. "Go back a little. I can see what Charpentier's motivations were, but I don't understand Vachey's. Why was he after Charpentier's neck? Froger's, yes—they'd been enemies for years—but what did Charpentier ever do to him?"

I plastered a last slice of bread with pate and bit into it. "To René Vachey, the feud with a windbag like Froger was nothing. I'm sure he looked forward to making him look a little silly over the Léger, but Froger was small fry, and anyway he never claimed to be a Cubist expert."

I swallowed, full at last, and wiped my fingers on a paper napkin. "But Charpentier ..."

Charpentier, on the other hand, did claim to be a Cubist expert, and Charpentier, unlike Froger, had deeply wounded Vachey. It had started when he'd twice ridiculed Vachey's early "neo-Cubist" efforts. "Derivative, shallow, pallid, uninformed," he'd called them, but that much Vachey might have lived with; honest criticism from a straightforward if curmudgeonly critic. But a few years after that, he'd *praised* Vachey's controversial Turbulent Century show, his collection of works purportedly by Braque, Picasso, and others.

Why should that upset Vachey? Because, as several of the other reviewers had surmised, some of the attributions in The Turbulent Century were suspect. In fact, Clotilde had told us, they were more than suspect: all four of the Cubist paintings—a Braque, a Picasso, a Léger, and a Gris—were actually by Vachey; a one-man tour de force that was afterward relegated to the basement, where they'd probably remained concealed until I'd made Christian show them to me the day before.

And several years after that, Clotilde had gone on, Charpentier had verified the authenticity of that unknown Léger in Basel, only—and by now, of course, I was ahead of her—it wasn't a Léger, it was another Vachey counterfeit. It had been given to a friend in fun, but somehow wound up a few years later on the wall of a restaurant, and subsequently on the block at one of the big London auction houses. According to Clotilde, Charpentier had later verified a second Vachey-cum-Léger that had found its way into the art market in Vienna, valued at several million dollars.

Where these paintings were now, God only knew (which is, of course, why we straight arrows get so exercised even about forgeries made in fun).

Thus, Charpentier had consistently valued in the millions of francs the excellent forgeries to which Vachey had affixed the signatures of Braque, or Gris, or—especially—Léger. Equally consistently, he had heaped contempt on the paintings Vachey had produced under his own name. It was more than enough to rouse the ire of any painter-forger who had a high regard for his own merits, which Vachey most assuredly had.

"And so," I said, "he set this whole thing up to bring Charpentier down a peg. He knew Charpentier would accept the Léger as real—"

"How could he possibly know that?"

"He'd fallen for every one of Vachey's 'Légers' up till then. Why should this be any different?"

"That's so. And he was right."

"Yes, it would have worked. When that self-portrait came to light, Charpentier's reputation would have been in worse shape than that gesso."

Wordlessly, she offered me the remains of the baguettes. When I shook my head, she threw them to the appreciative swans. "But what about *Vachey's* reputation?" she asked. "Everyone would find out he was a forger."

"No, what everyone would know was that he was good enough to make a chump out of France's most eminent Cubist authority. Nobody would think of him as a forger, any more than people thought of him as a thief when he stole those paintings from the Barillot. He was having another one of his jokes, that's all."

"Only Charpentier didn't see the humor in it," Anne mused. "And now they're both dead."

A dreary gray cloud sheet had moved in, and with it had come a cold, fitful wind. Piles of neatly raked brown leaves at the junctions of the paths began to come apart and skitter over the gravel. We both got to work gathering up the food.

"One more thing, Chris. I see why Vachey couldn't let the Léger be tested, but why keep you from testing the Rembrandt? You don't think there could be something ..."

"Not a chance. No, he applied the restrictions to both pictures because if he did it to one and not the other, it would have given the show away. Charpentier wouldn't have gone near it."

"Well, I still don't understand what SAM has to do with all this. Why—really—did he donate the Rembrandt?"

I shrugged. "I suppose, for the reason he said. To make good on that old promise to Ferdinand de Quincy."

"But if he wanted to give you a painting, why not simply *give* it

to you? Why involve the Seattle Art Museum in this other mess?
And the Louvre, for that matter?"

"We're back to guessing, but I assume he wanted to have the
biggest, splashiest show he could. Partly because that's the way he
was, and partly because he wanted to expose Charpentier's blooper
as publicly as possible—right in the middle of the big exhibition."

"Whew." She shook her head. "It's pretty complex, isn't it? Messy."

"Vachey was a complex man."

I put the last of our leavings in the paper sack they'd come
in, and threw an olive that had fallen on the bench to the swans,
which weren't interested.

"Didn't you say he was murdered in the Place Darcy?" Anne
asked abruptly.

"Yes, why?" I glanced up to find her gazing at a blue-and-white
street sign on one of the concrete gate posts along the park fence.
PLACE DARCY, it said.

We looked at each other. Vachey had died here, his body found
in this pond. Perhaps he'd been sitting on this very bench . . .

I put down the sack. "Let's open the wine after all." She nodded
and got out the plastic glasses again. I poured, and we raised our
glasses. "To a complex man," I said.

CHAPTER 21

The temperature in the Galerie Vachey at five o'clock was a properly cool sixty-eight degrees, the humidity a comfortable fifty percent. But the "little gala" planned by Clotilde had failed to materialize. Initially contrived by Vachey, it was to have been his moment of triumph, when his brilliant outmaneuvering of the dean of France's Cubist authorities would be revealed to an astonished world. Even with Vachey dead, the loyal Clotilde had intended to go on with the show. But now, with Charpentier dead, too, any remaining pizazz had gone out of it.

Instead, there was a quiet signing at a folding table set up in front of the Rembrandt, followed by a subdued cocktail party in the reception area for no more than a dozen people. The sole press representative was a reporter from *Le Bien Public,* the Dijon newspaper, who left after taking a couple of pictures of Christian and me stiffly shaking hands in front of the painting. Questions on Charpentier's death and the faked *Violon et Cruche* were turned brusquely away by Sully; these matters would be addressed at a press conference to be held at the prefecture at nine the following morning.

My mission to Dijon completed at last, I was headed to the modest buffet table, where Calvin and Anne were drinking champagne and browsing among the hors d'oeuvres, when an unusually pensive-looking Lorenzo placed a hand on my arm.

"Ah, Christopher? Is it true? *Violon et Cruche* was painted by Vachey himself?"

"It's true, all right."

"And he painted many other such paintings? Derains, Delaunays . . . ?

"Apparently." According to Clotilde, there were at least sixty forgeries described in meticulous detail in the scrapbook.

Lorenzo chewed the corner of his lip. His Adam's apple bobbed. "Christopher, you don't think . . . that is to say, between my father and myself, we've bought a number of pictures from him, many of them Cubist, none of them tested. You don't imagine he would actually have . . . that some of them might be . . ."

I clapped him on the shoulder. "Lorenzo, what are you worrying about? Look at things postexistentially, that's all. Why do you want to get hung up with this immaterial contextualism?"

Sure, it was mean, but I just couldn't help myself. Sometimes these things come over me.

Naturally, I felt awful as soon as I said it. I tightened my grip on his shoulder reassuringly. "Actually, I don't see what there is to worry about. As far as anyone knows, he never tried to sell any of his fakes."

He looked a little less stricken, a little more hopeful. "No?"

"No, he did them for his own satisfaction. When he was finished with them, into the cellar they went."

"You're telling me the truth?"

I was and I wasn't. They might have gone into the cellar, but they hadn't remained in the cellar. When I'd been down there with Christian the day before, there had been about twenty-five of them lined up on the lower rack of the storeroom. That left a round figure of thirty-five unaccounted for—thirty-five fakes by a master-forger capable of fooling some of France's greatest experts. Who knew where they were now? Two of them had found their way to the big auction houses. Were the others hanging in the living rooms of friends? On other restaurant walls around Europe? Had some even found their way to museums, perhaps? Or to Lorenzo's collection?

But I couldn't really imagine Vachey hoodwinking his customers—not for profit, that is. "Of course I am, Lorenzo. There's nothing for you to worry about. Anyway, a dealer would have to be out of his mind to try to put one over on you or your father."

He brightened immediately. "Ah-ha-ha, well, yes, that's true enough, anyway. Well, hello, Christian, very nice affair." And on his way he went, restored to his normal good cheer.

Christian Vachey obviously wanted to talk to me privately. When Lorenzo left, he motioned me to a corner away from the ears of others, and draped a comradely arm over my shoulder. "Ah, say, Chris . . . Lefevre hasn't said a word to me about. . . well, you know ..."

"Pushing me out the window?"

He flinched and glanced furtively around. "Well, yes. I was starting to think maybe you changed your mind about telling him?"

At that moment I got one of the best ideas of my life. "I didn't change my mind, I just wanted to talk to you first. Maybe we can make a deal."

His eyes, no more than a foot from mine, narrowed appraisingly. I was speaking his language. "What kind of deal?"

I took a deep breath. "You give Mann that Flinck, and I won't say anything to Lefevre."

It wasn't what he'd been expecting. His arm came away from my shoulder. "No deal."

"Okay," I said, and began to turn away.

"All right, deal," he said.

I felt like cheering. Instead, I let out what was left of that deep breath. "I'll call Mann tonight. I'll tell him he can expect it next week."

"Next week—! Oh, hell, all right, next weekm you win."

But I could see that he thought he'd gotten off cheap—I thought so too—and I decided to push my luck a little, in my own interests. "There's one other thing, Christian. That self-portrait of your father under the 'Léger.' I'm assuming Froger isn't going to want to touch it, which means it would go to you."

He kept his eyes fixed on mine, like a wary fighter in the ring. "Yes, so?"

"It doesn't have any value. I'd like very much to have it."

He was surprised, but he couldn't have been much more so than I was. The idea had popped into my mind without forethought. I wasn't even sure why I wanted it, I just knew I did.

Christian folded his thick arms and tipped his head to the side. The earring gleamed. "*I'll* make a deal with *you*. You promise me not to go around blabbing about those paintings downstairs . . . and you can take it back with you when you go home."

"You mean those old Dutch and French pictures?"

"No, I mean the modern stuff."

That was what I thought he meant. I understood by now why Christian had been so eager to get his hands on the scrapbook. He wasn't interested in protecting his father's name or anything like it; he was interested in burying the evidence that the twenty-five or so modernist pictures in the cellar were all counterfeits, painted by René Vachey. Christian Vachey, unlike his father, wouldn't hesitate for a moment—could hardly wait, in fact—to start selling them off to the overeager or the undercautious as long-lost originals by Léger, Gris, et al.

And once that happened, they would be around for decades, periodically surfacing to foul things up in the auction houses, in scholarship, and in the art world in general. "Sorry, I can't do that," I said, "but I'll tell you what I can do." I almost laughed as I said it. I was starting to sound like an M.B.A. myself.

What I could do, I told Christian, was to put him in touch with a London gallery that sold forgeries *as* forgeries, clearly marked. (Yes, truly, there are such places.) When the forger was famous and the forgeries notorious, the pictures could sell for fifteen or twenty thousand dollars. Considering the tangled story of upper-crust revenge and murder that was about to hit the world's presses, these could well be worth even more, which meant that Christian himself could probably clear fifteen thousand apiece on them.

His eyelids whirred, probably from the calculations going on behind them. Twenty-five pictures at $15,000 came to $375,000, whereas he'd been hoping for the millions that would have come from slowly passing off the fakes as originals. But he knew I wasn't going to let him get away with that.

The whirring stopped. "All right, deal," he said again. "You son of a bitch."

"I'll call you," I said.

"I can hardly wait."

As he left, Calvin and Anne came up. Anne handed me a glass of champagne.

"Not that we meant to eavesdrop—" Anne said.

"Hey, perish the thought," said Calvin.

"—but did we or did we not just hear you talk Christian out of Vachey's self-portrait?"

"You did," I said, highly pleased with my performance overall. I was imagining Mann's reaction to the news about his beloved Flinck.

"What for?"

"What for do I want Vachey's picture? To hang in my office."

Anne blinked. "Christopher Norgren is going to have a *Léger* in his office—and a fake Léger at that?"

I laughed. "As a reminder," I said.

She made a face. "Of what?"

I hardly knew how to explain. "I don't know . . . of an extraordinary man, of a weird few days, of getting out of here alive, of—"

"How about of how fundamentally full of crap all these art experts are?" Calvin volunteered.

"Calvin—" I began indignantly.

"Sometimes," he quickly added.

I considered the emendation. "Calvin," I said, "you got it."

ABOUT THE AUTHOR

Aaron Elkins is a former anthropologist and professor who has been writing mysteries and thrillers since 1982. His major continuing series features forensic anthropologist-detective Gideon Oliver, "the Skeleton Detective." There are fifteen published titles to date in the series. The Gideon Oliver books have been (roughly) translated into a major ABC-TV series and have been selections of the Book-of-the-Month Club, the Literary Guild, and the Readers Digest Condensed Mystery Series. His work has been published in a dozen languages.

Mr. Elkins won the 1988 Edgar Award for best mystery of the year for *Old Bones*, the fourth book in the Gideon Oliver Series. He and his cowriter and wife, Charlotte, also won an Agatha Award, and he has also won a Nero Wolfe Award. Mr. Elkins lives on Washington's Olympic Peninsula with Charlotte.

OPEN ROAD
INTEGRATED MEDIA

Open Road Integrated Media is a digital publisher and multimedia content company. Open Road creates connections between authors and their audiences by marketing its ebooks through a new proprietary online platform, which uses premium video content and social media.

Videos, Archival Documents, and New Releases

Sign up for the Open Road Media newsletter and get news delivered straight to your inbox.

Sign up now at
www.openroadmedia.com/newsletters

Made in the USA
Lexington, KY
20 July 2015